RONIN

JAN DOMAGALA

Ronin

Copyright © 2020 by Jan Domagala

Published by The Global Edit, a division of Red Penguin Books

New York

ISBN

Print 978-1-952859-84-7

Digital 978-1-952859-85-4

THE COL SEC UNIVERSE

COL SEC PERSONNEL

Kurt Stryder: Main character. He was born on Celeron and, when not on duty, still lives in his family home overlooking the coast. Stryder joined Col Sec because his father instilled within him a strong sense of necessity to do the right thing. He remembers his father telling him that for evil to triumph, all that is required is for good men to do nothing. That was his motivation for joining the military and later volunteering for the programme. He has blonde hair, cobalt blue eyes, and a warm smile accentuated by high cheekbones that give evidence of his Nordic ancestry. He's tall, just over 6ft, and has a lean, hardened physique from years in Recon Delta—the Special Forces of Col Sec (Colonial Security).

General Sinclair: Head of Col Sec. The general is in his fifties but still stiff as a ramrod from his years in the military. His brown hair is receding with age, creating a high forehead topped with a sharp widow's peak, and he has deep brown eyes were unfathomable. His resting stoic expression gives nothing away, and his thin lips rarely spread into a smile. It has been said that if he ever played poker, he could have made a fortune from his deadpan expression.

Doctor Baxter: Programme Head. In-charge of the experiment that would change the military forever—and the same one that Kurt Stryder volunteers for. He stands at 5'10 with a reed-thin body and razor sharp mind. The doctor also wears spectacles that he pushes up his nose when nervous.

Zara Hardy: Recon Delta Marine. She was born on Earth and sent to keep an eye on Kurt. Zara is tall and athletic with mocha skin and long black hair usually worn in a plait down her back. Her deep brown eyes and mischievous sense of fun bring her closer to Kurt, and they find a common sense of purpose.

Captain Anthony (Tony) Storm, callsign Guardian: Recon Delta Marine Captain. Captain Storm leads a team guarding Kurt on Research Station Five. He is 6'4 with close-cropped dark brown hair and steely grey eyes. His broad shoulders and chest are proof of his physical strength, but his real strength lines in his drive to put the needs of his men first above his own, hence his callsign: Guardian.

Private John Wayne, callsign Cowboy: Recon Delta Marine in Captain Storm's team. Private Wayne is as strong and reliable team member and friend to Captain Storm, Private Ives, and the other team members. His callsign "Cowboy" was chosen because of his father's love of 20th century western movies that starred John Wayne.

Private William Ives, callsign Hacker: Recon Delta Marine.

He is less physically imposing than his team mates, but with the unique ability to hack into any computer—a skill that earned him the callsign "Hacker." He is somewhat of an enigma because, despite his speciality being computers, he has the heart of an adrenaline junkie. In his free time he loves nothing more than base jumping, rock climbing, and anything that gets the blood pumping.

Matthew Hawk: Recon Delta Marine, on secondment to Colonial Intelligence. Being born and raised on a planet with gravity slightly greater than that of Earth gave him slightly thicker bone density and muscle mass than that of anyone born on Earth. That, coupled with his broad shoulders, 6'6 frame, and well-muscled torso, arms and legs, make him quite the force to be reckoned with. He also has cold, ice blue eyes that sparkle with a mischievous quality often mistaken for indifference.

Colonel Abraham Gemmell: Reckon Delta Marine and General Sinclair's right-hand man. The Colonel towers at 6'5 and is as fit as soldiers half his age due to the regular exercise routines he undertakes with those under his command. He is the type of officer who would not ask a soldier to perform something he is not prepared to do himself. His sharp grey eyes shine with a fierce intelligence and laser-like focus that he directs at every challenge he faces. His black hair has not lost any of its lustre, despite being in his late forties.

Joanne Watkiss: General Sinclair's aid. She is a physically plain and unattractive woman with a short, stocky build and dark hair. As such, she is unaccustomed to attention from the opposite sex.

ELYSIUM ALLIANCE PERSONNEL

Captain Pavel Norsky: Captain of the Alliance's Special Forces unit, the Black Knights. Captain Norsky is in his early thirties and known as a fast-track officer who wants to become a Major by the time his present mission comes to an end. Currently stationed on Celeron, his mission is to capture Kurt Stryder.

Captain Pavel Tchercovic: "Security Chief Captain James Howard." He is sent to stop the programme Kurt volunteered for. He is an undercover agent, seconded from the Black Knights, acting on intelligence gained from a mole inside Col Sec.

Captain Pavel Temic: Black Knights Captain. He is an undercover agent working under the guise of "David Grant." Tall and good looking, he is well-suited for his role.

Captain Nokorovic: Black Knight Captain. He is an aide to General Solon, the head officer in charge of black ops in the Elysium Alliance's Black Knights.

General Solon: Black Knight Officer-in-Charge. General Solon is the highest ranked officer and most decorated officer in the Alliance military. He is a staggering 6'6 with the body of a weight lifter and a white crewcut chopped tight to his skull in stark military fashion. His slate grey eyes are cold and cruel like a shark's, and a scar runs from his left eyebrow to the point of his cheekbone in a curved line. He is a master of close-quarter combat and still practises daily, despite now being in his sixties. His only directive is to shift the balance of power in the Alliance's favour, and he will go to any length to achieve that aim.

OTHER NOTABLE CHARACTERS

Alexander Bane: Owner of The Golden Palace nightclub. Bane is a reformed gangster now in his fifties and built with a layer of fat covering a hard body honed by years of learning the fighting arts under a master which helped him climb the ladder in the planet's largest gang. His face is scarred and he has a broken nose which he refuses to have repaired because he sees it as a testament to all the fights he'd fought to get where he was. His salt-and-pepper hair is combed straight back from a prominent forehead, below which deep brown eyes peer out at the world.

~

PLANETS

Earth: Home Planet of the Colonial Confederation. Col Sec Headquarters is located here, situated in New York City on the site of the old United Nations Building.

Mars: One of the first colonised planets in the Solar System the population live under domed cities as it was colonised before terraforming was made possible. It is also the headquarters of the Offworld Special Intelligence (OSI), a new branch set up by President Takagi to investigate the mysteries found on Tartaran.

Io: The fourth moon of Jupiter and the most geologically active object in the Solar System.

Celeron: Terraformed into an Earth-class planet over three hundred years ago and is the home world to Kurt Stryder. Its two main cities were named after the first two leaders of the colonists who arrived with the first colony ship: Jamestown and Jacksonville. Haven is a popular resort town on the coast near Stryder's family home.

Toldax: Situated twenty four light years inside the Confederation and Alliance border in Alliance space, Toldax is an E Class planet, one of the few that hasn't needed terraforming before the colonisation programme had begun fully. It has a population of close to four million and the military base is located far away from them on the opposite side of the planet, on the second largest of the two largest land masses.

Dalos IV: Over a thousand light years from Earth, deep in Alliance space, it is an E Class planet that serves as the headquarters for General Solon, Head of Alliance Intelligence and all operations concerning the Black Knights.

Canto: An E Class planet located fifty seven light-years from Earth, three systems away. It is highly populated with five billion people, several continents, and hundreds of cities. One of the larger mountain ranges called the Quad was formed by four mountain peaks simply called Q1 to 4. At the base of the Quad is a forest that is popular with visitors who prefer the outdoor lifestyle.

Cordoba: An E Class planet located forty three light years from Earth in the Praxima system. New San Fransisco is the capital city, located on a bay.

Tartaran Battlefield: A debris field of broken and damaged starships that fought for the planet Tartaran. It is close to the border of Colonial and Alliance space where a massive battle was fought for control of the planet.

Tartaran: An E Class planet thought to be destroyed ecologically during the battle fought over it. It sits close to the border between Colonial and Alliance space. The initial landing party fifty years ago performed an autopsy on a surviving indigenous life-form. The research gained from that expedition is the basis of the programme Kurt Stryder volunteered for.

Tula Rhan: An E Class planet. Famously home to Prince Aswan. It is an unaligned world that has economic deals with both Colonial and Alliance trading partners.

Pallisto: An E Class planet renowned for its sandy beach resorts. Situated nine light-years from the solar system, it has long been considered the vacation planet of the Confederation.

RH426: A barren world populated by a series of cavernous regions where Omega Command is located. The 'RH' refers to Roger Humphries, the astronomer who discovered the planet in the early years of colonisation. It is a barren rock orbiting a star like Sol, our own sun, and although it was barren of organic or indigenous life, it does hold a variety of rare earth elements used in propulsion systems of starships. The Confederation strip mined it until it had nothing left.

Tarsus Prime: An E Class planet colonised for a century. It has twelve million people living in the two main cities, and several smaller communities dotted around on the outskirts.

Tarsus II: A small planetoid orbiting Tarsus Prime.

Paradisia: An E Class planet and Home Planet of Elysium Alliance.

Osiris: An E Class planet with heavier gravity than Earth. Its existence is shrouded in myth, as the colony is believed to be mysteriously abandoned.

Genotia: An E Class independent world located several sectors out of Confederation space.

Talipso: An E Class planet with a population of approximately 150 million in 6 cities, with others dotted around the world on other land masses. Talipso is dependant on trade with other worlds to be sustainable. Previously an Orion Cartel stronghold.

Qaobos: An E Class planet orbiting a star several times more massive than Sol. It is the fifth planet in the system and only populated planet in the entire sector. Not much is known about this world, due to its secluded location far from any other inhabited systems.

C4515: (Morphos): An E Class planet and an independent world in a system that has three other inhabited planets. Morphos is considered the vacation spot in this part of the galaxy.

Pentonville Outpost: A small yet important colony near the border of Confederation and Alliance space.

Andor: An E Class planet near the border of Confederation and Alliance space. Andor is still very much a frontier world, since the colony that has been located there for the last decade is still developing.

Binda: An E Class planet that supplies the needs of the largest ship yards of the Confederation. It is in high orbit around the planet, which also serves as an R-and-R facility for the shipyard workers.

Titanus IV: An E Class planet and the fourth planet orbiting around the star Titanus. It is an independent world and home to the New Order who want to take control of the galaxy and have their home world as the centre of it.

Hi there, I'd just like to say a few words of thanks to you, the reader, for picking up this book and also a few words about what you are about to read.

As an author I write to entertain, nothing more, nothing less. A good story, well told, can transport readers out of their normal nine-to-five lives and into something truly wonderful. That, hopefully, is what you have before you.

That having been said, there's nothing left to add except– sit back, relax, and enjoy.

ACKNOWLEDGMENTS

I would also like to thank all the people who have inspired me to write: Jack Higgins, Matthew Reilly, Robert Ludlum, James Rollins, and many more too numerous to list. Thanks guys, hope I don't let you down.

No book is ever a success because of one person; it is a collaboration of talents. Here is the list of those who helped me make this book what it is now.

This book wouldn't be what it is now if not for the amazing talents of Vivian Head at Bookscribe.com for the editing and polishing. The cover artwork is down to the talents of Jessica Tahbonemah at Magic Quill Graphics. I couldn't have done it without you, thanks to you all.

Finally, for Matt who helped with ideas for this book. Sadly, you're no longer with us; but you are never far from our thoughts.

Miss you, dude; hope this turned out like you wanted.

FOREWORD

By the late twenty-first century, development in technology made it possible for starships to travel faster than the speed of light. With hyperdrive engines, starships could jump into hyperspace and exit light years from their point of entry.

The government of Earth, or EarthGov, established a colonisation programme; and suitable planets were sought out and inhabited. This was the first time Man had set foot on a planet outside of his own solar system.

Some planets needed to be terraformed to make them habitable for humans to settle. This took decades; but as advancements in technology were made, the time it took to terraform a new world was reduced. Unfortunately, unrest at how the colonists were picked began to grow; and a terrorist group called the Elysium Alliance tried to disrupt the programme. This Alliance gave hope to those who thought they would never have a second chance at life. Backed by many powerful and influential corporations who lost out on lucrative government contracts, the Alliance started building their own fleet and training personnel. Within a few short years, they had manufactured enough starships fitted with hyperdrive engines to start out themselves and become a legitimate alternative to EarthGov.

This, of course, created competition for the planets chosen for colonisation; and the Alliance made bold moves to reach certain planets first.

Conflict followed and inevitable–war. Many lives were lost over the next few decades until a cease fire was reached. A decision had finally been made and reason prevailed. The Elysium Alliance had colonised almost as many planets as the Colonial Confederation, as EarthGov was now known, and an uneasy peace reigned. During the cold war, the two sides kept watch on each other. Now, it's the mid-twenty-fifth century and the known galaxy still maintains an uneasy peace.

He stood on the Observation Lounge looking out at the vista of stars, waiting to die.

Out of the four volunteers for the special experimental programme, only he and Kurt Stryder were left alive. The other two, Summerfield and Watson, had died in circumstances too horrible to contemplate. Was this his fate, too, to die like them?

He knew there were risks involved in the programme, a fact of any experimental programme; but seeing those risks, observing the consequences up close and personal made him doubt the validity of both the programme and his eagerness to enlist in it. It was too late to pull out now though, for the final round of tests had already been completed. At least he had got that far, more than could be said for Summerfield or Watson.

Turning away from the large panoramic viewport, he decided to return to his quarters. It was after midnight station time, which was synchronous with Earth Central Time. At this time of night only the night shift was working keeping this station, Research Station Five, operational. He walked towards his quarters, nothing more than a cubicle with a bed, really, and he entered. He quickly disrobed placing his uniform in the wardrobe, the only other piece of furniture present in the Spartan quarters before climbing into the bed.

He was more tired than he had first thought, and sleep came to him quickly. However, after only a few hours sleep, he was awoken abruptly by a searing pain that ripped through his abdomen like a wildfire. Still wrapped in the duvet that restricted his movements, he tumbled out of bed. Though he tried to stand, a wave of nausea engulfed him like a raging tide washing over the shore. He stumbled and steadied himself against the wardrobe to prevent him falling on the floor, then activated the locking pad on the door. As it opened on a cushion of compressed air he threw himself out into the corridor beyond.

A series of hacking coughs wracked his body; and when his sight returned, he saw the wall he had leaned against for support was splattered with blood.

This was not good. This was how the other two started before they died.

Fear gripped him and he screamed for help before another coughing fit took control.

Falling to the floor, his stomach heaved, the pain escalating to an excruciating level. As he lay on the floor, he turned his head to see a pair of boots running towards him. He had never felt such pain, and he was so weak he could hardly lift his head.

Someone cradled his head and he looked up into a pair of worried eyes.

He coughed once more spraying the shirt of the security guard holding him with blood before succumbing to the darkness that had been creeping into his peripheral vision.

Still on his knees and cradling Captain Bell's head, Private Robert Whitehead accessed a comm. channel via his Neural Interface.

When the call was connected he said, "Sir, Captain Bell has just died."

CHAPTER 1

Kurt Stryder was taking a shower when his Neural Interface tingled telling him a comm. channel had been accessed and a call was coming through to him.

"Go ahead," he said. The NI automatically connected him to various networks wherever he was on a starship, station or planet, whether by comm networks or the main computer on board. Effectively doing away with the need for external devices, the NI gave remote access to the same sources. Most Col Sec personnel were fitted with these NIs along with certain private citizens who could afford the cost of surgery, and the device.

"Something's happened to Bell," General Sinclair said, his voice coming through as clear as if he stood next to him in the room.

"What, same as the others?" Stryder asked almost knowing the answer, which would make his own worst fear come true.

"I'm afraid so, just like Summerfield and Watson."

"How long have I got?" Stryder asked, for he was part of

the same project and now the only remaining test subject left alive.

"There's no guarantee that what happened to them will also happen to you. They assure me they're doing everything in their power to get to the bottom of this," Sinclair said.

"Excuse me, sir, if I don't feel reassured. What I don't understand is, if we all had the procedure at the same time, why have the others died at different intervals?"

"That's something they're looking into, I can assure you. I want you to come to the main lab right away. There are some tests they want you to perform, and I want you under close surveillance at all times until we get to the bottom of this."

"Right, I'll just finish my shower and be right there, sir."

"There'll be an escort waiting at your door when you're ready, Sinclair out."

Stryder continued with his shower now that the telltale tingle had left him as the connection was severed.

All he could think of was when would *he* die? He'd seen the reports of the first two deaths and they were horrible. He'd seen his fair share of death during combat and had caused enough of his own to warrant his participation in this project. This was supposed to help bring about the end of the needless bloodshed, or, at the very least, help reduce it. He had thought that if the results of this project helped to save one life in the field, then whatever they had to endure would be worth it.

Now he wasn't so sure. It didn't seem right to sacrifice three lives, possibly more, to save only one life. The balance was off and he had no idea how to redress it.

Finishing his shower, he dried off and quickly got dressed in his uniform of white shirt and dark blue trousers. The Col Sec emblem was on the patch pocket on his shirt directly over his heart, and the three pips of his rank of captain were on the epaulets. He glanced in the mirror to ensure he was presentable, but what he saw disturbed him. His blond hair was cut to regulation length, not too short but trimmed neatly around ears that lay flat against the side of his head. High cheekbones gave evidence of his Nordic ancestry, as did his cobalt blue eyes. His normal, warm smile was missing now, replaced with a worried frown. Trying not to think about what could lie ahead, he went to the door.

As the door opened he saw his escort, two Marines from Recon Delta. Delta was his old unit, the elite of Col Sec, which meant the General was taking this development seriously. The Marines promptly fell in behind him as he left his room.

Arriving at the main lab, he was met by General Sinclair and Doctor Baxter, the two main men heading this project. General Sinclair was in overall command of Col Sec, along with Recon Delta and Intelligence Division. Doctor Baxter was in charge of the lab.

"There you are, Captain," Sinclair said as Stryder entered the lab flanked by his escort. Sinclair was in his fifties but still ramrod stiff from his years in Col Sec. His brown hair was receding from a high forehead leaving a widow's peak. Below that his deep brown eyes were unfathomable, as was his normal, stoic expression. Thin lips rarely, if ever, spread into a smile. It was said in some circles that if Sinclair had ever indulged in playing poker, with his normal deadpan expression he could have been wealthy beyond his dreams.

"Yes, sir, I see you've beefed up the security somewhat," Stryder replied with a sardonic smile.

"Yes, I thought it about time."

"Granted, but don't you think it smacks of closing the stable door after the horse has bolted, just a little?"

"Your opinion is thus noted Captain, but Baxter here doesn't share your sense of doom. Tell him, Doctor."

Stryder turned to the doctor not daring to hope. He said, "Tell me what, Doc?"

Baxter was smaller than the other men in the lab who were all professional soldiers standing between six feet one and six feet three inches tall, with lean, hard physiques that had been honed through years of hard training. Baxter, however, was five feet ten inches tall, with a thin, reedy body that had rarely seen exercise. His mind, though, was as sharp as any blade known to man.

"Well, Captain, you know as well as any on this project that what we've witnessed has been unprecedented and, quite frankly, simply should not have happened…" he said, his slate grey eyes aglow with excitement. He ran his hand through his thinning, salt and pepper hair, and then pushed his spectacles up his aquiline nose, a habit of his when he was nervous or excited.

"But it did happen, sir, three times now and it's the same every time. What I need to know is, when is it going to be my turn and can you prevent it?" Stryder asked.

"But that's just it…the same every time. All three died in exactly the same way," said Baxter, thrusting his hands into the pockets of his white lab coat.

"I understand that, Doctor; but what's your point?"

"You know the basis of what we're doing here, right? We've injected you all with a serum that alters you genetically—to enhance your immune system, to give you the ability to heal faster, and to aggressively attack toxins."

"Yes, sir, I was briefed fully at the induction. We all were."

"And you agree that no two people's DNA is exactly the same?"

"Yes, sir."

"So why would the treatment affect three people in exactly the same manner, at different intervals, when it has been proven that there are no toxins present in the serum?"

"I don't know, Doctor, you tell me. You're the expert. No wait…you suspect foul play. How is that possible? I thought the facility was locked down tighter than an airlock in deep space."

"It is, but considering we are in deep space, that comment is redundant. Having said that, it's the only explanation that fits the facts," Baxter replied.

"So what're we going to do, sir?" Stryder asked, glancing at the General.

"You are going to continue with the programme and leave the security of this facility to me," Sinclair replied confidently.

"Do you have a list of suspects, sir? I'd like to know so I can keep an eye out. Or am I to be the bait?" Stryder asked.

"We're looking into it, Captain," Sinclair said, giving nothing away as usual.

Stryder watched as Baxter turned to the General and said, "Tell him."

"Tell me what, sir? What is it you're keeping from me?" Stryder asked suspiciously.

Sinclair stared at Baxter for a second, his eyes boring into him with repressed anger. Baxter was a civilian scientist working for Col Sec, but not directly under Sinclair's command, otherwise his little outburst would not have happened. He looked away from the doctor then turned to face Stryder. There was a battle going on inside his head, Stryder could see that. When he came to a decision he said, "Okay, we suspect that Captain Howard may have something to do with all this."

"Howard? Isn't he in charge of security here?"

"Yes, and we have to handle this carefully. If he has ties to the Alliance, then we need to find out. We'll have to keep him under close surveillance but without alerting him to the fact we're on to him. If he is our man and he gets wind of our suspicions, there's no telling what he might do."

"One thought has occurred to me, sir, why is he going to so much trouble when this project clearly doesn't work?" Stryder asked.

"Excuse me?" Baxter replied indignantly, staring at the taller man as if he had insulted him.

"Well, sir, if this serum is supposed to increase our immune system to make us more able to fight off toxins, how is he killing us off one by one? All the testing we've undergone so far has been to see if it affected us on a physical level. As far as I can see, our immune system has not been tested yet. Surely if a poison or toxin of some sort has been used, shouldn't the serum have neutralised it?" Stryder explained with no trace of malice.

Baxter's expression softened a little. "That, again, is something of a mystery. You were right to point out about the testing. We had to ensure that the serum had no debilitating effects on your abilities to perform as a soldier. In fact, in your case Captain, it had quite the opposite effect; it actually increased your strength and stamina. I'm sure you're aware that your endurance levels have increased by twenty-five per cent."

Stryder expressed mild surprise and a little bewilderment "To be honest, Doc, I thought you were taking it easy on me, well on us, actually. I never realised it was just me; we were never tested together. I just put it down to my training in Recon Delta being harder than what you put us through." He paused then asked, "But why me?"

Baxter had no answer for him other than a shake of his head and a bemused expression. When he spoke, his voice displayed his frustration.

"We've encountered so many variables that were, to be honest, unexpected. Each test subject has had a different reaction to the serum, however small. You, it seems, Captain, are the only one to exhibit any positive reaction to the serum. It seems the serum did not affect the immune system of the first three. In fact, once the autopsy results are in on Bell, I'm sure it will confirm my earlier findings, that their immune system actually saw the serum as a threat and destroyed it."

"How is that possible, sir; and what does it mean for me? Am I in danger from it?" Stryder asked, a little concerned.

"On the contrary, it seems to have increased your metabolism, now all we need to do is to get it to increase your immune system. We need to get it to attach itself onto your DNA to affect your immune system genetically; otherwise, it could be perceived as a threat by your body's defences and be destroyed by the very thing it seeks to improve."

"And how on earth do you intend to do that?"

"I've developed a nanoserum–billions of tiny robots programmed to attach the serum to the specific strand of your DNA. We just inject it into your bloodstream and they get to work. We should see results within a very short time." Baxter said, smiling and almost rubbing his hands together in glee at the prospect of this new development.

"Billions of tiny robots, Doc? I'm no scientist, but how have you programmed so many in such a short space of time?"

"We've been working on nanobots for many years. They're used extensively throughout the medical profession, as I'm sure you're aware. Programming them was relatively easy; they work in a series, you see. If you programme one, it passes that data along to the rest almost instantaneously."

"When are you planning on…?" Stryder stopped short when he saw Baxter reach for a syringe.

"Right now, Captain. Roll up your sleeve, please."Before

he knew it, the injection had been administered and he was pulling down his sleeve again.

"How soon Doc, before you know? What can I expect?" he asked, unsure of what would happen next.

"Not sure really, but the nanobots should get to work immediately. As to the question of whether you'll feel anything, I wouldn't expect so. Remember, this is taking place at the genetic level so the changes should go unnoticed until the immune system is threatened."

"So what you're saying, basically, is that I won't know if it's worked until I get injured?" Stryder asked.

"Well, I suppose that's somewhat true, yes," Baxter replied seeming a little unsure.

"You don't sound too confident, Doctor." Sinclair said.

"We're not dealing with absolutes here, we're into uncharted waters. This has never been attempted before and, quite frankly, until we get some sort of results, until we can test this, I don't know what to expect."

"Forgive me, Doc, if I don't feel reassured," Stryder said.

"If it works though, just think of the potential. Think of the lives we'll be able to save," Baxter said, pushing his spectacles back up his nose.

"Going back to my earlier question about Howard, sir, why is he going to so much trouble to kill us all off? Does he know something about this that we don't, or is the Alliance so afraid that we may be on to something that they're desperate to stop us at any cost?"

"It's no secret that they are desperate to prevent us gaining any sort of advantage over them; and if they can't duplicate our research, then the safest thing to do is either discredit or destroy it," Sinclair said.

"If he's in charge of security, won't he be pissed off that you brought in Recon Delta to take over?"

"Oh, I do hope so," Sinclair said with an uncharacteristically smug smirk.

"I get it, you want to rattle his cage and force him to make a mistake."

"Of course," Sinclair said.

"So, not only am I a guinea pig, but I'm bait now as well," Stryder said.

Baxter looked from him over to Sinclair, then down to the floor, unable to maintain eye contact with him. The General, though, had no trouble at all looking at him straight in the eyes.

"Don't feel guilty, Doc. I'm first and always a soldier, this comes with the territory," Stryder said, never taking his eyes off Sinclair.

"You got that right, Captain; this is what you signed up for," Sinclair said coldly.

"Yea! The life in Recon Delta, it's not just a job, it's an adventure," Stryder replied.

CHAPTER 2

Captain James Howard was in his office when the news of Bell's death filtered through to him. Instead of feeling panic or concern over a further death he and his men had been unable to prevent, he felt pleasure.

He had taken another risk in eliminating Bell–the third risk–and he would take one more to complete his mission to destroy this project. He could not allow the Confederation to gain such an advantage over the Alliance. For that reason, whatever risks he took, would be worth it.

This posting had been a recent promotion for Howard. He had worked hard to get there, starting out as a lowly Constable and, gradually, through effort and initiative, making his way up through the ranks until he reached Captain. This posting was the most prestigious of his career, in charge of security on Research Station Five, the largest research facility that the Colonial Confederation had. Situated out in deep space, fifty-seven light years from Earth, it was where all the major testing of new weapons and equipment was undertaken, along with any new research and development, such as this project.

The real Captain Howard would be so proud, but this Howard was in fact Captain Pavel Tchercovic of the Elysium Alliance's equivalent of Recon Delta, an elite unit known as the Black Knights.

When the Alliance learnt of this project through a mole planted within Col Sec a full year before testing began, they started researching the personnel of Research Station Five. It was somewhere they had never been able to infiltrate, until now.

The posting of Captain James Howard six months prior to the start of the project, came as a godsend. No one on the station had ever met him, and his official file was the only record they had of the man. It was a simple matter for the mole to gain access to the official records database and exchange Howard's photograph for one of Tchercovic so that when he arrived to start his tour of duty he was, to all intents and purposes, Howard.

He had done his research before arriving at the station so he knew as much about the project, those in charge and those participating, as the mole had been able to learn. Once there, and when the testing began, he surreptitiously entered the main computer to check on the progress. He became aware early on of the doubts Baxter had and of the dangers inherent in the project. However, instead of sabotaging the serum, he decided the best tactic would be to play on the dangers. If the test subjects all died, they were more likely to abandon the project.

If that were to happen, and with the death of Bell he was hoping that would be more likely now, he planned to steal the research data and transmit it to the Alliance via a secure burst sub-space signal, where they could duplicate the programme with better results and thus gain the advantage Col Sec was hoping for.

When he was informed of the arrival of the detail from Recon Delta to supplement his security, he wasn't sure how to act. His first reaction was a mixture of pleasure and frustration. Pleasure at the prospect of pitting himself against an adversary supposed to be his opposite and equal, yet frustration at the knowledge that they intended to continue with the project and not abandon it as he had hoped.

More to the point, though, how would the real Howard have reacted? He would have been incensed, to be sure, that his authority had been superseded by Recon Delta. He would probably have lodged an official complaint to General Sinclair personally.

Deciding that was the best action to take to ensure his cover remained in place, he left his office and made his way to the main lab where he knew Sinclair would be. He arrived just after their conversation about him had ended.

"General Sinclair we need to talk, sir, in private," Tchercovic said as he burst into the room, anger etched across his face.

"Ah, Captain Howard. Here to discuss the new security arrangements I've implemented to assist you and your men, no doubt," Sinclair said, to take the sting out of Tchercovic's assault.

"That's not what I've been told, sir. As I understand it, Recon Delta has taken control of the security of your project. My men and I have been locked out." Tchercovic said, making a show of barely-contained anger.

"That's right; have you a problem with that, Captain?" Sinclair asked.

"If you had a problem with how I run the security of this

station, I would have preferred you come to me with it, rather than go over my head."

"You may be in charge of the security of this station, Captain, but I am in command of this station and everyone on board. I don't need to refer to you on any of my decisions. You are under my command here, Captain; don't ever forget that. Dismissed," Sinclair said with a tone of finality in his voice.

Tchercovic was barely able to control his anger at the rebuff; real anger this time, not feigned. He wanted to tear the General's head off but, to remain in character, simply said, "Aye, sir," then turned and left.

Outside the lab Tchercovic had to pull himself back under control. That was close; he had never come so close to losing it like that before. He prided himself on being the consummate professional. Always under control, but just then when confronted by Sinclair, he felt that control slipping. Just a fraction but it had happened. He only hoped that no one had noticed.

Getting to the last test subject, Stryder, would be harder now that Recon Delta had been brought in, but that would not prove too much of a problem. Everyone thought that Recon Delta was the elite, the best of the best, but he knew different. The Black Knights were superior in every way imaginable, and he would prove it.

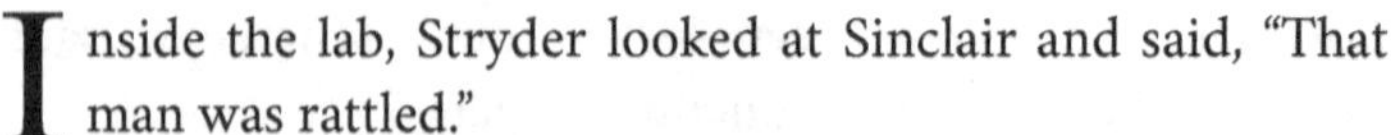

Inside the lab, Stryder looked at Sinclair and said, "That man was rattled."

Smiling, Sinclair said, "That *was* the point."

CHAPTER 3

Over the next few hours, Tchercovic watched through the surveillance monitors as Stryder was tested at the lab before returning to his quarters.

At no time during this period was he left alone. There were at least two Marines with him, or close by, at all times. Getting to him through this barrier was not going to be as easy as he first thought.

While he was studying the monitors, another plan began to formulate in the back of his mind.

As he watched Stryder settle down for the night, he realised what he must do. He must steal the research data and destroy the station. All the witnesses, test subjects and the much-vaunted Col Sec, with their esteemed Recon Delta, would be destroyed. They would be unable to testify as to who was responsible, or have the ability to rebuild.

Being the head of station security afforded him certain privileges, such as having all the station's security protocols.

Entering the station's main computer, he logged into Engineering where he programmed the core reactor to go critical in one hour.

That should be plenty of time to sabotage the life pods, download the research data and get the hell off the station, he thought.

Once that was done, he hacked into the main lab's internal computer and entered the master decrypt code that unlocked all the files. All security chiefs on Outpost Research Stations are issued with the code key. Each key is specific to one station and is only to be used during major emergencies to retrieve important data so that it cannot be destroyed or stolen.

Not bothering to sift through all the files for the pertinent data, and so that he didn't leave anything behind, he downloaded them all onto a data card.

All that remained was to sabotage the escape pods and all the docking bays so that no one could leave, except him, of course. The best way to do that was to restrict access to the docking bays, effectively locking them off. As for the life pods, he programmed them all to vent atmosphere thirty seconds after release from the station.

Confident that he'd left nothing to chance, he locked down the main computer with an encrypted command that would take over an hour to crack. By that time, it would be too late.

He left his office and headed towards Docking Bay Six, the only one not locked down, and where a ship was berthed. It was his escape route.

The clock was ticking. There was less than forty-five minutes left before the station's core went critical and destroyed everything and everyone on board.

No one knew what was about to happen, he had covered his tracks too well. They were all going to die and he was the only one who knew.

Slowly, he began to walk towards his ship and his way out.

~

Sinclair was asleep when the silent alarm went off. Tchercovic had disabled the alarms when he programmed the reactor core to go critical but, thinking he had completed his task, failed to check if the audible alarms were the only ones activated.

A warning light shone directly into the face of the sleeping General from above his bed; a bright, intense white light guaranteed to wake anyone. Scrambling out of bed, he quickly pulled on his pants then said, "Computer, status."

"Station's main reactor will reach critical mass in forty-three minutes, twenty-seven seconds," replied the calm female voice of the computer's simulated interface.

"Reverse the action immediately," ordered Sinclair as he continued dressing.

"Unable to comply," said the computer.

"Explain?" Sinclair asked as he stopped dressing, a bad feeling swarming over him.

"To initiate that action, an activation code is required."

"Command override, Alpha One, authorisation code Sinclair, General, Col Sec," Sinclair said quickly as he frantically resumed getting dressed. Somehow, he knew his override code would not be accepted, but he had to try.

"Unable to comply, code not recognised. Countdown will continue," replied the computer.

Through his NI he said, "Engineering, what's your status?"

Almost immediately a voice came back on to say, "We're a bit busy just now, sir. We're attempting to re-initialise the reactor safeguards, but the main computer's locked us out. We'll get back to you."

Sinclair knew this was bad and he knew who was behind

it. It had to be Howard. Next, he contacted Stryder. When he came back, it was obvious he'd been asleep.

"Yes, sir?" he said, his voice thick with fatigue having just been woken up.

"Howard's sabotaged the station. The reactor will go critical in forty minutes and he's locked us out of the main computer," Sinclair told him urgently, yet calmly.

Stryder was instantly awake on hearing the news. "If that's the case and he's disabled the alarms, it's safe to assume he's covered his tracks. He'll have downloaded what he needed from the computer and probably made sure we couldn't get off the station, should we somehow be alerted before we blew up," he said, surprising himself by just how alert he was so quickly.

"We have to stop him getting away with the project data," Sinclair said.

"Computer, locate Captain Howard," Stryder said.

"Captain Howard is on Deck Eight, en route to Docking Bay Six," was the reply.

"You get the evacuation started, sir. I'll get Howard," Stryder said. Before Sinclair could even think about replying, the link was severed and Stryder was leaving his quarters having gotten fully dressed during the call.

Two Recon Delta Marines met him at the door; one of them wore the stripes of a captain. He was slightly taller than Stryder with wide shoulders and a broad chest. His dark brown hair was clipped into a buzz cut, identical to the other Marine standing next to him. Steel grey eyes stared at Stryder as he appeared in the doorway.

"Excuse me sir, where are you going?" he asked.

"No time for details, but this station is going to explode in little over half an hour. I'm going after the guy responsible before he escapes. He has the key that allows us back into the main computer that'll prevent it, otherwise we'll have to evacuate. Now get out of my way soldier."

The Marine weighed up what he'd heard, saw the intense look in Stryder's eyes, and came to an immediate decision.

"Okay sir, we're with you," said the Marine.

"Good, but General Sinclair might need some help with the evacuation, I can handle this on my own," Stryder replied.

"With respect sir, I'll stay with you," replied the Marine who then turned to his team mate and said, "Cowboy, locate the General and work with him. Rouse the rest of the squad and get them up to speed. The clock's ticking, let's go boy."

"Aye, sir," Cowboy replied. He was thinner than the captain with lighter hair and darker eyes. They both wore sidearms and had the Remm assault rifle as standard issue. Cowboy slung the rifle over his shoulder as he ran off to carry out his orders.

"Okay then it's just you and me, but remember we need this guy alive. Is that clear?" Stryder said, not waiting for a reply, for he was off and running down the corridor. After all, like the man had said, the clock was ticking.

CHAPTER 4

Tchercovic was halfway to his escape route when he heard, "Howard, hold it right there."

The voice was unmistakable, that asshole they sent Recon Delta to protect, Stryder.

"How in the entire galaxy did he find out what was happening?" he thought, as he wondered what to do next.

As he was so close to his ship and the countdown about halfway through, he couldn't allow himself to be brought back, no matter what the reason. Therefore, there was only one course of action open to him.

Drawing his pistol, he spun around and fired.

The Sig P996, the standard sidearm for security personnel, was based upon the Sig Sauer P200 range of semi-automatic pistols from over four centuries ago. It was a short pistol with a slide on top, which primed the battery clip that fitted into the butt. It fired a bolt of plasma, ionised energy, in a pulse to minimise the blooming effect, which would cause the energy to spread over a distance minimising its effectiveness. It had two settings, 'stun' and 'full power'. The 'full power' bolt struck Stryder high on the right side of his chest as he desperately twisted his body trying to avoid being hit, only spotting the pistol at the last second.

The force of the bolt accelerated Stryder's motion and sent him spinning to the floor, leaving a trail of blood arcing through the air to trace his path.

The Marine was caught off guard also. His reactions were a millisecond slower than Stryder's. By the time he'd switched his gaze from Stryder to Tchercovic, and thought to bring up his assault rifle, Tchercovic had already altered his aim.

The second bolt struck the Marine in the centre of his chest, sending him flying backwards down the corridor. His life was saved by his body armour, which was designed to handle more powerful charges than that.

Tchercovic, seeing his handiwork, holstered the Sig, turned and sprinted off down the corridor towards Docking Bay Six.

Shaking his head to clear the cobwebs, the Marine got to his knees and looked down the corridor at the fleeing form of the security chief as he disappeared around a corner.

He looked over to where Stryder was lying, blood over his clothes from the wound high on his chest. Kneeling down beside him he checked for a pulse, finding it immediately, strong and even.

Stryder opened his eyes and took in a massive gulp of air, like that of a diver coming to the surface.

Startled, the Marine asked, "You okay, sir?"

Checking himself mentally, Stryder said, "I think so." Then he checked his wound, which to his amazement was closing up before his very eyes. It was healing itself at a remarkable rate.

"That is so very weird, yet also very cool," the Marine said, not quite knowing whether to be repulsed or amazed.

"Seems like the project is a success," Stryder said with a surprised smile.

"Sir, I don't want to know, let's just go get the bad guy," the Marine said, getting to his feet.

Stryder stood up unable to take in what was happening to him. He knew what the projected results were, but actually seeing them work, feeling his body heal at such an alarming rate, was something else.

What did this mean to him, to Col Sec, to the future of the Confederation? He had no idea. What he did know though, was if they didn't stop Howard then it was all for nothing, all the sacrifices, everything would be in vain. They would all die and the Alliance would have won. Not just this, but much, much more and with that victory, how many more deaths would come as a result?

That was something he was not about to let happen.

Pushing himself into run and trying not to focus on the decreasing pain but on what must be done, he pursued Tchercovic.

By the time he'd reached the bend in the corridor his wound had healed, with no visible scar.

Docking Bay Six was in sight for Tchercovic when the station's alarms went off, sounding a 'Red Alert' status.

He knew that within minutes station personnel would be falling over themselves in order to get to the life pods. That meant he had to get to his ship, and fast.

The entrance to the docking bay was just another few hundred metres along this corridor, around the next bend. He was thinking, planning ahead, when a plasma pulse rifle was fired from behind him.

The bolt struck the wall close to his head, impacting on the wall and blasting a hole larger than his head showering him with sparks from the mini explosion.

Instinctively, Tchercovic dropped to one knee spinning

and around drawing his sidearm, all in one motion. Holding the Sig P996 out in both hands, arms outstretched, he was ready to return fire but what he saw stopped him.

"That's the only warning shot you get. Drop your weapon and put your hands on your head, or I fire," said the Marine as he aimed his assault rifle at him, the blast burn on his body armour hidden by how he held and aimed the assault rifle.

What stopped him though was the sight of Stryder standing at his shoulder, the hole in his bloodstained shirt showing the flesh beneath, clean and unblemished.

But if the shirt was showing signs of being hit, the hole with the singed edges, the blood spatters, why wasn't the man wearing it showing the same?

The only explanation was that the serum worked, and a hell of a lot better than expected, which made it more important than ever that he get away with the data.

But first he had to get rid of these two. Knowing the Marine would not dare fire on him gave him an edge. By now they must know that the reactor core was reaching critical and as they could not reverse it without his authorisation code, they needed him alive.

The Marine saw that Tchercovic was about to call his bluff and moved just in time as the first shot went past him. He knew as he pressed himself against the corridor wall, that the next time he wouldn't be so lucky.

Stryder cursed himself for not being armed. He saw the first shot miss and knew that if he didn't do something, the next shot would not.

He was not about to stand by and watch as his fellow Recon Delta Marine was gunned down in cold blood, but what could he do? He was unarmed, standing at least thirty-five metres from the shooter, but he knew he had to do something, anything.

The corridor was empty except for those three figures

and there was nothing he could utilise as a weapon. He was powerless, unable to stop what was about to happen and he felt a rage, fuelled by frustration build up inside him as he watched Tchercovic/Howard bring his sidearm to bear on his target.

He could stand it no longer; he had to do something. He hurled himself at the shooter in an act of sheer desperation, yet one that worked. He covered the distance in one single leap cannoning into Tchercovic, sending them both crashing to the floor.

The Marine couldn't believe his eyes as he saw Stryder leap at the shooter and land on him. He was so amazed at the sight he almost dropped his assault rifle.

Stryder was the first to his feet, knocking the Sig from Tchercovic's hand, sending it spinning across the floor. The Black Knight repositioned himself, lying on his back, and then lashing out with both his feet at Stryder, striking him in the stomach. Stryder staggered backwards a few paces leaving room for his attacker to flip himself back onto his feet.

Facing each other, the two combatants had their guards up and were balanced lightly on the balls of their feet, ready to move.

The Black Knight was the first to attack, coming at Stryder with a clubbing right aimed at the top of his head.

A strange way to attack, thought Stryder as he blocked, grabbed the wrist, and twisted his hips into his attacker ready for the hip toss. Too late he realised why.

As Tchercovic allowed himself to be thrown, he landed right where he had intended, close enough to his sidearm to be able to grab it.

Snatching up the Sig, he turned to Stryder and fired a rapid two-shot burst aimed at the wall close to his head.

As the bolts struck the wall, the blast's impact showered

Stryder with sparks and pieces of shrapnel, forcing him to duck his head and cover it with his arms.

The Black Knight used the distraction as he had intended and sprinted past him.

"Damn!" shouted Stryder, angry with himself for being played like that and gave pursuit followed by the Marine.

They reached the docking bay just in time to see their quarry disappear through the open doorway.

Carefully, they followed him, mindful that he could be waiting to open fire on them from anywhere.

The docking bays were large, open plan chambers where cargo could be stored, either to be shipped out or after having been shipped in. At the far end was the hatch leading to the walkway umbilical that was attached to the ship, in this case Tchercovic's ship.

"Give it up Howard, you're not going anywhere," Stryder said, as the two of them crouched down behind several containers. He had hoped that their quarry would respond, thereby giving his position away. It seemed though, that he was too wily for that one to work.

From their position, over by the left hand side of the door, they could see quite clearly all the way to the large hatch. He was nowhere in sight.

If he wanted to escape to the waiting ship, he would have to go through this chamber. There would be no point in going to either of the two upper levels. Around the chamber above them, were balconies that were attached to the walls that gave some access from the decks above. Staircases strategically placed on the balconies linked them both with the floor.

It was inconceivable to think he would enter down here, only to leave on a deck above, when his transport was below.

No, he had to be here, somewhere, waiting to make his move.

~

The Recon Delta Marine, whose call sign was Cowboy, had located General Sinclair straight away but not before rousing the rest of the squad. They rendezvoused five minutes after they got the call, suited and booted.

"We need to evac the station a.s.a.p. What's your name son?" Sinclair asked once Cowboy arrived and apprised him of the situation regarding Stryder.

"Private John Wayne, sir, call sign Cowboy. Apparently my namesake made a few western movies back in the day," was the reply from the young man with the sparkling eyes, easy manner and even easier smile.

"Right, I need you to round up all the research staff and get them safely to the nearest docking bay. Take as many of your men as you need but I also want someone down in Engineering to help there, and the rest up here trying to regain access to the main computer. That must be a priority. Without access to the main computer no one gets off this station."

"You know your men, Cowboy. You allocate who you think is best suited to each task and I'll coordinate all your efforts from here, in Command and Control," Sinclair said.

The alarms would rouse the rest of the station personnel. He'd managed to activate them manually whilst Cowboy was waking his squad.

Cowboy, a little surprised to find himself in a position of authority, rose to the task, issuing orders to the rest of the squad. Moments later, they set off to complete their tasks leaving behind one Marine.

"What's your name son?" Sinclair asked.

"Private William Ives, sir, call sign Hacker," was the reply.

"No need to ask why, just get to it Hacker. Pick any

workstation you want, just get me access to the main computer," Sinclair barked.

"Aye, sir," Hacker replied, then headed for the Ops workstation and got to work. He sat down at the station and began to manually input commands via the manual interface at the same time monitoring the results via his NI. His eyes glazed over as his entire focus was on the task ahead. He became oblivious to everything that was happening around him as he lost himself in the virtual world of the computer.

Sinclair paced around the C and C deck like a caged tiger, feeling more and more ineffective. Everyone seemed to be doing something, everyone except him.

That was the burden of command he supposed, to make the decisions, to give the orders and to shoulder the blame, should it all go wrong.

In this instance though, if it all went wrong, countless lives would be lost. Not just those on the station but those opposing the Alliance, should they manage to put the research to good use.

He looked at the station chronometer above the large central view screen. Less than ten minutes left.

"Come on Stryder, it looks like it's all up to you son," he said quietly.

CHAPTER 5

Inside Docking Bay Six Stryder glanced at his chronometer.

"We've got less than ten minutes to find and subdue him before this station goes kablooey," he said to the Marine at his side.

"If time's running out for us, it's the same for him. He'll want to get to that ship pretty soon so he can escape before it does," he replied.

Again he scanned the floor area for possible hiding places but there were just too many. Over by the hatch to the right and left, were a group of cylindrical containers, similar to those they were hiding behind. Over by the left hand side of the chamber the loading vehicle was parked with its array of grabs, next to another group of containers. The right hand side of the chamber floor was littered with three more groups of containers.

Tchercovic could have been behind any one of them or even the loading vehicle, the eloquently titled Multi Grab and Lift Loading Vehicle. The staff simply called it the Loader.

"We'll soon be out of time, we need to do something fast. Make sure when you get the shot you take it, but remember, we need him alive so make sure your rifle's on a stun setting," Stryder said.

"Whoa! Hold on, what have you got in mind?" asked the Marine.

"I'm going to try and draw him out, so the second you see him, take him out, got that?" replied Stryder, getting himself ready to move.

He sprung out from behind the containers they were using for cover before the Marine could reply and ran towards the hatch.

Positioned behind a group of containers to the right of the hatch, Tchercovic saw Stryder come running towards him. He knew it was a ploy to draw him out but he thought he could use it against them. Time was running out, so he had to act fast.

Bringing up the Sig P996 to aim, he stood up and fired straight at Stryder.

The Marine saw the movement but Stryder's trajectory put him directly between him and his target, Tchercovic. He had no clear shot.

Stryder saw him get to his feet, weapon in hand, aimed directly at him. Instantly he knew the mistake he'd made, there was no way the Marine could get his shot off, he was directly in his line of fire. He saw the movement, heard the gunshot too late.

The blast struck him on his shoulder as he turned trying to avoid it.

As the gun went off, the Marine stood up, bringing his assault rifle up to his shoulder sighting down the barrel but just a millisecond too late, for as Stryder was hit and twisted out of his line of sight, Tchercovic fired a second time, almost a double tap, the two shots almost as one. The pulsed plasma bolt struck him in his chest again sending him backwards to collide with the wall, sending his assault rifle spinning from his hands. The special body armour he wore absorbed the impact of the bolt, which meant the energy in the charge didn't get through to him. However, the force of the impact was like being hit by a solid object at a thousand feet per second. That's what sent him crashing into the wall, his breath knocked out of him. For a moment he was unconscious, but a moment was all Tchercovic needed to make his escape.

With both men down, his way to the hatch and his escape were clear. Glancing at them, with a sneer of contempt on his face, he turned towards the hatch.

The pain from the plasma bolt was intense as it seared Stryder's flesh. He had tried to ride it, twist out of the way, but even though he knew his reflexes had increased he was still not agile enough to dodge something that fast. He hit the floor, not only in pain from being shot, but from knowing he'd failed. Being shot at such close range meant he would go into shock, lose consciousness and most probably die. There was no way he could stop Tchercovic now. He had failed and everyone on the station would die.

Even as those thoughts were going through his mind, so was another thought, a realisation … the pain was fading.

Stryder hit the floor, heard the second shot and knew the Marine had been hit. He just hoped it wasn't a headshot.

He glanced up and saw Tchercovic walking casually towards the hatch, like he hadn't a care in the world, which at that point, he hadn't.

Remarkably the pain was receding and as he looked down at his wound, Stryder saw again that his body was repairing itself.

The consequences of this, the potential, was beyond his imagination at that moment. All he could think of was that he still had a chance to stop him, a chance to avert a certain disaster and save the lives of everyone on board the station. Sorting out the ramifications of his new ability could wait until everyone was safe.

After getting to his feet, Stryder strode after the figure disappearing through the hatch, feeling stronger with every step.

~

Back in the C and C, Sinclair was still pacing across the deck. As he glanced at the chronometer, he realised they had less than five minutes remaining before the station's reactor core went critical and blew them all to Hell and back.

Stopping at the ops station he said, "Hacker, what's your status son?" his voice calm as always, although that was the exact opposite of how he felt.

Without lifting his eyes from his task Hacker said, "Sir, I think I may have something. He's good, he's very good but then so are we. He's locked the main computer into a ..."

"Son, the short version," interrupted Sinclair.

"I've managed to gain partial access. I can now access Engineering and return control to them, sir," Hacker replied.

"Do it," Sinclair ordered. Then through the NI said, "Engineering we're about to return computer control to you. Reverse the reactor to normal parameters immediately. Advise us of your progress, Sinclair out."

To Hacker he said, "Good work son, now see what you can do about freeing the docking bays, we're not out of the woods, just yet."

"I'm on it, sir," Hacker replied as he continued to work feverishly at his console, his shoulders relaxing slightly with the knowledge that the main threat had been averted.

"Engineering here, sir, we've managed to get the reactor

back under control. It was close, damn close, sir. Another thirty seconds and no matter what we did it would've blown," said the voice of the Chief Engineer, his voice breathless with relief at them pulling back from the brink of disaster.

"What's your status now then Chief?" Sinclair asked.

"All reactor levels are dropping back down to normal now, sir. We should have things back on track within the hour. I would suggest that we take all non-essential systems offline for the time being sir, so that I can run a full diagnostic on the reactor, just to be safe."

"Good idea Chief, but I'm afraid we have a situation here that requires all the station's resources. It should be cleared up in the next few minutes though, and as soon as it is, I'll inform you and you can go ahead. Good work Chief, Sinclair out."

Sinclair stood erect, his back ramrod stiff, showing no sign of the tension he had been feeling. Just a few loose ends to tie up then we can all relax he mused. The biggest loose end of them all though, was Tchercovic. They might not need his access code anymore but he was still in possession of the project data. Until that was either returned or destroyed, they were all still at risk.

"Cancel the Red Alert, Hacker," he said and the alarms were cut.

CHAPTER 6

Stryder followed Tchercovic through the hatch. He saw him go through the outer hatch into the walkway umbilical that led to his ship, when suddenly the station's alarms went silent.

Startled by the sudden quiet Tchercovic spun around and saw Stryder standing there, large as life in spite of having been shot twice.

Stryder's NI tingled and he said, "Kind of busy right now."

Sinclair's voice came through clear, as he said, "We've managed to regain control of the computer and reversed the reactor from going critical. You just need to retrieve the project data now."

"I'm on it, sir," Stryder replied. He smiled because some of the pressure was off, although his task was still far from easy. He was still facing a determined, armed enemy with no means of defending himself. It could get interesting.

"I had no doubt that you would be able to crack my code, although I never thought you'd have had the time," Tchercovic said, bringing up the Sig P996 to point directly at

Stryder. "No matter, I've got what I need, and there's nothing you can do to stop me," he added.

"You've shot me twice Howard, and I'm still here, so there seems to be nothing you can do to stop me," Stryder replied.

"Is that a fact? Perhaps a headshot might stop you. It should at least slow you down enough so I can reach my ship," Tchercovic said as he aimed the Sig carefully at Stryder's head.

The walkway umbilical was basically a tunnel. It was large enough for the loader to transport cargo from the docking bay to a waiting ship, or vice versa, but a tunnel nonetheless. There was effectively, nowhere for him to hide.

It had already been proven that he couldn't dodge the plasma bolts, so he knew he was in trouble.

His only chance lay in the fact that Tchercovic had said he would try for a head shot, the most difficult shot to make with a moving target. Even a marksman would find it tricky, as it was the smallest target to hit, so he planned to make it even more difficult for him.

Seeing it as his only option, he adopted a fighter's stance. Dancing from one foot to the other, his weight evenly distributed as he balanced lightly on the balls of his feet he began to bob and weave. He moved up and down, then left and right, presenting a frustratingly elusive target. Then he started to approach the Black Knight.

Tchercovic saw what Stryder was trying to do, so he fired.

His first shot missed, the plasma bolt searing the hair on Stryder's head as it passed harmlessly on the left. He fired again, more carefully this time and again it missed.

Stryder was getting closer with every shot; soon he would be within arm's reach. He had to stop him.

He fired again and again as he began to allow panic to set in. His aim became more and more erratic, and then finally, his battery clip was empty.

In desperation he threw the useless weapon the fifteen or so feet now separating them. Deftly Stryder caught the Sig in his right hand and tossed it straight back catching Tchercovic full in the face.

Stryder closed the distance between them before the Black Knight had recovered from the blow.

Stryder grabbed him by the front of his shirt then delivered a thunderous right punch, hitting him flush in the face. As his nose broke blood spurted out, cascading over his face and, for good measure, Stryder hit him again.

Releasing his grip, Stryder allowed him to fall to the floor stunned.

Quickly he searched his prone form and found the data card that was loaded with everything from the project. Getting up, he started to walk back towards the hatch.

Tchercovic began to revive and saw Stryder walking away. He knew he must have the data card and, seeing his Sig within reach, took his chance.

Picking up the fallen weapon and ejecting the spent battery clip, he inserted a fresh one from his back pocket and then pulled back on the slide to prime the clip. This gave him another twenty shots, which would be more than enough for what he needed.

Getting to his feet he prepared to shoot Stryder in the back.

Stryder heard the battery clip being ejected and another rammed up into the grip of the Sig. Then he heard someone shout, "DOWN!"

As Stryder dived for the floor a high energy plasma bolt shot over his head and struck Tchercovic full in the chest, throwing him several metres back towards the outer hatch on the walkway umbilical. Blood from his wound traced an arc through the air.

Stryder looked up and saw the Marine standing in the

doorway of the hatch sighting down the barrel of his assault rifle. As he brought the weapon down he looked at Stryder and smiled.

"The alarms went silent, which meant we were out of danger from the reactor core going critical and you were walking from him holding a data card. I assumed it safe to say you didn't need him alive any more. Was I right?" he said, his smile fading slightly.

Getting to his feet Stryder smiled and said, "You were right, and thanks."

"Stryder to General Sinclair, the data card has been retrieved and Howard is dead, sir," he said using his NI.

"Good work Captain, bring the data card here and I'll debrief you."

"Sir, can the debrief wait? I'd like to get back to bed," Stryder said.

Laughing, Sinclair said, "Okay Captain, I think you've earned it. See you at o eight hundred."

Stryder looked at the Marine. "I'm bushed. Hey, I never got your name."

"Captain Storm sir, call sign Guardian," said the Marine.

"Guardian?" Stryder enquired.

"Yes sir, my men gave it to me, said it was because I always looked out for them," Storm told him.

"Well, I can certainly vouch for that. Now if you'll excuse me, there's a pillow on my bunk that's got my name on it," Stryder said as he led the way out of the docking bay.

Over a thousand light years away, deep in the heart of Alliance space on the planet Dalos IV, one man was eagerly awaiting news from Research Station Five. That man was General Solon, late of the Black Knights, himself now head of Special Operations, which meant he was in charge of all covert missions against the Confederation.

Sitting at his desk, he was going through some mission reports. Still in his prime despite being over sixty years of age, he had been head of Special Operations for the past ten years. His hair was completely white, which was possibly the only indication of his true age. A face devoid of wrinkles, except those around the eyes, looked intently at the computer screen before him on his desk. Large fingers deftly worked the keypad controller as he scrolled through the reports.

He was a large man in every way, tall, standing at just over six feet six inches, and muscular. He had the physique of a weight lifter, still toned despite his age. He was undoubtedly courageous, being one of the most decorated soldiers in Alliance history. His nose was slightly askew, a feature he chose not to correct as it reminded him of all the battles he had fought over the years. He was an expert in close-quarter combat and, even now, practised daily. His eyes were slate grey and at times, cold, like those of a shark. A scar ran from his left eyebrow to the point of his cheekbone in a curved line, another testament to his many battles.

The door to his chambers opened and Captain Nokorovic walked in, a grave expression on his average features.

"Yes, Captain, what is it?" Solon asked, his deep bass voice booming out from his barrel chest.

"Sir, we've just received a coded transmission from our informant at Col Sec Headquarters," Nokorovic said, his normal voice sounding positively anaemic next to Solon's rich, textured, bass voice. Nokorovic was average in every way – looks, build and personality. It was a mystery how he got to be the great man's aid to everyone except the great man himself. Solon had heard of Nokorovic's undercover work for which his plain, mediocre appearance made him well suited. He had asked for him personally to be his aide, after his cover had been blown and he had become a known face to the analysts at Col Sec.

"And?" enquired Solon.

"There's been an incident at Research Station Five, sir. Tchercovic has been reported killed, sir."

"Killed, how?" Solon asked, a feeling of dread beginning to spread through him.

"They're saying it was an accident sir, but our informant says that they knew Tchercovic was a traitor. They don't know his true identity and they may never know. One good thing's come out of this though, sir."

"What's that?" Solon asked, hoping for something, anything, positive to come out of this debacle.

"Col Sec has abandoned the project sir. It seems it's too dangerous to pursue any further."

"And do you honestly believe that Captain? It's more likely that they were successful. Find out all you can about this project from our informant. If they were successful, I want to know. Find out the names of any surviving test subjects. If the informant can't tell us what we want, we'll go directly to the source and grab one of them."

"Aye sir, I'll get right on it."

~

Stryder lounged on his reclining chair on the front veranda of his house, which had a magnificent view of the bay below.

Over the past two weeks since his debrief and departure from Research Station Five after being granted permission for leave, his skin had darkened to a rich tan. His blond hair had lightened under the hot sun and his body had become stronger through his regular exercise routine, interspersed with hefty doses of relaxation.

The property he called home was a two-storey detached villa constructed of white brick. On the ground floor were the garage, kitchen, gym/armoury and utilities room, which housed spare equipment and also served as a laundry room. Upstairs the entire floor was given over to living space. There was a spacious lounge with glass patio doors opening out onto the veranda, and large enough to accommodate a table and chairs for a six-place setting, plus enough lounge chairs for the same. There were also four bedrooms, two bathrooms and a study.

Stryder had inherited it from his parents after a tragic road accident took their lives three years previously. They had all lived there together as a family. When his parents took early retirement after selling the family business for a hefty profit, they took to travelling in a luxurious ground car, until the day of the accident. Their car had been forced off the road by a driver who was on the run from the local Constabulary, causing them to fly off a cliffside road only to meet their death on the rocks below.

Out of all the locations they could have chosen this was the one they finally decided upon. Celeron was one of the first planets the Confederation had settled over three hundred years ago, and after terraforming it into the planet it was now, it had, over two centuries, developed a vibrant culture of its own.

Similar in climate to that of Earth, Celeron boasted four large landmasses surrounded by oceans. On the landmasses grew the two major cities, Jamestown and Jacksonville named after the original colony leaders.

Stryder's parents were born and raised in Jacksonville and his father had proposed to his mother where the villa now stood. That area of the coast had become an attraction for holidaymakers, not only from that planet but also from all over the Confederation.

Stryder was assailed with memories of his parents every time he returned there. It was almost as if their very essence imbued the place.

Whenever he felt he needed to recharge his batteries there was no other choice, he returned home every time.

That's how it had been this time. After the incident on Research Station Five and his realisation of how the project had altered him, he made a decision, one he had been thinking about ever since he returned home.

After retrieving the data card from the traitor Howard he began to wonder about the harm that data could do – not the good, but the harm.

If the Alliance knew it was still out there, to what lengths would they go to obtain it? If it were returned to Col Sec, would they develop more experiments like the one he'd endured to perfect the Super Soldier? Where would they stop? How far were they willing to go?

And then there was the effect it had had on him and would have, in the future. The Confederation would not leave him be if they knew the extent of the changes taking place in his metabolism. He would be forever under scrutiny, under examination or worse, some sort of super agent sent on covert ops where the chance of survival was usually nil, but now of course that had all changed.

That was why when Sinclair told him that all the data had been downloaded onto the card and deleted from the memory core, he told him that the card had been damaged and the data corrupted and therefore he had destroyed it.

Sinclair was furious, obviously, especially when Stryder told him that there had been no changes after the last run of tests he had undergone.

To all intents and purposes, the project was dead in the water.

He knew Sinclair didn't believe him, but his leave was granted anyway. Stryder knew that Sinclair still wanted him working for him, but he wanted him voluntarily and not having been coerced.

As he lounged on his veranda overlooking the coast, with the verdant blue seas and sailing boats below, he took out the data card and looked at it again. On the small table at his elbow was a long, cold drink that he lifted with his free hand and took a sip. It was white rum and pineapple juice over a mound of ice cubes. Savouring the taste of the blended flavours he pondered the small object in his other hand.

What should he do with it? Should he return it so they could continue their research and take the consequences, or destroy it as he had said?

There were potential advances in medicine to be gained from this research. Many lives would be saved if they could harness it, but also, as with any great discovery, there was an equal potential for harm.

It was a dilemma that had plagued him this past fortnight. He was no closer to an answer now, than he had been at the start.

"Hello in there. Is there anyone home?" said a female voice from below the veranda.

Hurriedly putting the data card away in the pocket of his shorts, Stryder got to his feet and went to the railing at the edge of the veranda.

Wandering around below, looking about her was a young woman. As she turned to look up she wore an expression of frustration on her lovely face.

She was tall, standing around five feet ten, with an athletic figure and a full bosom. She was wearing a tight, low-cut white tee shirt and khaki shorts that showed off her shapely legs. On her feet she wore open sandals. She was dark skinned and her complexion was almost perfect.

Her dark eyes were like limpid pools in which a man could drown, given time. Although dark skinned, her nose was slender rather than squat and her lips were full and sensuous. Her hair was braided, long and pulled back from around her face and tied off at the nape of her neck.

When she spoke her voice was soft and smooth as silk.

She said, "Hello, can you help me please, I seem to be lost?"

Although she was asking for help, he got the impression that this was a situation she was unaccustomed to. She gave off the air of being very self-sufficient.

"Certainly, hold on I'll be right down," Stryder said. As he passed through the lounge he made a quick detour to his wall safe where he deposited the data card. Then he continued to the staircase, which would take him down to the front door below the veranda.

As he opened the door she was facing the other way, her back to him as she took in the amazing view.

"Hi," he said. As she turned he added, "I'm Kurt Stryder, please come in. Can I offer you something to drink?"

"Thank you, but it's really not necessary. I just need you to point me in the right direction," she replied.

"If I can, I will, but first some refreshment to speed you on your way, Miss err…?"

"If you insist, my name's Zara Hardy," she said reluctantly, stepping into the villa.

"There's no need to worry Miss Hardy, I don't bite," Stryder said with a smile, as he followed her back inside.

He indicated for her to go upstairs and when she reached the top of the landing she said, "Very nice Mister Stryder."

"My friends call me Kurt," he said coming to stand next to her.

"But I hardly know you," she replied coyly, smiling at her host.

"Well, let me get you that drink and we can rectify that now, can't we?" he said going over to the mini bar by the wall.

He poured two fingers of white rum into a tall glass tumbler then poured a good measure of pineapple juice over it topping it off with a handful of ice cubes.

"There you go, that should refresh you a little," he said as he handed her the drink.

After tasting it she said, "Very nice."

"Join me," he said as he walked through onto the veranda. She followed him and took the offered seat next to his.

"Now this is very nice. You'll have to be careful Mister Stryder, I may not want to leave," she said smiling.

"Kurt, call me Kurt," he insisted.

"Okay, Kurt," she agreed with a nod of her head.

"Tell me where you're looking for?" he asked.

"I'm actually trying to find my way back to Jacksonville, but I must've taken a wrong turning somewhere along the way."

"Jacksonville's not that far away actually I'll give you directions when we've finished these drinks and you can be on your way."

"Thank you, I appreciate it, really. If I can ever repay the favour, you only have to ask."

"That implies that we'll keep in touch, or is it one of those gestures that people make just to be polite but that they never intend to keep?" Stryder asked. Then after a short pause he added, "I'm sorry, I put you on the spot there."

"No, it's fine, honestly, and no, it wasn't an empty gesture," she replied.

"Okay then, how about dinner tonight? I know of a wonderful restaurant. You tell me where you're staying and I'll pick you up at, say eight. How's that sound?"

Smiling broadly she said, "That sounds great. I'm staying at the Wyatt Hotel, room 3121."

"It's a date then," he said. Then he stopped what he was doing abruptly, his drink halfway to his mouth, all his senses on overdrive. Something was not quite right. He'd heard something that had alerted him, but to what? He wasn't quite sure; it just felt wrong somehow.

"Are you okay?" Zara asked becoming concerned at his sudden change of mood.

"It's nothing," he said, not wanting to alarm her. It was then that the danger presented itself in the form of three armed men; all dressed in black from head to toe and armed with Arnov mini assault pistols. They had rushed upstairs and were in the middle of the lounge aiming their Arnov's straight at Kurt and Zara.

"No one needs to get hurt here. If you just do as we say then it'll be over before you know it. Slowly, put your hands on your head, you're coming with us," said the gunman in the middle.

"It seems that dinner may be delayed a little," Stryder said calmly.

CHAPTER 8

"You, Stryder, are coming with us," said the leader of the trio.

"Okay, that's fine by me, as long as you allow the girl to leave unharmed," Stryder said calmly yet assertively.

"I can't do that I'm afraid."

"Why not? She only just arrived, she's lost, came here for directions. Whatever this is about, she's not part of it and is no threat to you," Stryder argued hoping they would let her go.

"Do you expect me to believe that? How cosy you two are, yet you say you've only just met? I don't think so," countered the leader of the gunmen with a sneer.

"Then what do you intend to do?" Stryder asked, probing to learn just how much trouble they were in.

"My orders are to bring you along, it says nothing about your friend here," was the reply. Stryder wasn't about to leave it there; it was too non-committal.

"Well, if you can't let her go, there's only one other option. Think about it, if she's lost that means someone's waiting for her. If she turns up dead then the authorities will be all over you like a rash, not only that but Col Sec too. You do know who I am and why they told you to snatch me, don't you?" he said.

Glances were exchanged between the other two gunmen. When the enormity of what they were involved in struck home, the leader spoke, having thought it through.

"My orders never said anything about killing anyone, so it looks like you're coming too Missy. I'll let them sort out what to do with you later. I'm not getting paid enough for all this shit," he said.

"I knew I should never have accepted that offer of a drink," Zara said in a tense voice.

Stryder turned to look at her, stared into her eyes then said, "Don't worry, this is going to be fine, trust me. You don't think I'm going to let you get out of our dinner date that easily do you?" He smiled and saw some of the tension in her eyes smooth away a little.

"Very touching, but before you two lovebirds can get to that dinner date, we have the little matter of … what was it again … oh yes, you're coming with us. Now move it," the gunman said sarcastically.

"You're a funny guy, I just might tell my boss to go easy on you," Stryder countered.

Prodding him in the back with the mini assault pistol the gunman barked, "I said move it!"

"I said I might tell him to go easy on you, that could change you know," Stryder said.

The gunman stepped in front of him and gave him a slashing blow across the face with his pistol. The blow opened up a cut on Stryder's left cheek.

"That's just in case you forgot who's in charge here. Now move," said the gunman.

"I've changed my mind," Stryder said.

"Oh, really."

"Yep, you… I'll kill you myself," Stryder said and his eyes bore into the gunman's letting him know that there was no doubt in his mind he would carry out his threat. He froze beneath the stare and a moment later, when he regained his composure he smiled, a little more nervously this time. He waved his pistol in front of Stryder then beckoned towards the stairs for them to leave.

Zara said, "Are you always such a hothead?"

"We'll be fine, trust me," he replied.

"You keep saying that," she said. She stopped abruptly when she spotted something that made her catch her breath.

The cut on Kurt's face healed almost immediately and the lead gunman saw it too. He leaned in closer to get a better view, unable to believe his eyes, saying, "What the fuck?" and that's when Stryder made his move.

As the gunman leaned in, his guard was momentarily down. Stryder and Hardy, as instructed, had their hands on top of their heads. Stryder hit the gunman on the side of his face with a thunderous right cross from the top of his head that travelled downwards at a forty-five degree angle. He twisted his hips as he delivered the punch to put maximum force into it.

The gunman's head was snapped sideways viciously as the blow connected and, as he was leaning forwards, had no chance to either cover up or ride it. The force of the punch stunned him causing him to rock back on his heels. His eyes rolled up inside his sockets as his senses left him.

Stryder grabbed the mini assault pistol from his grasp before the gunman fell to the floor, out cold.

Bringing up the Arnov, he strafed the other two gunmen before they had a chance to react.

The burst of plasma fire caught the gunmen across the chest sending each one flying backwards in a mist of blood as the bolts tore up their bodies.

They were dead before they hit the floor.

Quickly Stryder went over to them to check their vitals. Reaching down to each one he felt for the pulse in their necks. Finding none and satisfied they posed no further threat, he returned to the first gunman who was beginning to recover from the punch to the head. Hardy had watched the events of the last few moments without so much as a flicker and, as Stryder was checking the two dead gunmen said, "Wow, you're good."

Stryder stood over the prone gunman watching intently as he showed signs of recovery and, without taking his eyes off him, said, "Thanks. You're a cool customer yourself. What are you really doing here?"

"I don't know what you mean," she said remaining composed.

"What are you, local Constabulary, Col Sec, Recon Delta? We've just been confronted by three armed men. You watched me neutralise one, and then take the other two out without as much as a gasp. No screams, no histrionics, why is that do you think? If you were who you said you were, just a passing tourist looking for directions, then surely what just happened here would've caused you at least some concern, unless you are used to being 'under fire' as it were?" Stryder said as he stood astride the gunman. As he began to move a bit more, Stryder placed his right foot between his shoulder blades and holding the Arnov in his right hand, pressed the muzzle against the back of the intruder's skull.

"Don't move," he said. Then, secure in the knowledge the gunman was, for the moment under control, he turned his head to look at her.

"Well, who sent you?" he asked.

As he looked at her he watched her expression change suddenly from blank to surprised and he knew immediately that something had happened behind him.

He turned to see two more gunmen had reached the top of the stairs. Armed also with Arnovs, they were preparing to fire.

Stryder brought the Arnov he was holding up as fast as he could and let loose a burst of plasma fire. Never expecting to hit them, the salvo had the desired effect of making the newcomers retreat down the stairs using the wall for cover.

"Quick move!" ordered Stryder as he struck the gunman at his feet to the head with the pistol to prevent him following. Pushing Hardy towards the veranda he quickly closed the patio doors behind them.

"Oh great, that'll stop 'em," she said.

"Toughened glass," he replied.

"Where do we go from here?" she asked becoming uneasy, thinking they were trapped with no cover.

"We jump," Stryder said and headed for the railing. He climbed over it and facing away from the house prepared to jump to the ground some fifteen feet below.

"Are you crazy?" she asked her voice going up an octave. Just then plasma fire struck the patio doors as the gunmen fired at them.

"A little, yes," Stryder replied then jumped.

"Oh shit!" she exclaimed as she followed him over the railing. She steadied herself, and then also jumped.

Stryder dropped the fifteen feet with his feet together and on landing, allowed his legs to bend at the knees to absorb the impact, then rolled as he had been taught by his parachute instructor back in basic training.

Getting to his feet as quickly as he could, he prepared to help Hardy on her landing which he had no doubt she would make with no trouble at all. He had detected within a very short time an iron resolve in the young woman.

She followed him to the floor and, making a landing

similar to his, got to her feet with only a little urging from him.

"Okay, where to now?" she asked hurriedly. It seemed to her that they had only delayed the inevitable.

"Now we get out of here," he replied walking to a door that at first she hadn't seen.

Stryder placed his hand to what, at first glance, seemed to be part of the design on the wall. A light shone beneath as a sensor read his palm print. One section of the wall slid upwards and around the inside of the ceiling of the chamber it revealed.

"Impressive," Hardy conceded as she followed him inside the spacious garage. Stryder was climbing inside the driver's console of the vehicle on the right. Of the two vehicles inside the garage this one looked the fastest. It was a bright red CIV sports hatch, one of the fastest vehicles on the road. The Celeron Independent Vehicles sports hatch was capable of speeds up to two hundred miles an hour.

Hardy got into the passenger seat alongside Stryder who had already primed the fuel cell that powered the sleek ground car.

"Hold on," he said as the engine roared into life and as he pressed the accelerator the sports hatch sped out of the garage.

Hardy was pressed back into the racing-style bucket seat as the sports hatch left the confines of the garage. It slammed sideways as Stryder threw the car into a power slide navigating a tight turn along the narrow track that led onto the road that ran past his villa.

She reached for the harness and strapped it on once the car was going in a straight line again.

As the car sped past the front of his villa, Stryder saw the other two gunmen exit his home, followed rather groggily by the leader of the first group. They got into a CIV Marauder

SUV and sped after them, tyres spinning on the track until they gained the proper purchase needed from the road.

"What happens now?" Hardy asked, her voice calm despite the tension of the situation.

"We get away, then figure out who those thugs are and who sent them," Stryder said as he concentrated on his driving. The road was narrow, twisting and therefore inherently dangerous.

There was a small coastal town a few miles from the villa, after which the road widened to three lanes before it reached Jacksonville.

"I never saw your ground car as we left my villa," he said not looking at her.

"It was up the track some distance away," she replied.

"You never answered my question. Who sent you?" he asked again.

"Are you always this suspicious of callers asking for directions?" she countered.

Stryder glanced at her, and then returned his concentration to the road ahead. It was obvious to him that he would not learn much from her if he pushed too hard. Ahead of them was the small town of Haven. It stretched out along the coast with an array of shops and restaurants, many of the latter actually on the beach.

The main narrow road snaked its way through the town with several streets branching off and leading farther inland.

They were a few hundred feet from the town's limits when plasma fire struck the rear compartment of the sports hatch.

"They are getting serious about us not getting away," Hardy said, becoming concerned when the plasma fire made the car buck and stutter across the narrow road.

"Losing some of their team has a tendency to do that," Stryder replied.

He corrected his steering towards Haven and once more plasma fire rocked their car.

"Now they're beginning to piss me off," Stryder snarled.

"But what can we do about them?" Hardy asked.

"This," Stryder said, and grabbing the emergency brake, he pulled it on and spun the wheel throwing the car into a sideways skid which he controlled perfectly, bringing the car to a stop across the road and effectively blocking it.

He opened the glove box and reached inside to find a Sig P996 before opening the driver's door and tumbling out of the vehicle.

"Come on," he told Hardy and quickly she unfastened her harness and climbed out after him.

The following SUV just had time to screech to a halt to avoid slamming into Stryder's vehicle. The three gunmen tumbled out of the SUV still holding their Arnov mini assault pistols.

Stryder by that time had positioned himself at the side of his car using it as cover. He stood with his arms outstretched on top of the sports hatch holding the Sig in a two-handed grip resting his arms on the roof of the car to steady his aim.

Having already checked and primed the battery clip in the Sig, he was ready to rock and roll.

Once the gunmen appeared out of the SUV he didn't give them any warning. They had already opened the hostilities so he simply aimed and fired a two-shot burst at each gunman.

The full power pulsed plasma bolts struck each gunman in the face knocking them backwards in a mist of blood as their heads were obliterated.

They were dead before they hit the ground.

"Remind me never to piss you off," Hardy said as she looked across at him.

He smiled at her when he saw her reaction to the cold

way he had dispatched the three chasing gunmen and then said, "We're going to have some trouble explaining this little incident to the local Constabulary."

"I agree," she said looking across at the SUV and the three dead bodies lying there.

"As much as I hate to admit it I think we're going to need some help with this," he said activating his NI.

CHAPTER 9

After he made the call and put Sinclair in the picture as to what had happened, Stryder returned to the villa along with Hardy to await the arrival of the clean up squad.

The clean up squad was split into two teams. The first team dealt with the most urgent issue of an abandoned SUV with three dead bodies alongside it on the road just outside one of the most popular resort towns on the planet and everything that entailed, whilst the second team went directly to the villa where they found Stryder and Hardy waiting patiently.

The team, consisting of four men, entered the lounge and fanned out to reveal a fifth member, General Sinclair.

Stryder was standing on the veranda, the blast-scarred patio doors wide open to allow the smell of death to escape, leaning against the railing his back to the ocean, his powerful arms folded across his chest. When he saw them arrive he smiled and said, "Why am I not surprised?"

"Afternoon Kurt, seems you've had a busy day," Sinclair said smiling.

"General, I should've expected you to show up soon, especially considering all the trouble you went to placing Hardy here," Stryder said.

Looking down at the two dead bodies Sinclair said, "Any idea who these people were or who sent them?"

"None, sir. Why did you send Hardy to keep tabs on me?" he asked after leaving the veranda to stand next to the General.

"Who?" asked Sinclair in his dull monotone voice, giving nothing away.

"The young girl over there. You might as well tell me General. She's good from what I've seen so far. Now we can play games with this if you want; I can pretend it's purely coincidence when I keep running into her over the next few days until this is sorted. Or you could recall her, and try with someone else. Or you could come clean and leave her with me and the two of us could work together, it's your call."

Sinclair glanced at Hardy, then back at Stryder. Placing the girl on Celeron had been a hasty decision, he had to admit, but one that he had been forced to make. He had wanted her to get to know Kurt before the Alliance made their move. She was supposed to act as his back up and as a liaison to Sinclair personally, should they have trouble keeping tabs on him. The attempt to take Kurt out came as a bit of a surprise to them all. His plans had not taken root and now it seemed were in danger of unravelling. It went against his best instincts but he came to a decision.

"Okay, she can stay."

"What's Hardy's security clearance for this, sir, has she been briefed on the project?" Stryder replied, remaining where he stood. Hardy was sitting on a lounger on the far side of the veranda out of earshot, nervously clasping her hands as if unsure what to do with them.

Sinclair barked a few instructions at the clean up team

then walked out onto the veranda leaving them to get on with their work.

"Not thoroughly," he said as he came and sat next to her.

"Don't you think you should, considering you sent her to keep tabs on me?" Stryder said following the General onto the veranda.

Hardy looked up at Stryder and a hint of a smile fleetingly crossed her lips, which she quickly suppressed.

"Excuse me?" she said, keeping to her cover story as she looked from Stryder to Sinclair.

Sinclair gave an almost imperceptible nod of his head, which told her that the game was up. "It's okay Miss Hardy, he knows the truth," he said.

"Are you ordering me to stay, sir?" she asked.

"I've already told you that you won't get out of our dinner date so easily," Stryder said with a smile.

She looked away turning her gaze to the floor and still trying to process what she had seen earlier. Had she really seen Stryder's face heal in the blink of an eye, or was it just a figment of her imagination brought on by the adrenalin rush of the action? She had an idea that whatever it was she had been ordered into was something strange and that she would soon learn what she needed to know.

"Yes, I suppose so, seeing as you're in place and that you two seem to be getting along. Kurt, I authorise you to bring her up to speed," Sinclair said.

"Okay then, well in that case we have to consider that the Alliance had something to do with these guys. I mean they would've learnt fairly quickly that Howard was dead and it wouldn't take much for them to learn that the project had been abandoned."

"And what, you think they sent someone to find out if that was true?" Sinclair probed raising an eyebrow.

"Most definitely. Who else was on the project they could

get near to? All the technical staff have been reassigned, the other test subjects have died, so that just leaves me, and I'm at home on leave. You don't have to be a genius to work that one out, sir."

"I'm glad to see your thinking processes weren't damaged by the project," Sinclair said. Stryder smiled then said, "But of course you already came to that conclusion, hence Hardy being here."

"Just needed to see if you'd figured it out as well," Sinclair said with a hint of a smile, then added, "Have you figured out what their plan was?"

"They were ordered to take me some place where presumably whoever was paying them would take me off their hands. From what I can gather they were expecting me to be on my own; they were thrown a little by Hardy being here, but I got them to concede they were just ordered to make a smash and grab. The weapons were just to intimidate. When I told them it would be foolish to kill her, they said that their orders didn't include killing anyone, but that they'd take her along and let whoever was paying them decide her fate. It was only when I pushed them that the weapons came into play, when they had no other choice."

"So whoever paid them is going to be rather upset that they got stiffed on the deal," Sinclair said with a smile.

"Upset is putting it mildly I'd say, and I would expect them to try again. I can't imagine them giving up just like that. If it *was* the Alliance, they will have to verify our claims."

"That puts you two in the firing line. I'll assign a detail to watch over you," Sinclair said.

"That won't be necessary, sir. I know somewhere we can go and be safe," Stryder said with a wave of his hand.

"Do you think that's wise Captain?"

"I think it would be best if we appear to act as normal as possible, sir. If the Alliance send anyone else, seeing a team protecting us will tell them two things – firstly that we need protecting because the project worked, and secondly, that we're on to them. If we act normally, carry on as if it was just a burglary that failed, we get to draw them in and force them to make another move. Then we nail them."

"I'm sorry, Captain, I cannot allow that to happen."

"And why not, sir, might I ask?"

"You know the reason; you're a soldier with the Confederation Recon Delta for heaven's sake. If that wasn't enough, your knowledge of the project makes you a very valuable asset and one I cannot allow to be taken captive by a hostile force."

"Damn it, I knew this would happen. I'm no longer Kurt Stryder. Now I'm a commodity, an asset. Well I quit. I formally tender my resignation sir, effective forthwith. As of this instant, General, I'm a civilian."

"Okay, if that's how you want it. I'll order the team to put the bodies back, and I'll inform the local Constabulary you're ready to make a statement about them and those you killed up the road. Hardy, you're with me. Seems we're no longer needed here!" Sinclair said and turned to leave.

"Do you really want me to make a statement with all the juicy facts about the project I'll be forced to divulge under oath?" Stryder asked. They each knew the other was bluffing but neither could or would back down. It was left to Hardy to come up with the answer.

"Sir, what if I went along with the Captain here to his secure place? I could send you sit-reps through the NI via an encoded channel. That way you don't have to worry about him going rogue on you and you'll be informed of our situation. Kurt gets his freedom and you keep a modicum of control, so everyone wins."

"Okay with me," Stryder said, knowing that Sinclair would be more likely to agree if he agreed first, giving the

General the final say and not making it appear that he had given in; diplomacy.

Sinclair stopped, turned around to face them and said, "Okay, but you have to keep the sit reps coming in on time. We'll process these goons and see if we can't learn something from them. It's fifteen hundred now, let's say you make your first sit rep when you arrive at your destination then every twenty-four hours thereafter," and without waiting for a reply he turned and left the room.

Hardy turned to Stryder and joined him at the railing.

"Well, that was easy," she said. "Never thought he'd go for it. I thought he'd want to know where we are at all times," she added.

"He will," Stryder replied.

She looked at him and smiled as the realisation dawned on her.

"Our implants," she said. All Recon Delta Marines NIs were fitted with a nano chip homer initiated straight out of Basic. The chips could only be read by certain sensors; something the Alliance had not been able to crack.

"He knew there was nowhere we could go without him knowing exactly where we are," Stryder said.

"We just got played," she said, beginning to realise why Sinclair was so highly respected.

"Oh yes, the General is indeed a master of the game," Stryder said. There was something else he had wondered about again came to mind, which was, how had the project affected his implant? Had it affected his implant? Was that why Hardy had been sent to him with orders to keep him close? Were they finding it difficult to read his nanochip? It would make sense of Hardy's orders to stay as close as possible.

These thoughts he kept to himself for future reference. He might need to make use of that knowledge in the future, but for now he would act like he was unaware until he could test its validity.

"Come on, let's get moving," Stryder said.

He packed a few things into a travel grip and said, "What will you do for clothes?"

"I have some in a bag in my car not far from here, we can pick them up on the way," she replied.

"Okay, then let's go," he said and led the way downstairs to the garage.

"Are you thinking of taking the sports hatch? I mean, it's a little conspicuous, don't you think?" she asked.

"No, we'll be taking the ATV, it's possibly better suited for our needs," he replied.

When they entered the garage she noticed the ATV. The first time she had entered the garage under different circumstances all her attention had been focused on survival. This time though she was quite relaxed and noticed a lot more. She could see that the beautiful red machine Stryder had indicated was their way out of there.

The garage was just that, a garage. A room large enough for his two vehicles, with enough space around them should the need for any maintenance arise. In one corner was a workbench with an array of tools arranged on shelves and that was it. She noticed the garage didn't take up as much space as she'd imagined and wondered what else was on the ground floor.

Stryder noticed her expression and said, "I'll give you a proper tour of the villa when all this is over if you'd like?"

Hardy smiled when she realised he'd read her mind and said, "Yes thanks, I'd love that."

"Okay then, let's get moving," he replied and threw his travel grip into the rear compartment of his CIV Champion ATV and climbed aboard on the driver's side.

Hardy looked at the All-Terrain Vehicle they were going

to use. The CIV Champion was based on the military version called the Juggernaut, which was almost exactly what it was because once in motion it could handle almost any terrain. The Juggernaut was manufactured by the Rand Corporation, possibly the largest corporation in the Confederation who leased out patents to the manufacturers such as Celeron Independent Vehicles but retained control of the rights.

The Champion was not as large as its military counterpart, for there was no need for the troop carrying facility or weapons in the civilian version, but it could still seat seven comfortably. Sleeker than the Juggernaut, with more rounded edges, the Champion nonetheless still exuded power and stability and when Hardy climbed aboard and strapped herself into the large, comfortable front passenger seat, she felt safe.

Stryder turned to her and asked, "Ready?"

"As I'll ever be," she replied and actually found herself smiling. In spite of the danger they were in and all the threats to their safety they were about to face, she found herself enjoying it all. "Okay then, here we go," Stryder said as he gunned the powerful engine and pulled out of the garage.

CHAPTER 10

On Dalos IV, news of the failure to capture Stryder reached Captain Nokorovic, and he was furious. He'd, personally, picked the agent for the mission, and from these results he began to think his judgement might have been faulty.

If General Solon learned of this he would have his head, of that there was no doubt. He would have to see if this was salvageable before he informed the General.

As he sat at his desk pondering the situation, he reviewed his options. Undoubtedly this Captain Stryder and his new companion would have gone to ground somewhere they deemed safe. The asset he had in place had lost them and all the mercenaries he chose to use in his operation. This Stryder was fast becoming a serious pain in the ass and the harder he proved to capture, only bolstered the belief that perhaps the project had been a success after all.

If the asset on the ground couldn't locate them, then perhaps what they needed was some extra help.

It was well known that Recon Delta Marines were each implanted with a nanochip tracker, which, so far, Alliance technology couldn't duplicate or crack the codes enabling them to be tracked.

What he had in mind was risky but as he viewed his situation, he decided he had little choice.

Through his NI he accessed a secure comm channel and contacted Captain Pavel Temic.

Col Sec Headquarters was on Earth, the centre of the Confederation in New York. Over the last five centuries, the city had changed beyond all recognition, but Col Sec HQ was situated approximately where the old United Nations building used to be.

The HQ was a sprawling complex that stretched out over five city blocks. It had to be so vast because all Colonial business was conducted there. Its full name was actually the Colonial Confederations Headquarters. Col Sec, Colonial Security, the section that dealt with the security of the Confederation was, as the name implied, just a part of it and was situated below ground away from the prying eyes of everyday personnel and shielded from sensors.

Col Sec itself was divided into two sections: Starforce, which was entirely military, and Intelligence Division, which was staffed by members of Starforce but was completely separate.

General Sinclair was in charge of Intelligence Division.

The mole secreted inside HQ was Joanne Watkiss and she worked in Intelligence Division. At the age of fifty-four she had never been married, never seriously dated anyone and still lived at home with her parents. She concentrated on her work, important work, which gave her access to Top Secret files, as she was a senior aide to General Sinclair.

Thinking her life was exciting enough, something happened whilst on leave that proved she was wrong. She met a handsome stranger who swept her off her feet.

Being away from work on her annual vacation, she had let her guard down.

She was short at only five feet four, with a stocky build and dark hair and eyes in a face that was plain and therefore unaccustomed to having members of the opposite sex pay any attention to her. She was caught off guard one night when a tall, good-looking stranger asked if he could sit next to her at the bar. Thinking that he was waiting for someone, she agreed. When he struck up a conversation with her she was literally lost for words.

Totally charming, he soon put her at her ease and he introduced himself as David Grant. They spent a wonderfully relaxed evening, talking, laughing and she was quite surprised when she noticed the time was close to two in the morning. He, being the perfect gentleman, offered to see her to her room. Finding herself more than a little tipsy and in a euphoric mood, she agreed.

The night, of course, didn't end there though. At her door, not wanting what was possibly the best night of her life to end, she plucked up enough courage to ask him inside for a nightcap.

"I thought you'd never ask," he said his voice rich and husky.

Once inside any thoughts of a nightcap were quickly dispelled when he leant forward and kissed her on the lips. One thing led to another and soon they were in bed, their swiftly discarded clothes tangled on the floor.

That night she experienced what she had been missing for most of her adult life as he brought her expertly to orgasm after orgasm until, finally, they both drifted off to sleep, exhausted as dawn was breaking.

The rest of her vacation was much the same and by the time she had to return to work she was hooked.

Totally in love with a man she hardly knew, she found it

unbearable to be away from him. Nevertheless they parted and she went back to work dreaming of what might have been and waiting for the call he had promised to make, but somehow never did.

After three months of waiting she had reached the point where she'd decided that their time together had been one of those things she'd often heard about but never experienced – a holiday romance. She had resigned herself to the fact that she'd never see him again when he made the call.

They met and spent the night together in a hotel and she knew then that she would do anything, give anything, for it not to end.

By the morning he knew he had her.

David Grant was in fact Captain Pavel Temic of the Elysium Alliance.

He began to ask her about her work on their weekly trysts. At first it was general interest but before long the requests for data started, small insignificant details at first to test her. When she refused he failed to turn up for their next date. The following week, though, she was there waiting with exactly what he'd asked for.

Now over a year later they had worked up to Top Secret data and she was finding it more and more difficult to cover her tracks. When this last request came in, she knew she was in trouble.

His requests for data had become more and more difficult to get away with. Acquiring what her lover wanted was not the problem as being a senior aide to the head of Intelligence Division afforded her unlimited access to Top Secret material. No, the problem was concealing her tracks so that no one would be aware that the material had even been looked at, let alone stolen.

When Grant had asked her for the Recon Delta codes it

was towards the end of her working day so there was no chance to retrieve it from the computer, cover her tracks and pass the information on to him. She spent the night wondering about the consequences of her actions over the last few months. Passing on data about the project being conducted on Outpost Station Five had been a blessing and afforded her a full weekend of uninhibited sex with no thought or concern of the consequences. Later she learned that all but one of the test subjects had died. That wasn't her fault, surely?

She was no fool, she soon became aware that her beloved David Grant had ties to the Alliance, but by that time she was past caring.

Then he asked for the whereabouts of Captain Stryder, the only survivor of the project, which she knew from various reports, had been deemed a failure. But she also knew of Sinclair's doubts, a little fact she had kept from Grant. *Why was that?* She often wondered. *Had her conscience started to reaffirm itself?*

The attack on Stryder at his home could only have meant one thing; that it was directly due to her passing on his whereabouts to Grant, of that she was now certain. It was the first time she had been confronted with the consequences of her actions. Those consequences almost cost the lives of Stryder and Hardy, the young Marine they sent to keep tabs on him, and did cost the lives of five men who tried to capture them.

Where would it end?

Wracked with guilt she decided not to pass on the information.

Out of habit, when the opportunity arose, being left alone at a terminal, she searched for and then downloaded the data onto a data card.

Having arranged to meet him for lunch she barely made it

in time. She was determined to tell him, face to face, that this was a request she couldn't fulfil.

One look into his eyes though and she melted as usual and handed over the data card. The sex that followed was great, as always, but when she returned to work the guilt returned and she spent an hour in the toilet crying.

When someone found her in such a state she hurriedly made up the excuse that she'd had some bad news about a relative and was sent home.

As soon as Watkiss left the hotel room, Temic passed the codes onto Nokorovic via an encoded subspace burst transmission.

On receiving the data, Nokorovic smiled with relief. Now he had something of value to pass onto General Solon, which would counter balance the abortive snatch attempt on Stryder.

Now, no matter where the elusive Captain went, they would find him and this time they would capture him.

Nothing would stop them now.

CHAPTER 11

The asset stationed on Celeron, Captain Pavel Norsky, was awaiting further instructions from Nokorovic. He was in his early thirties, what was known as a fast track officer, and hoped to be a major at the end of his mission there. He was tall, lean and handsome with black wavy hair and dark flashing eyes. His looks and easy charming manner had secured him a position in bed with many of the opposite sex.

He had come to Celeron posing as a trade negotiator who was mixing business with a little pleasure. In that way he could warrant his frequent visits into Jacksonville to recruit the troops he thought he might require and his visits to Haven, the local tourist resort. The decision to recruit local muscle rather than import some with him was a sound one at the time. Local muscle worked for money and was already on site, whereas to import some with him threw up more problems, such as having to deal with customs. What he hadn't considered, though, was just how good Stryder turned out to be.

When he received no contact from his team, he had to

figure the worst. Waiting at the rendezvous point at the other side of Haven, he learned of the failure through the local news report of an accident that had occurred on the road to the resort. The local Constabulary presumed: *the three dead men found at the scene had been killed by rival gangs and an investigation was underway.* He knew at once that Col Sec had doctored that statement having pulled a few strings with the Constabulary.

Although the failure was no fault of his, he knew it would be viewed as such due to his choice of agents.

There was nothing he could do but wait for further instructions. Having driven past the villa and finding it deserted, he knew Stryder had gone to ground and would be more than a little difficult to find, especially as Col Sec would be keeping a close guard on him. They might have even taken him off world; there was no way of knowing.

So he decided to concentrate on the second portion of his cover story, relax, take in some sun and behave like a tourist. Enjoy it while he could for he knew it could not last.

~

Stryder drove the CIV Champion farther up into the hills overlooking Haven down below on the coast. Hardy had picked up her things from her rental car on the way and sat back with no idea where he was taking her and with no other recourse than to sit back and enjoy the ride.

"Where are we going?" Hardy asked after half an hour of driving. Stryder had been quiet the entire time and she wasn't sure if it was because he was concentrating on driving the large ATV or because he was working on some strategy.

"As you probably know, all Confederation worlds have safe locations which only certain personnel get to know about," he replied.

"You're referring to the Col Sec safe house."

"Yes, there are four on Celeron, two in Jacksonville and two in Jamestown."

"We're going to one of those?"

"Yes, for tonight, until I can think this through."

"So that's your secret place; why didn't you tell Sinclair?"

"Because I honestly expected to be on the run and didn't want him to know I'd be using Col Sec facilities."

"But with the nanochip tracer he'd have known anyway."

"Yes, but by the time he'd sent anyone there I'd have gone."

"That was your plan?" Hardy said, her voice dripping with sarcasm.

"Don't start, I'm making this up as I go," Stryder countered.

Hardy just shook her head, "We're doomed."

Stryder glanced across at her then concentrated on getting them to the safe house. *Not far now*, he thought.

By the time they reached Jacksonville it was getting dark. The safe house was in a quiet district on the outskirts of the main metropolis. All the houses were well tended in that neighbourhood and had sufficient space around them so that they were not overlooked on either side. Privacy was the watchword there and it seemed everyone who lived there observed it.

There were no families, no children running around playing in the street, which also meant no prying eyes from inquisitive youngsters. The owners of each property, mostly business people, young professionals or military types, had all been checked out by Col Sec before a decision was made to use the property, to ensure they would most likely keep themselves to themselves.

When Stryder drove up to the large wrought iron gates barring the driveway, he operated the remote code through his NI, activating the lock mechanism. The gates swung open allowing access to the tree-lined driveway.

The house was visible in the distance at the end of the driveway and, as the gates closed behind them, Hardy noticed the surveillance cameras sitting atop the gateposts.

"Bit obvious, aren't they?" she pointed out.

"They're for show, everyone here has them. The real surveillance equipment you can't see," Stryder explained as he drove up to the house.

All the security measures were set on auto and once the gates had been activated by the correct code they became active. The car was scanned as soon it entered through the gates and the details such as DNA, vital signs, retina patterns, dental records and the like were checked against those on file. If they hadn't been recognised they would've been neutralised before they had reached the house.

"This is gorgeous," Hardy commented as they pulled up in front of the house. It was a large, detached building built to resemble a Georgian style house from Earth's history. Three stone steps led up to the front door, which was flanked by two stone columns. From outside it looked to have two large windows on the ground floor and the same on the upper floor. As they got out of the car she asked, "What about security?"

"We were subjected to a full body scan when we came through the gates. We'd be unconscious by now if we hadn't been recognised and probably in custody. The Constabulary have an understanding with Col Sec. If anyone did manage to get inside, the security would neutralise them and immediately send out an alert to the Constabulary who have a special unit standing by at all times. They would hold whoever it was until someone from Col Sec arrived to take control," Stryder explained. "Come on grab your things, let's get changed," he added.

Hardy looked at him slightly puzzled. "Excuse me?" she said.

"I've got an idea," was all he said as he grabbed his travel grip.

"Would you like to elaborate a little more please?"

"Let's get changed, I'll explain on the way," he said cryptically.

"On the way to where, exactly?" she said trying to pin him down.

"Why, I'm taking you to dinner, of course," he said as he left her by the ATV looking confused. At the doorway to the house, he turned back to her as she stood looking at him and said, "Well, are you coming or not?"

~

Captain Pavel Norsky was in his room in the small hotel in Haven just finishing his shower when his NI tingled. He wrapped a towel around himself and padded through to his bedroom, his feet leaving wet footprints across the carpet and said, "Yes."

"Good evening Captain. I trust I find you well," Nokorovic said.

"Yes, sir," Norsky replied as, even though they were of equal rank, Nokorovic's post as General Solon's aide afforded him a certain amount of authority.

"I have something that might prove useful in locating Captain Stryder and his companion. I have the codes that will enable you to access the satellite tracking of the implanted nanochips in every Recon Delta Marine. Use this wisely Captain and handle this personally. There can be no more slip-ups. Do I make myself clear? I am sending you the codes now," Nokorovic said. He felt he'd made his point by the tone of his voice alone and before Norsky could reply had terminated the contact.

Norsky stood there waiting as the codes came through entrusting them to memory, something all soldiers learned in basic training. When there is no time or way to write down codes or instructions you had to learn how to memorise things immediately, it was literally the difference between life and death and he knew exactly what Nokorovic had meant. If he failed to capture Stryder this time, it was his head on the block.

Still, now he had an edge, he would be able to locate him and plan his capture. It shouldn't be too difficult.

Reaching for his bag he took out his remote computer terminal. Normally to access a satellite he would use his NI, but for this he would need to cover his tracks and consequently would need a bit more power.

Before long he had logged onto the network, re-routing his signal through various relay points to disguise it and was about to enter the codes.

"Okay Stryder, let's see what you and your lady friend are up to tonight," he said in anticipation.

~

As Stryder and Hardy got back in the ATV, each having freshened up with a shower and a change of clothes, Hardy said, "Well, are you going to tell me where we're going to dinner or should I guess? If you'd given me more time and warning I could've dressed a bit better."

"There's a little club I know. It's owned by Abraham Bane, probably the biggest gangster in Jacksonville," explained Stryder.

"Oh, if I'd known we were going upmarket I'd have brought my best cocktail dress," Hardy said sarcastically. She was dressed in a plain white blouse over which she wore a dark blue trouser suit finished off with a pair of black high heels. A simple gold necklace with a matching bracelet, were the only accessories to her outfit. With her face freshly made up and her sleek hair down to her shoulders she looked stunning and Stryder had a hard job keeping his eyes off her and on the road ahead.

To accompany her he wore a white shirt and black tie over which he wore a tailored black suit. The comment she made raised a thought, which he quickly suppressed. He couldn't allow those kinds of thoughts to distract him from what he knew he must do. He said, "You look gorgeous just the way you are."

She smiled then turned her head to look out the side window. "So should I be worried, should I be carrying?" she said.

"No, we're just going to talk. I only want to find out if Bane knows of anyone recruiting muscle," Stryder replied.

"And what if he doesn't want to tell you?"

"We'll just have to persuade him."

"And how do you intend to do that with only two pistols?"

"Two pistols?"

"Yes, I brought my Sig," she said reaching behind to retrieve her pistol from where it had been secreted in the waistband of her trousers in the small of her back. "And I presume you brought yours too," she added replacing the Sig.

"I never saw that when you got in the ATV," he said.

"If you'd taken your eyes off my ass long enough you might have," she said with a knowing smile.

"Oh really," he said.

"Really," she said smiling. "So Kurt, you think I look gorgeous?" she added and in spite of everything, he found himself smiling at her playfulness in the midst of danger. He found it refreshing and realised that he quite liked her, which could become a problem later. He had to stay detached from any personal involvement with her, with anyone, until he had sorted out what the changes he had undergone meant for his future.

"You'll do, but let's concentrate on what's ahead," he said finally.

"Just what is ahead? Presumably you've thought this through. You've studied the layout of this club. You know where all the exits are, what the security's like and how many of the opposition we're likely to find there," she said and waited for a response. "Oh my God, you haven't thought this through at all, have you? You are making this up as you go along aren't you? I thought you were joking when you said it earlier, but you weren't, were you?" she said in exasperation.

"Don't worry about it. It'll all work out fine, trust me."

"Are you kidding me?" she said, her voice going up an octave.

"Take it steady now. We're just going to go there, be nice, have something to eat, ask a few questions then leave, okay? Easy, right? No worries," Stryder said, his voice low and calm.

"Oh easy, yeah, easy? You think you can just waltz into a club, walk right up to the owner and ask him if he knows of anyone hiring any muscle?" she said her voice still at a high pitch.

"Why not?" Stryder asked seriously.

"Oh, this I just have to see. In fact if I wasn't actually going to be there, I'd pay money to see this," she said finally, her voice returning to normal.

"There you go then, you should thank me. I've just saved you some money and got you ringside seats," Stryder said keeping a straight face.

Hardy looked across at him and for a moment couldn't

make up her mind if he was joking or serious until she caught the mischievous glint in his eye.

She suddenly found herself laughing in spite of her exasperation, and said, "Oh you're a funny guy. If nothing else, this should prove to be a night I won't forget in a hurry."

"I know how to show a lady a good time," Stryder said smiling.

"Yea, well let's not go doing anything stupid to get ourselves killed 'eh? I've got a feeling we won't get much chance to enjoy this dinner date and I'm not going to let a little something like you getting yourself killed get you out of taking me for dinner. You got that soldier?" she said, the last four words delivered like a mock drill sergeant.

"Copy that, sir," Stryder replied, saluting.

CHAPTER 12

Norsky had entered the codes into his computer, giving him access to the Col Sec satellite. Within seconds he had the locations of each and every Recon Delta man or woman on the planet. The number was staggering, he had no idea there were so many stationed there.

It took some time to scroll through all of them until he found the one he wanted – Stryder. He was still with the woman Hardy and they were on the move.

The detail from the satellite was impressive and he couldn't help being a little amazed. It gave clear visual representation of their real time locations and when he saw where they were, his blood ran cold.

The Golden Palace was owned by Abraham Bane and it was Bane who had given him the name of the gangster Alexander Brown, supplier of the ill-fated team hired to get Stryder.

Why were they at that particular club? Did Stryder know he'd been there, was he looking for him? Was his cover about to be blown?

When he'd got his breathing under control once more, he tried to reason it through. It was safe to assume that Stryder knew those guys were local guns for hire. It was also safe to assume that he knew they must have been recruited, and it was a well-known fact that nothing happened on Celeron without Abraham Bane knowing about it. Would Bane know who he was? Doubtful, but he could tell Stryder what he looked like and no doubt the club was full of monitors that would have recorded their meeting. As much as he'd disliked the idea, he'd had to agree to the meeting, as Bane never made a deal unless it was face to face. How had he explained it? Oh yes, if the deal went south he would know who to come looking for.

Was Stryder there to ask Bane who those goons worked for? Possibly.

Would Bane tell him? Doubtful, but could he take that risk?

He had to do something, but what? Then an idea began to form in his mind.

It was well known in gangland circles that Alexander Brown coveted Bane's position as top dog in the underworld. He would probably embrace any chance to usurp him and the loss of five of his men might be just the incentive required for what he had in mind.

Through his NI he contacted Brown.

~

General Sinclair was just about to go to dinner at his hotel when his NI tingled. His Interface automatically informed him that it was an encoded transmission.

"Go ahead," he said, the NI automatically encoding his reply.

"Captain Reynolds here, sir," came the reply. Reynolds

was in command of the Col Sec starship on which Sinclair had arrived and which was in orbit around the planet.

"What is it Captain?"

"Sir, we've been monitoring comm chatter and it seems that someone has accessed one of the communication satellites but not the civilian ones, this was a Col Sec satellite, sir."

"That's not too unusual. As you know we've quite a contingent of Marines planet side, so I assume there's something more."

"Sir, whoever it was covered their tracks which means it was unauthorised. They input the Recon Delta codes. They now know where all the Recon Delta Marines are on Celeron, sir, but they concentrated on just one."

"Captain Stryder," Sinclair said, his blood running cold.

"Yes sir, but it also means no Recon Delta Marine is safe anywhere. Someone's just painted a bull's eye on every one of them."

"I'm aware of that Captain. This is one monumental mess. How the hell did this happen? How did they get hold of those codes in the first place?" Sinclair said, his anger flaring but keeping his voice under control. "Captain, I need whoever you have available from Recon Delta immediately. It would take those already on the ground too long to get in place, your people can get there quicker by shuttle. Stryder is going to need serious back-up and I can't rely on the local Constabulary being up to the task," he added as he thought through the problem at hand.

"Aye sir, I'll send the best we have."

"Order them to Captain Stryder's location, I'll meet them there personally," Sinclair said. Then he broke the connection.

This was dreadful. How in the entire galaxy had the Alliance got hold of those codes? They were supposed to be the one item in Col Sec security that was inviolate and yet, somehow, someone had got hold of them. The two main questions he needed answers to were, 'who?' and 'how?' The 'why?' was obvious, the 'how' would become clear too, once they learn the 'who'.

That would have to wait though, for the time being they had more pressing matters to attend to, like keeping Stryder alive.

~

Stryder and Hardy found the club with no problems. The Golden Palace was lit up like a Christmas tree with flashing lights around the doors and windows and the club's name on the front, high above the entrance in letters three feet high.

"Tasteful, I must say," Hardy said as they approached the entrance.

Stryder said, "Abraham Bane was never known for his subtlety."

"Seeing this it's no wonder why," she added.

A doorman, a well-muscled individual who looked like he'd been carved out of solid rock, showed them in. Once inside they were shown to a table by the Maître d'. The interior decor was a little more understated than the exterior appearance. The lighting was subdued with wall lights giving off just enough illumination for the customers to see what they were doing. The floor was home grown oak panelled and the large bar ran the entire length of the room. Tables were dotted around and a dance floor was over on the opposite side to the bar, situated just before a modest stage where a small band accompanied a young woman singing. All in all quite tastefully done, they both thought as they walked to their table.

"Is he here?" Hardy asked once they were seated and the waiter had left them with the menu to peruse.

Stryder had quickly taken in every single face in the large room on his way over to their table. He'd done it without appearing to allow his gaze to wander away from his partner for the evening, even though the lighting was subtle and subdued. He didn't know how he'd managed to do it; he just knew he had.

"Yes, he's in a private booth over by the far wall in what I can only imagine is the VIP area," he replied never taking his eyes off hers. "Third booth from the right," he added.

"But you're sitting with your back to them, how can you possibly know that?" she said, quickly glancing over his shoulder to where he'd said.

"Careful, don't let them see you checking them out, not yet at least," he said.

"How did you know where they were? You didn't take your eyes off my ass the whole time we walked over here, so you must know this place already. How often have you been here Kurt?" she asked.

"Including tonight?"

"Yes."

"One time, tonight, and what makes you think I was watching your ass?"

"You're a guy."

"Well it is a mighty fine ass."

"So you admit it, you were watching my ass the whole time we've been in here."

"I'm not watching it now, am I?"

"Only because I'm sitting on it. Go on Kurt, tell me. How did you know?"

The smile faded from his face as he pondered her probing question. How much could he tell her? Could he trust her? Should he let her into his little secret and if he did would she be able to handle it or would she freak or worse still inform the General?

He wasn't sure if he was ready just yet to inform Sinclair, unsure of where his future would lead once the General knew.

One thing he was sure of though, and the realisation hit him like a ton of bricks, was he could trust her! He didn't know how he knew, he just knew.

"What? What's the matter Kurt? What's troubling you?" she asked becoming concerned.

"I've a confession of sorts to make. You know how I told you about the project on Outpost Station Five, the one that failed?" he said easing his way into it.

"Yes, I read the report once my clearance got upgraded."

"Well, I wasn't quite accurate when I said in my report that there were no changes."

"Go on, how inaccurate were you?"

"Well, my speed, strength and stamina have all increased like the reports stated, but by a bit more than they realised. Up until now I've not been able to quantify by just how much, but that's not all."

"Go on, I'm listening."

"My other senses have all increased, my hearing, my sight, smell and touch; in fact all of them. I can walk into a room and almost instantly know details about all the occupants in that room. The main change though, the one I've kept to myself, the one the project was set up for, was a success, a total success."

"Your immune system, they increased it?"

"Yes, now I'm more resistant to toxins and disease but something else too. Simple cuts and abrasions heal almost instantly while anything larger or more serious takes a bit longer. Again, I've not been able to quantify this either. I don't know all the science behind all this, I just know it worked."

"I saw your face heal almost immediately back at your villa. I thought I was seeing things at first, but that explains so much," she said quietly. She looked at him, smiling and said, "So that's how you knew so much about where Bane was, even though you were staring at my ass the whole time."

"It's a nice ass."

"Nice? A second ago it was a mighty fine ass, now it's just nice. Are you going off me already Kurt?"

"No, I…" he stammered then saw the mischievous glint in her eye and knew he'd been had. He smiled then said, "You don't seem fazed by what I just told you, why is that?"

"I *was* fazed, one minute I've a mighty fine ass and then it's just nice."

"You know what I'm talking about."

"Yes, I do, but it's no big deal."

"Excuse me? Would you mind explaining that? This whole situation is because of the results of that project. The Alliance wants to duplicate it, Col Sec wants to reproduce it, everybody wants it and the only viable specimen they have to work with is here," he said tapping his chest. "So it is a big deal. There are so many potential advances we could make with this, but as with any great discovery, someone always turns it around and uses it for harm."

He looked at her allowing his guard to drop and she saw all his anguish, all his fear come flooding out.

"I don't know what to do," he said finally.

She glanced down at her hands then up to look him in the eyes once more, taking that moment to process it all.

She said, "You know Kurt, there are some things we're not meant to know."

"Are you saying I should keep this to myself?"

"I can't tell you what to do, that's a decision only you can make, but whatever you decide I'll back you up all the way if you want me to. What I meant was that there are certain things that we shouldn't tamper with, we're not Gods. We're mortals and what they've done to you and would do to others is beyond the realm of mankind." She looked away for a moment then turned to him once more, "But hey! That's just my opinion, what do I know right, I'm just a grunt, a Marine?" she said and her smile was back in place, a little shaky, but it was there.

Stryder looked at her and realised his feelings for her were just a little deeper than friendship.

"Let's order, I'm starved," he said with a smile. He knew then that whatever he decided, whatever he did, he would not be alone. This woman would stand by his side through thick and thin.

"Me too," she said and they both looked at the menu.

CHAPTER 13

Norsky arrived at the Golden Palace and injected himself with a short-term dose of facial reconstruction nanobots, the effect of which would be temporary but dramatic. They would work on the soft tissue in his face altering his appearance to whatever design he had pre-programmed into them. Nothing too drastic, but different enough so he wouldn't be recognised from any mug shot data file.

He was admitted into the club and shown to a table close to Stryder and Hardy. He took great pleasure in the knowledge that he was within earshot of them and they had no idea. From his vantage point he could watch what was about to happen with complete impunity.

The call he'd made to Alexander Brown had had the desired effect. Knowing that the five men he'd supplied had all been killed had incensed Brown. Bane supplying his name was even worse, almost like it was his fault, but finally knowing that the killer would be at Bane's club eased him a little. It was a chance to get revenge, kill the guy responsible and if Bane's club got trashed, even better. It was all good.

Norsky could see no downside to this. Stryder was obviously capable, having taking care of five local thugs, but then he would expect that of Recon Delta, they were supposed to be the best Col Sec had. Now he had the chance to see him in action, so that when it was time for him to make his move against him, he would be better prepared. And, if in the process he kept the two main gang leaders at each other's throats, perhaps start a little turf war causing a little unrest in this city, then that was good too.

The Alliance would be pleased.

Stryder and Hardy seemed content to remain at their table waiting for their meal. So far they had made no move to contact Bane or even appeared to know that he was there. Perhaps he was wrong, perhaps they were just out for dinner and not there to see Bane after all. It would be a while before Brown arrived, plenty of time for him to enjoy himself first. The club had a reputation for serving excellent food, no matter who the owner was. He looked at the menu and decided to order.

~

They had both enjoyed their dinner; the food had been excellent. Stryder had opted for Beef Bourguignon with local vegetables whilst Hardy had chosen Rack of Lamb. To wash it down they had chosen a half bottle of Savary Rose from a local vineyard. It had an excellent reputation and supplied all the clubs, restaurants and other outlets on Celeron and recently had also begun to supply off world after winning a prestigious wine tasting contest.

The two of them had declined any starters opting to go straight to the main course, not knowing if they would be interrupted.

"What happens now?" Hardy asked once the waiter had cleared their plates away.

"Now it's down to business," Stryder replied.

"I was afraid you'd say that."

"It's time I asked Mister Bane a few questions," Stryder said as he calmly got to his feet, turned towards the VIP area and started walking over to where Bane was seated.

Hardy was at his shoulder in seconds and, slightly surprised, he glanced at her as she said, "What, you thought I'd let you go over there on your own? Hey, we're a team, where you go, I go," which brought a smile to his lips.

"Okay, partner, here we go," he said as they continued across the floor.

~

Norsky had almost finished eating when he saw Stryder and Hardy get up and walk towards Bane.

"Oh shit!" he thought as he checked the time. Brown should be here by now, where the hell was he? He needed to do something to stop them from getting anything from Bane, but what?

~

Before Stryder and Hardy reached the VIP area, they were stopped in their tracks by a huge man mountain.

"Where do you think you're going?" he said placing a hand the size of a shovel on Stryder's chest.

Stryder looked down at his chest where the beefy hand was placed, then slowly looked up at the man standing before him making eye contact. He had to look up slightly for the guy was at least five inches taller than him.

"Over there, I want to talk to him," Stryder said glancing past the man mountain to where Bane was sitting.

"Mister Bane sees no one while he's having dinner, unless they've made an appointment, and you don't have an appointment," the guard said.

"Oh, he'll see me," Stryder said confidently.

"I don't think so," the guard said with a smirk.

"Why's that?" Stryder asked.

"Simple, to see him you've gotta get past me."

"Is that all?"

"Never gonna happen," said the guard leaning his face closer to Stryder's adding menace to his words.

Stryder placed his left hand on the guard's wrist and twisted it free of his chest. The guard went down on one knee, his face contorted in a kind of rictus of alarm from the pain in his wrist.

Stryder released his grip and stepped over the guard towards the VIP area.

The guard was up straight away coming after Stryder. He placed a hand on his left shoulder to stop him. Stryder grabbed it with his right hand and brought it over his head turning towards him. The guard's arm was held rigid giving Stryder the advantage, he placed his left hand on the guard's shoulder to gain further control and because the arm was twisted against the joint there was nothing he could do to prevent what was happening.

Stryder again forced him to the floor, let go and walked past him.

This time when the guard got to his feet he bellowed his rage and frustration wanting to tear Stryder apart.

Stryder turned to face him and put up a finger to halt him. The effect was almost comical, the giant guard pulled up short unable to believe what was happening.

Calmly Stryder said, "Look, all I want to do is talk, so be

kind to yourself and introduce me to your boss before you make me hurt you."

The guard was completely flabbergasted, didn't know what to do or say, he just knew he wanted to destroy him.

Bane's attention had been grabbed when his guard went down the first time and he continued watching avidly, since he couldn't help but notice the stunning beauty with the man giving his guard so much trouble.

"Tony, why don't you bring them over here, you're scaring the customers," he said before anything else could be done or said.

Tony, the man mountain, grudgingly tore his eyes from Stryder's to look around him at his boss.

"Okay Boss," he said; then returning his gaze to Stryder said, "This ain't over."

"You just name the time and place and I'll be there," Stryder replied calmly locking eyes with him.

Tony, unused to not being able to intimidate, didn't know how to react to Stryder's calm indifference. Finally, he broke eye contact and gestured towards the booth where Bane sat.

"Go ahead," he said.

Stryder, flanked by Hardy, walked towards the booth and stood at the entrance waiting for Bane to invite them in. He allowed Bane to keep some semblance of control here on his own turf. The display with Tony showed that he was not to be messed with, but by waiting for the invite from Bane, he demonstrated some respect for the man. Stryder would not make him lose face in front of his men.

"Okay, so you got my attention, I just hope it was worth it. Who are you and what do you want?" Bane asked after a short pause during which he finished his meal, carefully wiped around his hard mouth with a napkin then slowly pushed his empty plate away. He was in his fifties with a large frame that still looked in good shape for his age. Salt and pepper hair was combed straight back from a prominent forehead, below which deep brown eyes looked out at the world. A long, flat nose lay close to his face, a testament to a fight he lost in his youth. It was the last fight he ever lost. He became a student of a fighting arts master and used his prodigious strength and thirst for knowledge to learn what he could to gain revenge on the man who had bested him. He quickly climbed the ranks of the criminal underworld to become the leader of the largest gang in Jacksonville.

"My name is Kurt Stryder and I used to work for Col Sec. What I want is a little more complicated," Stryder said by way of introduction.

"Go on, you still have my attention, you'll know when you don't, trust me." Bane said.

"Can I, trust you, I mean?"

"What's that supposed to mean?"

"It means I need the truth from you about something that happened recently, something you possibly had a hand in or at least knew about. Can I trust you to be truthful about it?"

"Why don't you ask, and then decide when, or if, I choose to answer?"

"Okay, earlier today, five local muscle were sent to my house to force me to go with them and be handed over to whoever hired them. I chose not to go."

"And?"

"What I need from you is the name of the guy the muscle worked for."

Bane looked at Stryder trying to figure him out. Finally he said, "What makes you think they didn't work for me?"

"Well, whoever sent them would've come to you looking to hire muscle for a job. Now I figure he'd be someone you didn't know so you wouldn't trust sending your own people. You'd pass him onto someone else, possibly a rival, and let them take the risk. That way you've given this guy what he wants, where to get the muscle he needs. You get what you want, your fee and, if it went sour, you retain your safety and your rivals forces are depleted."

"Sound reasoning, but why would I tell you anything?"

"I used to work for Col Sec, I still have contacts there and they will want to know what happened, so if you don't tell me I can't guarantee you won't have them crawling all over this place looking for answers."

"That sounds like a threat to me, have Col Sec crawling all over this place wanting to know what happened," Bane said getting a little angry, but Stryder knew it was mostly for show. He knew he could ill afford to have Col Sec mount an investigation centred on him.

"What did happen anyway?" he asked finally.

"To the five men, the muscle?"

"Yea, what happened to the muscle, they in the cells?"

"No, the morgue," Stryder replied.

"The morgue?" Bane asked as if he'd misheard.

"Yes, I killed them," Stryder said calmly.

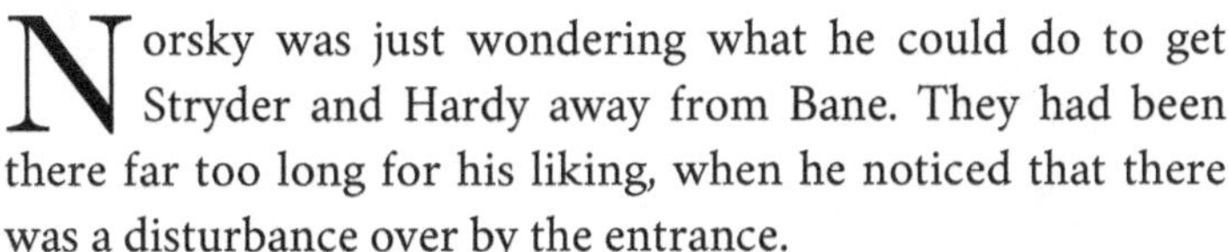

Norsky was just wondering what he could do to get Stryder and Hardy away from Bane. They had been there far too long for his liking, when he noticed that there was a disturbance over by the entrance.

Alexander Brown and a number of his men had arrived.

All hell was about to break loose.

CHAPTER 14

"What the hell is going on now?" Bane said as he spotted the group of men force their way past the Maître d' and into the club.

When he saw who was leading them he said just one word, "Brown."

Stryder and Hardy both turned to see to whom Bane was referring.

"Who's Brown?" Stryder asked, spotting the guy in charge of the large bunch of intruders.

"Alexander Brown. He hates me and if what you've just told me is true, you killed five of his men," Bane replied.

"Why are they here?" Stryder wondered.

"Why don't you go ask him?" Bane asked calmly.

"No, I mean why are they here now, at this particular time? Don't you think it just a little strange they turn up just as you and I start talking?" Stryder said, elaborating his point a little. "Almost as if someone didn't want us to meet," he added.

Bane looked at him wondering how the hell he'd come to

that conclusion. Yes, it was a bit of a coincidence, but Stryder seemed utterly convinced he was right.

How?

Just as Bane was silently asking himself those questions, Stryder was doing the same. He didn't know how, he just knew that Brown had turned up to kill him in revenge for his five men, and to trash the club.

Knowing that fact threw up another series of questions such as, how did Brown know he'd be there? Whoever hired him must've contacted him with the information, but how did that person know where he was? How had they been discovered when he'd covered his tracks so carefully?

The only possible explanation he could come up with at such short notice was that they had a mole in Col Sec somehow leaking data to the Alliance asset on the ground, but that didn't explain how they found him. Only Hardy knew where he was, and he'd kept her in the dark until they left the safe house for the club.

There could only be one explanation of how the Alliance had learned of their whereabouts; they were under surveillance, possibly even now. He could be in the room with them at that very moment.

Stryder scanned the faces of those people at the tables. They were all looking towards Brown and his men, all except one.

Norsky had seen Brown and his men push through and thought that it was about time. He'd watch what was about to happen and see for himself just how good this Stryder was. He would need this information for when he made his move against him. The Alliance wanted him and he was under orders to handle it personally. Failure was not an option, so he would have to watch closely.

He was watching Stryder, trying to gauge his reaction to the intrusion and gain some measure of the man when he did something quite unexpected. He turned from Brown and looked straight at him.

As their eyes locked, Norsky knew in that instant he'd been made.

Stryder knew who he was and panic, irrational and uncontrollable, ran through him churning his insides so that all he wanted to do was escape.

With a Herculean effort of will he remained seated and stared back at him. Stryder might know his face but this face was temporary and would be gone in a few hours. Stryder would be looking for someone who didn't exist, if he survived the next few moments that is. His attention would be on his own survival and not on Norsky.

~

"That's him," Stryder said.

"Who?" Hardy asked tearing her gaze from the large number of angry men heading directly for them.

"Kurt, what're we going to do?" she asked.

"That's the guy who sent them after me," Stryder said.

"Who? These guys? I don't understand!" Hardy asked, more than a little confused at his apparent rambling.

"No, the first five at my house, he's the one who wants me captured. He's the one who works for the Alliance," Stryder explained, his eyes still locked on Norsky's.

Hardy tore her eyes from Brown's advancing mob and followed Stryder's gaze. "That's the guy who's behind all this?"

Bane, overhearing what was said between the two of them glanced over to where they were looking. The guy staring back at them wasn't anyone he recognised and he said so.

"That's not him, that's not the guy who I met," he said.

Stryder turned to him and asked, "Are you sure?"

"I never forget a face," Bane answered.

"Er… guys, can we talk about this later, we have another more urgent problem to discuss right now, like what do we do with an angry mob," Hardy said, bringing their attention back to the approaching group of men.

"Not my problem, it's you they want," Bane said calmly.

The group was half way across the room and the farther they got into the club the more panic they caused. Guests started to move out of their way, some hurriedly heading for the exit. When Bane saw that he said, "Okay, they're intimidating my customers, now it's my problem too. Tony, you and some of the boys go tell Brown and his party we're fully booked."

"Yes, boss," Tony said, pressing a finger to his ear where his comm unit was inserted. When he spoke the others in the circuit could hear and he summoned some back up from other rooms in the club.

In total five men came from the other rooms and stood with Tony who said, "We're a bit short staffed tonight boss."

When Stryder saw the odds were in Brown's favour he knew he had to do something. Bane would be a useful ally to have on his side and if he was going to make that happen he had to do something to prove he was worth the trouble.

Stryder stepped around Tony and his reinforcements and walked towards the advancing group.

Before the changes due to the project had occurred he would never have even considered facing off against a group of this number. It was clearly foolhardy and yet as he stopped in front of them he felt no fear, a tingle of excitement perhaps, but mostly he felt supremely confident.

"Alexander Brown, I think it's me you're looking for," he said looking at each face in turn.

"I'm Brown and if you're the guy responsible for the deaths of five of my men then, yes, it's you we're looking for," said the oldest guy in the group. Where the rest were well muscled, hard looking customers, Brown looked soft, but mean. Not as tall as his men and in his fifties, he had a body that at one time had been lean and hard, now though, it ran more to fat than muscle. His hair was still jet black but his face was worn, like that of a prize fighter long past his prime. Battle scars lined his face like a road map of his life. Eyes full of hatred stared at Stryder and when he had finished speaking his thin lips formed a sneer of contempt.

"I'm responsible, they came looking for me and found trouble instead," said Stryder.

"You don't look that hard," said the guy standing next to Brown.

"I'm sure that's what they thought too and yet I'm here and they're in the morgue," Stryder said looking him square in the eyes.

"Now, if you're still interested in talking to me then we can take this outside. There's no need to scare the customers any more is there?" Stryder added to Brown.

"Oh, there's every reason. If it hadn't been for Bane passing my name on to the guy who wants you, then I wouldn't have lost five of my crew," Brown replied full of malice.

"You do know that that guy was an Alliance agent, don't you? If Col Sec find out about you helping him, I don't think they'll look too kindly on you. Treason is the term they use," Stryder said.

"The Alliance you say?" Brown said, slightly taken aback.

This had added a new dimension to the situation. He thought about it for a second then said "Well, I'll never tell, I'm sure Bane won't either and you won't be able to once we've finished." He gestured with a wave of his hand for his men to grab him.

Stryder saw the gesture and his reactions went into hyper-drive. All movement around him seemed to slow down a fraction, whereas he was outside of it moving as always, so that when the first attack came he saw it coming and could take action.

The group had bunched around Brown, standing to the side and behind him as he spoke with Stryder. As soon as the guy standing next to Brown made his move the rest of them surged forward allowing Brown to retreat behind them to safety.

The blow was a simple straight right to the jaw except that Stryder saw it coming from the first twitch of the attacker's shoulder.

He simply moved to the right allowing the punch to sail past his head. Then, dipping his right shoulder, he hit the thug with a right uppercut that lifted him off his feet to sail backwards and land on his back, although Stryder didn't have time to actually see him land because he was kept busy with the rest of Brown's muscle.

Two more rushed him aiming punches at Stryder who deftly stepped out of the way of each blow dropping each man with a punch to the jaw.

Before he knew it he was blocking punches left and right, delivering blows of his own, both punches and low kicks at knees, as more and more of Brown's men threw themselves into the fray.

Already he had taken care of three of Brown's men, laying them on the floor unconscious, but the odds were stacking up against him. He was strong and fast but when surrounded by so many men intent on beating him to a pulp it was just a matter of time before the blows began to get through.

Hardy watched in fascinated horror as Stryder took on the entire group. Bane had come to stand next to her and watched clinically as if it was some prize fight. Tony and the reinforcements just stood ready to intervene if Bane judged it necessary.

Although the club had emptied once the fight started, so far there had been no damage so Bane was quite happy to just watch the show, to see what this guy had got.

Hardy couldn't stand by any longer and do nothing. She made to step forward but Bane placed a restraining hand on her arm and, without taking his eyes off the melee, said, "You don't want to go and get yourself mixed up in this, not a pretty thing like yourself."

She tore his hand away and pushed past Tony grabbing one of Brown's men who was about to attack Stryder from behind and, spinning him around, punched him flush in the face with a straight right. The guy's nose exploded in a spray of blood as his head was snapped backwards. Before he could vent his fury on her she kicked him between the legs, which wiped the anger from his face to be replaced with a rictus of agony. Then she finished him off by bringing up her right knee into his already damaged face as his head came down. The blow lifted him off his feet and sent him crashing to the floor.

Stryder turned, having sent another thug to the floor, to see Hardy finish off the thug behind him and he felt enormous pride swell inside him, but then his peripheral vision caught sight of another attacker coming at her from her blind side.

She saw Stryder glance at her and she smiled when she saw him smile, but then she saw his expression change to one of alarm.

The attack was from her blind side, but because she'd seen the direction of Stryder's glance she had an idea where it was coming from. The punch caught her on the left side of her face but as she rode it the effect was diminished, it just served to anger her rather than take her out.

Her attacker continued with a left cross to the stomach but by that time she had recovered enough to bring both arms up to cover her torso and deflect the blow. Then she hit him a terrific punch to the face with a left back fist, which he never expected, and this snapped his head around almost sending him to his knees.

Hardy followed up with a right cross to his jaw, putting all her body weight behind it and the man went down, lights out.

Stryder felt like applauding but instead he received a terrific blow to the back of his head as someone smashed a chair across his shoulders. Pain erupted across his back, shoulders and head as the chair splintered across him. The force of the blow sent him to his knees and within seconds there were three more men kicking and stamping on him.

He went down as the blows continued.

For the first time during the fight he was in a position where all he could do was cover up and try to defend himself.

Hardy saw him go down and literally leapt to his defence. She landed on top of the nearest thug who crumpled under the surprising weight. She kneed the thug beneath her on the side of his head then tore him away from Stryder sending him spinning across the floor to land at Tony's feet.

The guard turned to look at his boss enquiringly and Bane said, "Okay Tony, take out the trash."

CHAPTER 15

Having one of his attackers pulled off relieved the pressure on him somewhat, but Stryder still found it difficult to regain his feet. His opportunity came when one of the remaining thug's attention was diverted by Hardy turning to face them after tearing one of them off Stryder.

Seizing the opportunity the diversion afforded him, Stryder managed to uncurl a little and lash out with his foot at the thug who had looked over at Hardy. The blow wasn't powerful enough to incapacitate, but it did unbalance him and enabled Stryder to block the remaining attacker's blows. Before he could conjure up a counter attack, his assailant was suddenly sprawled out on the floor at the feet of the man mountain Tony.

"Thanks," Stryder said as he got to his feet. The fight was in full swing now with chairs flying through the air, bodies being thrown around and plenty of blood flowing from battered faces.

Stryder quickly looked around for the one man who seemed more interested in him rather than the group who had invaded the club. Finally he found him at the far end of the room leaning nonchalantly with his back against the bar watching the fight with intense eyes.

There you are. Time you and I had a little chat, he thought as he started to walk towards him.

Norsky, seeing Stryder approach him decided he'd seen enough and walked calmly towards the exit.

A sound behind him brought Stryder's attention back to the fight, the sound of a bottle breaking.

Turning he saw the bottle in the hand of one of Brown's thugs. He'd smashed it over Tony's head and was about to thrust the jagged edges into the dazed man's face.

Stryder stepped between them, grabbed the wrist just behind the jagged bottle, and twisted viciously. The sound of the bone breaking was drowned out by the man's scream of pain.

His misery was short lived though, as Stryder hit him full in the face with a straight right knocking him flying over a table. He was out cold before he hit the floor.

Stryder spun back around to look for the mystery man, but he'd used the distraction to exit the club. Thinking he would check him out later, he turned back to Tony who was recovering from the blow to the back of his head.

"You okay?" he asked as his eyes met Tony's. He was shaking his head, trying to dispel the drowsiness.

"Yea, I'm fine, thanks," Tony replied grudgingly. He'd never expected help from these two and it surprised him a little.

"Good. Time to end this I think," Stryder said and he searched the room for Brown. He saw him sitting at the edge of the floor, at one of the few tables not overturned, enjoying a free drink.

There were just a few strides separating them and he set off to close the gap.

A thug stepped in his way and was quickly dispatched with a punch to the stomach followed by a knee to the face. Nothing was going to stop him reaching Brown.

Brown got to his feet to meet Stryder, unnerved by the look of determination on his face. Before he could evade him, Brown found his throat grabbed by a hand with unbelievable strength.

Stryder pulled Brown towards him and reached for his pistol that was still secured in the waistband of his trousers in the small of his back. He saw terror in Brown's face then, a face rapidly turning blue from the lack of oxygen.

Stryder fired his Sig P996 straight up, the sound of which brought everyone in the room to a standstill. All eyes were suddenly on him, combatants separated, the fight suddenly forgotten for the time being.

Stryder placed the muzzle of his Sig to Brown's temple slowly so that everyone saw it and understood the implication.

"Okay, now that I have everyone's attention, how about you all drop whatever weapons you're holding and separate. Brown's men over by the exit and the rest of you over by Bane," he said, his voice sarcastic yet strident.

"Do it now or Brown gets his brain scrambled all over the floor," he added more forcefully.

Slowly the two groups began to separate, carefully. They knew not to make any sudden moves that would turn an already bad situation into one that could become much worse.

When he was satisfied with the result and loosening his grip slightly so Brown could breathe once more, Stryder said, "Now then Brown, we're gonna do something you didn't expect. You're gonna get your boys together, those that can still walk, and you're gonna grab those that can't and you're gonna get the hell outta here. You're not gonna get what you came here for, so I suggest you leave. At least that way you get another shot at me at a later date. If you stay here you're just gonna lose more of your men because if this carries on it'll turn ugly."

Brown said, "You said *we're* gonna do something. You've told me what *you* want me to do, what about the other part of this *we* thing, what're *you* gonna do?"

"Oh that's simple; I'm going to let you go," Stryder said.

Brown looked at him with mistrust in his eyes; he didn't say anything but Stryder knew it. "It's a onetime offer. I'd take it if I were you, before Bane decides he wants your hide."

That was plain enough, even for Brown. His shoulders relaxed with resignation. He knew he'd lost this battle but the war would rage on. Not here though, and not now. His time would come later. He vowed that one day he would see Abraham Bane on his knees before him, powerless, beaten and at his mercy and it was with that thought firmly in place that he gestured to his men that they were leaving.

It was over, for now.

Stryder carefully released him but kept the Sig trained on him as they all headed for the exit.

Hardy came to stand next to him once Brown and his group had left and she looked up at him with a smile saying, "Well Kurt, you sure know how to show a girl a good time."

"The night's not over yet," he replied and as they turned to look at Bane more figures came bursting into the club.

"Everyone, stand where you are, don't move and no one will get hurt," a voice said from the entrance.

"What now?" Stryder said as he turned to see who the voice belonged to. Standing in a row across the entrance were five Marines from Recon Delta, all armed with standard issue Remm assault rifles aimed at the group of people at the far end of the room.

"I should've known it!" exclaimed Bane angrily then added, "Brown should've killed you when he had the chance."

Stryder gave him a hard stare, cold enough to chill his blood, and then slowly returned his gaze to the Marines.

"What's this about?" he asked, although he suspected he already knew the answer to that one.

"We were sent to ensure your safety, sir," said the Marine in charge, who Stryder recognised as Guardian from Research Station Five.

"What exactly are your orders Captain Storm?" Stryder asked.

"To contain the situation and place you and Sergeant Hardy under protective custody until the General arrives, sir," Storm replied succinctly.

"I'm sorry Captain, but I can't allow that to happen," Stryder said calmly yet adamantly.

"Oh no, here we go again," Storm said. Then waving for his men to remain where they were he shouldered his assault rifle and slowly walked over to him.

"Good to see you again, sir. How've you been?" Storm said when he was in front of Stryder. He put out his hand and Stryder took it in a grip of steel.

"I've been good, but call me Kurt. There's no reason to call me sir," he replied. "Look, you don't need to place us in custody, the danger's passed but you could actually help us out here a little."

"How so?" Storm asked.

"How much do you know of what's been going on down here?"

"We've been kept appraised of the situation. The General requested that my squad and I be on board for this trip, said you might need us and because we were present at Outpost Station Five when all that business went down, he felt we would have a better understanding of it all. We were ordered personally to this location by Sinclair."

"Okay, good, that saves us some time. The person who sent those five goons to my house was here tonight; he caused this situation. I had a good look at him but I may need your authority to commandeer the visual records from this place."

"Can I ask you something?"

"Yeah sure, make it quick, time's running out."

"Okay, I'm presuming if he's Alliance he'd know about the monitors in here and would take precautions."

"That's right. When I spotted him, Bane, the owner of this club said that he wasn't the guy he'd met with. We both know Alliance agents work alone, so if I can get his face on disc I can get a retina scan, and no matter what he did to alter his appearance, he can't have changed that."

"Okay, let's go."

Bane was waiting for them and when they got there he looked around at the mess the fight had caused.

"Look at this place," he said anger boiling just beneath the surface.

I'm sorry about that," Stryder said, but Bane waved it off.

"Oh I don't blame you, don't worry. Brown would've used any excuse to try and ruin me; he's been trying for the last decade or so. He won't succeed though and payback is gonna be a bitch," he said.

"The monitors will have caught the guy behind it all, I need to see them."

"The Alliance guy eh? Look I may be plenty of things but traitor isn't one of them. I thought there was something funky about him when I passed him onto Brown. Of course you can have the discs but I don't know how much help they'll be, I've already told you he wasn't the man I met with."

"Thanks, but you let us worry about that, we just need to

see his face."

"Okay, this way, we can do this in my office."

As Bane, Stryder and Storm moved away, a thought occurred to Hardy. She went to say something then thought better of it. What she had in mind might be nothing but then again it might be something.

She walked towards the entrance where the four Marines stood guard.

"Hi guys, listen I think I may have an idea, but I need to get out of here just for a second," she said.

Private Wayne, call sign Cowboy, said, "Okay, the rest of you secure the room, I'll escort the lady."

"I'm no lady, I'm Recon Delta, same as you," she said with a smile. "Let's go," she added.

"I'm with you ma'am," Cowboy replied.

Norsky left the club and mingled with the crowd, which was in mild chaos as people hurriedly exited the club. A good many had arrived earlier in their own transport, and now made their way to the club's private parking lot. The rest waited around the entrance while they ordered transport. The moment the Marines arrived they decided that was enough and they all left to find some other way home. Brown and his men got lost in the crowd and disappeared.

Norsky had arrived in his own car and so he casually made his way to it, mulling over in his mind the events that had unfolded inside the club. Watching Stryder, he had learned a few things; mainly that he was no ordinary man. He was in fact, quite extraordinary.

To take on as many men as Stryder had, showed he was either supremely confident in his own abilities, or extremely foolhardy. Judging by the number of men he faced off against he would normally tend towards the latter, but having seen how he handled himself against them, he wasn't so sure.

As he'd watched the fight unfold, he saw the speed Stryder exhibited, both in avoiding attacks from those he fought and in executing counter attacks against the same. He was quite simply amazed by the apparent strength of the man. He also noticed that when Stryder stopped to look for him, once he'd got to his feet from underneath the group that was pounding on him, he didn't seem fazed by what had just happened. He'd had several guys punching and kicking him and when he got up it was as if it was an everyday occurrence, nothing out of the ordinary. He wasn't out of breath or unnerved by it at all. There wasn't a mark on him. He was just calm and collected with only one thought on his mind, the whereabouts of the person responsible for this situation and he had to admit that when their eyes met, that moment had unnerved him.

The only other thing he'd noticed was the certain bond between Stryder and the woman and as he sat in his car processing all that he'd learned, he wondered if he could exploit that fact in some way.

He was about to start his car and drive off to formulate a plan, when the 'some way' he had just thought about, presented itself.

~

Hardy and Cowboy hit the kerb outside the club. The only vehicles she saw were the Marines' transport shuttle, which had landed in the middle of the street, and a few cars scattered on the private parking lot across the street from the club.

"Right, there's a chance our guy came in his own car so

we need to know if all those belong to employees," she said indicating the parking lot.

"How do you intend to find that out?" Cowboy asked, not sure where she was going with this line of thought.

"Get one of the guards, he'll know, then we can check 'em out," she replied.

"Okay, wait a sec ma'am," he replied and accessed a comm channel. "Hacker, send out one of the bouncers ASAP," he said.

Inside the club William Ives, call sign Hacker turned to the nearest bouncer and said, "You... you're wanted outside."

When the bouncer just glared back at him Hacker said, "Now man, move it," and he emphasised his point by waving the muzzle of his assault rifle at him.

The bouncer still glared but moved towards the exit.

"Bouncer coming your way, Cowboy," Hacker said, then returned his attention to what was happening inside the club.

Norsky couldn't believe his luck, the woman and one of the Marines he'd seen arrive were outside the club. He'd almost panicked when the transport had arrived but thought he'd have enough time to get away. The only thing that had delayed his departure had been his mulling over what he'd observed of Stryder.

When he saw the Marine with the woman, panic began to return. He watched as she said something to the Marine then they seemed to be waiting for something. What it was soon became apparent when a bouncer from inside the club came out to join them.

At first he thought he'd been spotted, a thought quickly dispelled as they continued waiting on the kerb outside the club. Then, when the bouncer arrived, he knew they hadn't seen him. It was clear they planned on checking the cars in the parking lot and they needed the bouncer to tell them which belonged to the staff.

Peering through the window he watched as they carefully approached the parking lot. Slowly he opened the door after turning off the interior light so they wouldn't see his movement. Keeping low, he manoeuvred himself around the back of the small group.

Silently he came up behind her and placed the muzzle of his pistol, a Sig, to the back of her neck. He leaned in close so his voice would not carry and quietly yet with authority said, "Don't move."

Hardy went limp when she realised her mistake. She felt a hand take her pistol from the waistband at the small of her back and place the muzzle against her spine. Before the two men with her could react, Norsky shot them both at close range with his own Sig.

"Don't worry, I've only stunned them," he said. "Slowly open the door and get in," Norsky ordered, keeping his own pistol trained on her while tossing hers to the ground as proof that he had her when they came looking.

Once she was inside he came around the front of the car, his pistol aimed at her through the front windscreen and he got in beside her.

"Start the car and drive off, I'll tell you where to go once we're away from here. I've altered the setting on this thing to full power now. Don't make me use it."

She did as she was told.

Once they were clear he asked, "Are you Recon Delta

too?"

"Yes, why?"

"Then you know the risks involved and you know that when I say I'll kill you if you don't do as I say, I mean it, right?"

"Right."

"Good. Now use your NI and call Stryder. I want him to know I have you."

"Why?"

"So I can tell him where to come and pick you up."

"Why should I, you're going to kill me anyway, right?"

"Not true, my orders are to capture Stryder alive. They're very clear on that part; how I do it is up to me. I don't see the necessity of causing death needlessly, which I think I've already proved by not killing your friends back there. Don't get me wrong though, if I have to, if I have no other choice, I will kill you; so please, for your own sake, let's not let it get to that stage."

"Why should I trust you?"

"We are both soldiers you and I. We are both loyal to our causes and have been in combat where sometimes we have to take a life. That's what it's like and we accept that, it comes with the job description, but we are not murderers. We kill when we have to, not because we want to and I don't want to have to kill you, so please don't make me. One soldier to another, you have my word on it. Besides, like they say, where there's life, there's hope. So stay alive and you'll have hope that you can get him back."

"Okay then, one soldier to another, just so we understand each other, I'll do as you ask, but at the first opportunity, I *will* try to escape. I *will* try to help Kurt and if I have to, I *will* kill you, you have my word on it."

"Oh I think we understand each other just fine," Norsky said, then added, "Now make the call."

Stryder was standing next to Storm at the side of the desk in Bane's office. They had accessed the visual records from the interior of the club, zoomed in on Norsky's face, and then Stryder had accessed the orbiting starship's main computer via the Neural Interface and asked for the retina scans of known Alliance personnel. He'd asked for the data to be sent to Bane's computer so that the match could be made.

Within seconds Norsky's file was on the screen in front of them.

"Pavel Norsky, member of the Black Knights," Stryder said reading it off the screen.

"That's him, that's the guy I met," Bane said recognising the face on the screen.

"Go ahead Cowboy, what is it?" Storm said, as a call came through on the Marine's combat channel, a private frequency only those in the circuit could access.

Cowboy's voice came through loud and clear to Storm only, the combat frequency had been devised for use during a battle when the noise of weapon fire could drown out communications. The voice commands were routed through the NI and sent directly to the brain. It was described by one soldier, after trying it for the first time, as the closest thing to telepathy he had known. In that way communications between combat units wouldn't be lost or compromised as only members of those units could use it. It was also invaluable during black ops when silence was vital.

Cowboy said, "It's Hardy sir, she's gone."

"What do you mean, gone? Explain yourself soldier," Storm replied, hit by a sudden gut feeling that the mission had just taken a turn for the worse.

Cowboy explained about the two of them going outside, about him asking for a bouncer to be sent out and about them both being stunned. It was a short stun, because he and the bouncer came around just as Norsky was leaving the car park.

"Shit!" exclaimed Storm. Stryder had picked up what was going on, and then looked around for Hardy.

"Where's Hardy? Something's happened to her," he said. Then he heard her voice through his NI, she was using an open channel.

"Stryder, I'm with someone who wants to say something to you," she said as everyone in the room turned to look at him. Because she'd accessed an open channel they could all hear her and Norsky could also talk and be heard until she closed the connection.

"Captain Stryder, I really enjoyed watching you work tonight and I must say I was quite impressed," said Norsky.

"I'll accept the compliment, one Special Forces soldier to another Norsky, or can I call you Pavel?" Stryder replied.

"Once again you amaze me with your skill. I thought my true identity would remain hidden a little while longer." Norsky sounded genuinely surprised.

"Okay Pavel, we've established that you and I are soldiers

and have therefore accepted the risks. It's me you want, isn't it? Let the girl go, pick your place and I'll meet you there, alone."

"You forget, my friend, that Miss Hardy here has also accepted the risks as she too is a soldier, no? So, we are all soldiers together, risking our lives for the causes we believe in. Romantic is it not? So down to business. You will meet me at a time and place of my choice and if, when you arrive, I deem it that you have fulfilled your side of our little contract then, and only then, will I release the girl."

"Okay Pavel, just name the time and the place and I'll be there."

"I'm sure you will my friend, I'm sure you will. The time is not yet, the place is yet to be affirmed, but don't worry. I will be in touch with all the details you require through Miss Hardy here, so you can be assured she is safe and well. But be warned, if you do not adhere to my stipulations, Miss Hardy will surely die," and with that Hardy broke the connection.

"Seems this Norsky guy has got you by the balls," Bane said, breaking the silence that had settled over the small room.

Stryder looked at Bane and the look in his eyes made the gangster recoil a little for it was like looking into the depths of Hell itself. When he spoke his voice was cold and hard with no trace of emotion or humanity left in it.

"That's as may be, and he intends to squeeze until he gets what he wants, which leaves me no choice," he said.

"So what're you going to do?" Storm asked.

"The only thing I can do. What do you do when someone has you by the balls and is squeezing them?"

"Scream?" offered Bane.

"No. Squeeze back."

"Squeeze back against whom, may I ask? Would someone

please explain just what is going on here and where Hardy is?" General Sinclair said from the office doorway.

~

"I don't know what you hope to gain from this, but it won't work you know," Hardy said. Norsky had ordered her to drive away from the club to his hotel where they had ridden the elevator to ascend to his room on the tenth floor. The threat of the killing of anyone present if she tried anything made her reconsider any escape attempts.

"And why would you say that, my dear?" he replied rather smugly. He felt he held all the best cards in the game. The winning hand was his. Stryder would not endanger the woman's life by attempting to rescue her. Rather, he would wait until she was safe before attempting anything heroic. By that time though, it would be too late so he was also betting that Stryder was maverick enough to forgo any assistance and come alone.

"Kurt will find you and when he does, he'll kill you; it's that simple," she said, projecting far more confidence than she felt.

"And how do you think the multi-talented Captain will accomplish that feat, my dear?" Norsky asked, already knowing the answer.

Hardy thought about it for a second then, smiling, said, "How naive do you think I am? If I tell you how he'll find you it gives you the opportunity to cover your tracks. Let's just say that you'll have no idea how he'll do it but he'll do it alright and when he does, the fun will really start."

"Okay, so what say we start this off a little earlier than you expected?" Norsky said his smug smile still firmly in place.

"I don't follow," Hardy said, confusion showing on her face.

"If Stryder is as good as you hope he is, and there is no doubt he is a most remarkable man, then I see no reason to hang around to give him the opportunity to find us. We shall move on to the next phase of my plan," Norsky said as he collected his travel bag, already packed, from beside the table. When he saw her expression he said, "Oh I never unpack, I can't see the point. You never know when you'll have to grab your things and get moving again, like today for example."

He motioned for her to head towards the door and when she acquiesced he said, "What, aren't you going to ask where I'm taking you?"

"Nope, you'll tell me when you want me to know," she replied calmly. She'd decided not to play his game. She obviously wanted to ask him what his plans were, what he intended to do and where they were going. His "game" was the need to impress on her that it was he who was in control, that he held her life in his hands and that not even Kurt Stryder could rescue her. By not conceding to this scenario she was frustrating him and she hoped that the frustration would build until he made a mistake, something she could capitalise on to secure her release.

"And besides, I'll only have to wait for a minute or so and you'll tell me anyway. Your sort can't resist letting others know how clever they are," she added, hoping to sink another barb into his bloated ego.

"And what sort would that be, my dear?" Norsky asked, amused at her change of tack.

"You know the sort, the power hungry, the self-obsessed and the deluded. But if you're still in any doubt, just take a glance in the mirror," she replied calmly.

When he spoke, his voice was tight and clipped. Her

words had stung, had pierced his veneer and embedded in his ego, bruising it. He responded by saying, "You are wrong Miss Hardy. I am but a simple soldier fighting for what I believe in, much the same as you or Stryder. Would that our roles were reversed I dare say neither of you would do things any differently."

"That's where you're wrong. If I were in your shoes then this whole thing would be over by now. Mission accomplished, and I wouldn't need to brag about it either. Just get the job done and move on to the next mission."

"If you are successful and Stryder does manage to rescue you and kill the bad guy – me – will you truthfully be able to move on to your next mission? Is this a job, nothing more to you than that? I think not, I've seen the way you look at him, and him you. There's more there than just the job and I'm banking on that to make him play along and not endanger you. Now let's go. Don't worry, it'll soon be all over, one way or another."

"You got that part right at least," Hardy replied, with a smile full of scorn. As they exited the hotel she couldn't help wonder how much truth there was to his theory? Would Stryder sacrifice himself to secure her safety? Whether he had feelings for her or not, she was sure that he would do his utmost to secure her freedom and if that meant offering his own life as forfeit, she was sure he would pay that price. To her though that was too high a price to pay, so she vowed to do anything to make sure that didn't happen.

CHAPTER 17

"So you have a positive ID on whoever's behind this?" Sinclair said after he'd been brought up to speed on the situation.

"Yes, sir, but I don't see what good it'll do, not in time to get Hardy back anyway," Stryder replied. When he spoke there was steel in his voice, an icy, iron resolve and without asking, Sinclair knew what he intended to do. He would do whatever it took to get Hardy back safe and sound.

"You intend to wait until he contacts you, don't you?" Sinclair said.

"I don't see that I have any other choice, sir."

"I'll accompany you sir, my squad and I can be your back up," Storm said, offering before Sinclair could add anything.

"Thanks, but I don't think that'll be necessary or practical. Something tells me he'll choose somewhere that he'll have complete control over. Somewhere that we can't gain access to or place any back up units. That also means somewhere remote and isolated. Now you know as well as I do there are maybe hundreds of locations that could fit that bill. Now we don't have the time or resources to check them all out, so the only alternative is to wait for the call and play along."

"That is the most insane thing that I've heard in a long time," Sinclair said in exasperation.

"Yet it's true, sir, every word of it," Storm agreed, bringing Sinclair's laser-like stare fully onto him.

"I can't allow you to go through with this alone, there must be something that we can do," Sinclair said.

"Frustrating isn't it, having all the power Col Sec wields at your disposal and yet it means nothing? Well unfortunately, that's the truth of the matter. In the end its gonna come down to him and me, whoever wins that, wins the day," Stryder said reading Sinclair's expression expertly.

"My money's on you Kurt and I know it's safe," Storm said.

～

Norsky forced Hardy to drive to the spaceport where they boarded his shuttle. It was pre-programmed to return to the small starship he had placed in long-range geo stationary orbit above Jacksonville. It was equipped with stealth and whilst Norsky was down on the surface, all the equipment was powered down to a bare minimum to further reduce any threat of detection, however small.

Once the shuttle had docked they boarded the starship and Norsky spoke for the first time since boarding the shuttle.

"Welcome to my humble abode," he said.

"You live here?" she asked, incredulously.

"I move around a lot from mission to mission. I actually live on a planet not unlike Celeron but I hardly ever get to spend much time there so, yes, I suppose this is the closest thing to home I've got," he replied, a little surprised at allowing her that small insight into who he really was. Was he weakening, was he warming to this lovely woman and more importantly could he do what was required of him should the need arise?

Questions like those would only be answered when the time was right, so he chose not to dwell on them for fear of clouding his judgement.

"Come on, let me show you to your quarters, but first contact Stryder, like before on an open channel, so he knows it's you. I want them all to hear, okay?" he said injecting his voice with steel once more. This was business, time to get to work.

Hardy used her NI to access communication channels and was connected almost immediately.

"Kurt, are you there?" she said.

"I'm here, are you okay?" Stryder replied.

"She is fine Captain, I gave you my word," Norsky said before she could speak. "Now let's get down to business. You have one hour to reach the quarry north east of Jacksonville, I will meet you there. You will arrive there alone. If you bring anyone with you I will know and the woman will die. When I'm certain you are alone, I will release her," he added.

"How can I trust you?" Stryder asked, concerned for Hardy's safety.

"I have given you my word, as one soldier to another. That is all you need surely. Are you saying that if the roles were reversed and you gave me your word that I would have reason to doubt it?" countered Norsky.

"Touché Pavel, but just let me say one thing, if you don't keep your word, if you harm her in any way, I will kill you. You have no reason to doubt I'm telling the truth because I give you my word."

"You have one hour Captain, don't be late," Norsky said

finally. Then drawing a thumb across his throat he signalled Hardy to break the connection.

"You don't have to worry, he'll come, and alone. What you have to worry about is what he'll do once he gets here," Hardy said, trying to sound more confident than she felt.

"That, my dear, is why you will remain here on board."

"I should've known you wouldn't keep your word."

"My dear, you are my insurance policy, nothing more, nothing less. Your continued presence here ensures your boyfriend's good behaviour."

"Oh, I've no doubt you'll find some excuse to keep me here," she said with a sneer.

"This way my dear, I'll show you to your quarters," he said ignoring the look she gave him.

He led her down the corridor until they came to a door and he placed his left thumb to a panel next to the door, which then opened with a soft whoosh.

"Your quarters my dear," he said ushering her inside. As she came close to him he smiled then shot her with his pistol. The shot was on a stun setting but nevertheless, at such close range the force of the blast propelled her into the room. She was unconscious before she hit the floor.

"I'm sorry my dear, but I cannot allow you to contact Stryder through a combat channel to warn him," he said, although he knew she could not hear him. It was more for his benefit than hers.

～

Stryder had checked out the rendezvous point on the computer screen.

"There's no way you can go there alone. If he's already there he'll see you coming from miles away, you'll be a sitting duck." Sinclair said.

"So what do you suggest, sir, you've already tried to locate her via her tracker and failed. Wherever he has her is shielded and blocking the signal. Are you suggesting that I don't turn up and allow him to kill Hardy? If that happens, her death will be on your hands because you placed her here. Then what happens? Who does he kill next to get to me? No, this ends now, this ends here," Stryder argued.

"I take it you have something in mind? Please tell me you didn't buy into that one soldier to another soldier, you have my word crap? And please tell me you don't just plan on going there on your own."

"Okay then, I won't tell you," Stryder said and Sinclair, knowing it was useless to argue, quickly tried to think of another way to approach the problem. Just when he thought he had an idea Stryder added, "He said not to bring anyone along; he never said anything about having a starship monitor the rendezvous from orbit with a crack team from Recon Delta on standby ready to move at a moment's notice. An attack craft could reach any location within minutes. You can monitor my movements via the tracker in my implant."

Sinclair looked at him; the suggestion was identical to the one forming in his mind.

"I suppose that's a compromise that I can work with," he said with a smile.

"That's all we have, sir. Whether good or bad it'll have to do," Stryder said.

"I'll get the team prepped and ready to go. Scanners will be locked on to your tracker from the moment you are ready to leave. You already have transport. It might arouse suspicion if you arrive in a shuttle," Sinclair said.

"Sir, my team and I are ready to move on your command," Storm said eagerly.

"Good, that's settled then. We'll return to the ship and contact you when we're ready," Sinclair said.

"I'll be ready," Stryder said as he watched the General and Storm leave the room.

"Do you think you can pull this off?" Bane asked, amused by the whole situation.

"I have to," Stryder said, then he too walked out of the office.

Bane said, "Good luck."

"He'll need it," Tony said.

CHAPTER 18

Stryder knew where the quarry was and what it was like. Growing up in Jacksonville the quarry was one of those places that parents forbade their children to go near and so, obviously, it became their playground.

Stryder was no different; he and his friends had used the quarry for their childhood games. He knew it quite well and once he'd left the club he drove straight there.

"There you are," he said as he sat in the driver's seat of his ATV looking up at the quarry that opened out before him. There was not a lot to see, the only illumination coming from the stars overhead.

Having no portable scanner with him he was unable to tell if Norsky was already there, but one question arose in his mind, if he wasn't already there then where was he? The area was barren, long since abandoned and impossible to approach without being seen. It was a large hole cut from the side of a long, slow incline and was two hundred feet from top to bottom. Where he sat in his ATV was the only road into or out of it. The headlights of his vehicle illuminated the small portion in front, the rest remaining in almost total darkness.

"Okay Pavel, I'm here, where the hell are you?" he said out loud.

He checked his Sig for a full load then, tucking it into the waistband at the small of his back, slowly got out of his vehicle.

~

High above the quarry sitting in the pilot's seat of his shuttle, Norsky scanned Stryder. He'd seen him arrive and knew he was alone.

His scans showed he had one weapon with him as he got out of the ATV and that he'd made no calls on any of the open frequencies. If he'd used the combat channel to receive any messages it wouldn't do him any good because if his back-up was waiting outside of scanner range, ready to move in once Hardy was released, then they were in for a disappointment and were too far away to lend any assistance anyway.

He still held all the cards.

~

Sinclair was parading up and down the width of the bridge of the starship in orbit around Celeron, occasionally stopping behind the Op's station where the officer was keeping a constant lock on Stryder.

"Any change?" he asked on his latest flyby.

"None, sir, lock still holding. Captain Stryder is at the rendezvous point," replied the officer.

"Is there still no sign of anyone approaching, from any

direction, in any form of transport?" Sinclair asked, frustration giving his voice a certain edge.

"None, sir," came the reply. "Nothing on the ground for a radius of at least ten clicks and the skies above are clear also, except for authorised traffic in the commercial lanes," he replied.

"Okay, you let me know the moment anything alters," Sinclair said. Then turning to Captain Reynolds in the command chair in the centre of the bridge he added, "There's almost half an hour before the deadline, I'll be in my quarters. Keep me informed of any new developments Captain. My presence here seems to be adding to the tension, so I'll allow your men to get on with their jobs."

"Aye, sir, we'll inform you the moment Norsky makes an appearance," Reynolds replied. Sinclair gave a nod of his head then marched off the bridge.

This had always been the worst part of any mission for him, the waiting before the balloon went up. Remaining detached had never been a problem. Sending men to their deaths was just part of the job, something he had had to learn to deal with in order to survive in the military. That didn't mean that he liked it, or that he forgot about those who had died, quite the contrary in fact. The faces of the soldiers who had lost their lives were engraved on his memory and he, personally, contacted the relatives to inform them. It might not have helped the relatives who received the news, but he felt that it was the least he could do. To be able to do that meant he had to learn as much about them as he could and although the men under his command were unaware, he actually knew more about them than they realised.

It was because of this that his agitation levels had gone through the roof. He knew the project on Research Station Five had altered Stryder. He also knew it was his decision to go ahead with the project which cost the lives of four of his best men and changed the fifth forever. In spite of Stryder's protestations to the contrary he suspected the changes in him were as projected, perhaps even more so. Unfortunately he had to wait for Stryder to come to terms with those changes, accept them for what they were before he would be of any use to him.

He would be an incredible asset to the Confederation but conversely, if the Alliance got hold of him, he could also be a weapon to be feared.

As he returned to his quarters to await further updates on the present situation he said a silent prayer that Stryder would make the right decision.

~

Norsky watched as Stryder sat in his vehicle and waited. He'd had him on his scope since he'd arrived and was just waiting to see if he'd kept his word. If his actions so far had been any indication of the man's true personality, then he would keep to his word and come alone.

When Stryder got out of the ATV he knew it was time to make his move. There was nothing within a radius of three hundred clicks of them and anyone outside that limit, who wanted to help, would not reach them in time anyway.

He still had the winning hand because his ace in the hole, Hardy, was held in reserve.

Activating his NI he called Stryder through a combat channel. The frequencies were slightly different from Alliance to Confederation but he was sure he would make contact.

"Nice to see you kept your word Captain," he said.

Stryder looked around and could see no one even with his improved vision. He could see as well, if not better, than if he was using the latest generation of night vision lenses, a fact he'd only just begun to appreciate.

"Oh there's no need to look around for me, you won't be able to see me," Norsky said with a hint of glee in his voice. He was enjoying himself immensely, especially at how silly Stryder looked trying to see where he was.

"Okay Pavel, I'm here, what now? Where's Hardy?" Stryder asked not hiding his frustration very well. Then a thought struck him, if Norsky was in a position to approach him in order to pick him up but was out of sight, then it left only one possible location. He looked straight up and said, "Have you got enough landing room, I mean, I don't want you landing your shuttle on my head now, do I? It would sort of defeat the object of this whole exercise now, wouldn't it?"

There was a pause before Norsky could compose himself once more. When he'd watched Stryder look straight up it was almost like he was looking directly at him, as if he knew he was there, but that wasn't possible, was it?

"Very good Captain, it seems there is no limit to your talents. You have no need to worry though; you'll be quite safe, that I can assure you."

"That's nice to know," Stryder said, and he meant it because he knew it gave him some leeway. He was sure that the Alliance wanted him alive so that meant Norsky would have to ensure his safety. If it came down to a straight confrontation between the two of them, which he was sure it would, he knew he would have an edge over the other man because of his extra abilities. Norsky wanted him alive and that could make him hesitate, just enough to give Stryder an extra edge.

Norsky broke the connection and took the shuttle into a tight nosedive. The small, yet sleek, craft was equally at home flying either within an atmosphere or in deep space. It came soaring through the still night air at a hair-raising speed, until the very last minute when Norsky pulled it out of the dive, activating the landing thrusters to cushion the impact.

Stryder watched the craft come hurtling towards the quarry from high above, taking a keen interest in how it was handled upon approach. He hoped to learn as much about his adversary as was possible and seeing how he handled the shuttle, the aggressive way he brought her in to land, told him he liked to prove he was in charge. Perhaps Stryder's latest comments had rattled him slightly.

The door to the shuttle slid open revealing the aft section. No one was visible even to his enhanced vision, which meant that Norsky had reneged on his end of the bargain.

"Where's Hardy?" Stryder shouted.

Norsky appeared in the doorway with gun in hand.

"Lose the gun Captain," he commanded, his gun hand steadily keeping the pistol aimed directly at Stryder's chest. At that range he could hardly miss.

Reaching behind him Stryder brought the Sig into view.

"Slowly Captain, you don't want to make me nervous now do you? That way you'll never get to see the young lady again," Norsky said.

"Where is she? You said if I came alone you'd let her go," Stryder said striving to contain his anger.

"And I will, the moment you and I are safely away from here."

"So you're going back on your word then."

"Come now Captain, are you trying to tell me that if the roles were reversed, you would give up your insurance at the first opportunity? I think not, and by your expression I know I'm right. So, we go to my ship and I send her back down in the shuttle. That way you get to see her and know she's okay, and I get what I came for, so we're all happy. Now toss the gun."

Stryder did as he was told and waited for the next command.

"Slowly, come towards me."

Stryder thought about trying to jump him, wrestle the gun from his hand and take control of the shuttle, but he had no idea where his ship would be. Whether it would be cloaked, if there would be anyone else on board guarding Hardy, or any of the other variables that could endanger both their lives, so he decided to go along with him for the time being until he could get a better picture of what was going to happen. Then hopefully, he could come up with some sort of counter measure.

The Op's officer said, "Sir, a shuttle has just come out of the authorised lanes and landed near Captain Stryder's location."

Reynolds asked, "Have you a fix on Hardy's location?"

"Not yet sir," came the reply from the officer without looking up from his console.

"Keep me informed," Reynolds replied then said, "Captain Reynolds to General Sinclair, looks like the pickup is going ahead, sir. So far we've not confirmed the location of Hardy. How should we proceed?"

"Do nothing until Hardy is released then move in," Sinclair ordered.

"Ops, can you pick up anything on her whereabouts yet?" Reynolds wanted to know.

"Sorry, sir, there's no sign of her signature anywhere. If her tracker's active then she's either out of range, or dead."

"Let's hope for their sake that she's out of range, because I would not like to think what Stryder will do if they've killed her."

"There is one other possibility, sir."

"Are you gonna keep me waiting or do I have to guess?"

"Sorry, sir, the tracker might not be showing up if she's held in a ship with stealth. The cloak could mask the signal, sir."

"Is there any way for us to determine whether there's a cloaked ship out there in orbit somewhere before it's too late?"

"I very much doubt it, sir. By the time we'd reconfigured the sensors to search for a particular signature, and that's assuming we had the signature to search for in the first place, they'd be long gone."

"Okay, just keep a tight lock on Stryder and hopefully he'll take us to where the action is."

~

Stryder walked towards the shuttle his mind racing; formulating then disregarding options open to him. He realised that if he wanted to ensure the safety of Hardy he would have to go along with whatever Norsky had in mind, for the moment anyway.

Walking up the small ramp he entered the shuttle and the door 'whooshed' closed behind him, trapping him inside.

There was a sudden lurch as the thrusters lifted the small, sleek craft off the ground and into the air.

"Take a seat, this could get a little bumpy," Norsky said as he dropped into a seat across from him. A harness automatically strapped him in as the ship piloted herself.

Stryder took the seat across from Norsky and the harness secured him in place as the shuttle banked steeply into an almost vertical incline, her speed increasing to reach escape velocity.

Norsky never took his eyes from those of Stryder nor did

the muzzle waver from the centre of his chest. He had seen the Marine in action and he was not taking the chance of him getting an advantage.

"Obviously you came down here on your own, hoping that I would keep to my side of the bargain even if you had no intention of keeping to yours," Stryder said. "Which begs the question, are you alone? You possibly have one other with you who would be guarding your prisoner, that's assuming you haven't killed her."

"You're assuming an awful lot Captain. You insult my intelligence if you insist that you would not do the same if circumstances were reversed."

"Perhaps, but let me reiterate that if any harm has come to her then I *will* kill you," Stryder said, with a hard edge to his voice.

"You are in no position to make any threats Captain so just sit tight and enjoy the ride, it'll soon be over," replied Norsky calmly.

Stryder had no alternative but to do as he was told. He didn't have to wait much longer as the shuttle exited the planet's atmosphere and was in space moments after, at which time the craft's speed slowed considerably. The automatic pilot began docking manoeuvres as it approached a craft that suddenly appeared on the shuttle's scanners having dropped its cloak.

"You do realise that Col Sec is probably watching this, now that we've met up with your ship," Stryder said trying once more to rattle his captor.

"Yes, but I'm banking on them waiting for the shuttle to leave again with your Miss Hardy on board before they make their move," replied Norsky with a hint of a smile.

Stryder knew then what was about to happen. Norsky was right in assuming no one would make a move until they were assured of Hardy's safety. He'd made Sinclair promise that himself, and because of that, he'd sealed both their fates. Norsky had no intention of releasing her, because after all, she was his trump card and while they were waiting for her release, he could make his escape.

All this was his fault.

The outer hull doors clanged shut, the sound travelling even inside the shuttle, as they closed behind the smaller craft, hemming it inside the small docking bay and with it any hope Stryder had of escape.

"Okay Captain, I'll take you to your friend now," Norsky said as his seat released him. He still had his pistol trained on Stryder as he motioned for him to move out of his seat.

Stryder got to his feet and left the shuttle followed closely by the Black Knight. Even though he was behind him, Norsky led Stryder towards the room in which Hardy had been imprisoned.

"You'll find, my dear friend, that I kept my word about your lady friend. She is unharmed as I assured you she would be. It is unfortunate that it has to end like this but in every conflict there has to be a winner and a loser," Norsky said as they pulled up outside the room where he had left Hardy.

Operating the door release, Norsky opened the door and as it slid to the side revealing the room beyond, he said, "You'll find her in there."

Stryder took one step inside the room and as he saw Hardy sprawled out on the floor, turned in time to see Norsky aim his pistol and fire.

The blast, at close range again, sent him staggering inside the room to trip over the prone form of Zara Hardy. He hit the floor hard and lay there, unconscious.

"I'm truly sorry my friend, if it hadn't been for where we were both born, we could've been friends," he said as he left the room, closing and sealing the door with them inside.

Accessing the ship's computer through his NI, Norsky

gave the autopilot a command to leave orbit and return to Alliance space after engaging their stealth mode.

The ship banked sharply away from the planet, jumped into hyperspace and was gone.

~

"Any news of Hardy?" Reynolds asked the ops officer. "None at all, sir. Norsky's shuttle has entered the ship which suddenly appeared on our sensors, sir," replied ops.

"Keep a close lock on that ship. The second that shuttle leaves her I want a blast aimed at their engines. I don't want her going anywhere."

"Sir, they're gone," said the ops officer flabbergasted.

"What do you mean, gone?"

"Just that, sir, it was there one second and the next it'd gone. It made the jump to hyperspace, sir, we've lost it."

"Oh Christ!" Reynolds exclaimed as the importance of what he'd just been told sunk in. He thought for a second then said, "I want that entire section of space scanned for any residual energy signatures. We may be able to locate them if we know what to look for. I'm going to inform the General in person."

"Sir, you do realise that no one has ever been able to track a ship through hyperspace, don't you?"

"Yes damn it, but we have to try. We may just get lucky."

"Aye, sir," replied the officer as the Captain left the bridge. They both knew that all hope of finding Stryder and Hardy had vanished along with the starship, when it made the jump to hyperspace. He didn't envy his captain the task of informing General Sinclair of the fact.

CHAPTER 19

Stryder woke up to find he was lying next to Hardy on the floor of the room he'd been forced to enter at gunpoint.

He looked across at her and instantly knew that she was all right, unconscious but okay. She was close to coming round. He had no idea how he knew that, he just did, another indicator of the changes his body and mind had undergone.

He got to his feet and crossed the room to the door in a few strides. A quick inspection told him it was locked and secure, he wouldn't be getting out of there in a hurry.

He went back to Hardy and knelt beside her placing two fingers against the carotid artery and was pleased to feel the pulse, steady and pronounced. She would be fine.

She opened her eyes then and sat up quickly instantly regretting the swift movement.

"Ouch!" she said placing a hand on her head, "That hurt."

"Take it easy. If what happened to me is anything to go by, you were hit with a stun blast," Stryder said as he steadied her. She was a little shaky, having risen so suddenly.

"Wow, thanks," she said as she regained her equilibrium

and felt better. He released her and asked, "You okay?" concerned for her wellbeing. He knew that for them to escape they would both have to be at their best with no injuries. He knew that wouldn't be a problem for himself, but Hardy was another matter.

"I'm fine now, just a bit woozy there for a second. How about you, did you say you were blasted too?"

"Yep, but it seems I recovered quicker than you, probably due to the changes I told you about," he replied. Then a thought struck him and he started looking around the small room staring intently at the small recesses and the finer details.

"What're you looking for?" she asked, then she too realised he was looking for any sign that the room was bugged. If it was, then what he had just said could be the noose that hanged them.

"I can't see anything that would indicate there are any hidden lenses here, and there would be no reason for there to be. This isn't the brig; it's just a cabin like any of the quarters on board a thousand starships just like this one. If he'd planned on keeping us under surveillance then he would've put us in the brig. Everything about this pickup seems rushed to me, almost as if he made it up as he went along."

"You could be right there, especially seeing as how he watched you in the fight at the club. Watching you handle all those guys would make him revise his plans."

"They obviously want to extract whatever they can from me about the project so they can duplicate it for themselves."

"What do we do now then?" Hardy asked finally.

"I can't make any plans until I know where we are, but our priority has to be getting our asses out of here and as fast as we can," Stryder answered.

~

On the bridge of the starship Norsky was sitting in the pilot's seat, his fingers playing over the controls as he guided her through the vast reaches of hyperspace.

Everything was going according to plan; his mission had been an unqualified success. His capture of Captain Stryder almost certainly guaranteed his promotion and as that knowledge played around inside his mind he couldn't help but smile.

He'd outwitted the much-vaunted Confederation, captured their supposed prized possession right from under their noses and brought him here to Alliance space. Told like that in simple terms he wondered if Col Sec was the great force everyone was led to believe.

However, he had won and they had lost, it was as simple as that. Stryder was theirs now and there was no way they could get him back.

Personally speaking though, he couldn't see what all the fuss was about. Yes, he had to admit, that Stryder seemed to be a remarkable individual, but did he qualify for all the attention that was being lavished upon him? He supposed that only time would tell, and for him to gain the answer to that question he would have to get him safely to his destination.

An entry point to normal space opened in front of him, as the jump through hyperspace was completed, and the starship's deceleration back to real time speed took place.

He contacted Captain Nokorovic to inform him of his success.

"Congratulations Captain, this is excellent news. Go directly to our complex on Toldax and hand over your prisoners. Once that is done your commitment to this mission is fulfilled. You have some leave coming to you," Nokorovic said with obvious pleasure in his voice.

"Thank you, sir, I'll set course for Toldax immediately," Norsky said, hoping he had disguised the smug tone of his voice. He knew this victory would get him noticed by the high-ranking Generals of the Alliance.

"I'll inform them of your arrival," Nokorovic said, then broke the connection.

As Norsky programmed the autopilot for the change in course he couldn't help but plan what he would do with his newfound fame.

As the ship turned onto its new heading Norsky sat back in the pilot's chair a satisfied grin plastered across his face.

"Any news on finding that ship?" Sinclair asked as he strode across the bridge of the starship. He was battling to keep his anger under control. He had no idea how this situation had gone from poor to hell and back in such a short space of time. What was ten times worse, he had no idea how to gain anything from it. If they didn't find where Stryder and Hardy were, how could they even think of mounting a rescue operation? The answer was simple and short, they couldn't.

They had nothing to work on, no leads, nothing. It was hopeless. Stryder and Hardy were alone.

"None, sir," Captain Reynolds replied.

"Well, Captain, that's just not good enough!" stormed Sinclair. The bridge was plunged into silence, no one daring to utter even the slightest sound for fear of focussing his anger on them. It was unusual for the General to raise his voice like that. It was virtually unheard of and it caught them all off guard.

After a pause Reynolds said, "Sir, may I ask a question?"

Sinclair spun on him his fury blazing through his eyes,

but before answering he composed himself, aware that his normal shield of calm was slipping. He could not allow that to happen again. "What?" he said, his normal calm demeanour slowly returning.

"One thing's been bothering me for a while now, sir, and that's how the Alliance got hold of the codes for the Recon Delta tracking chips," Reynolds said.

"How is that going to help this situation may I ask?" Sinclair said, and then held up a hand to halt Reynolds, as he digested what had been said. "Yes, of course, if we can discover who gave them the codes, we might be able to exert some pressure to find out where they intend taking Stryder. Good point Captain, continue your search, I'll be in my quarters, I've things to sort out," he said. He turned on his heel and strode out of the bridge leaving Reynolds with his mouth wide open and the rest of the bridge crew to continue with their work.

After a short pause, Reynolds regained his composure and said, "You heard the man, let's continue the sensor sweeps."

~

Toldax was an Earth-type planet, one of the few that hadn't needed to be terraformed before the colonisation started. The Alliance found it before the Confederation even knew of it. It was situated twenty-four light years from the border of Confederation and Alliance space on the Alliance side.

Norsky took his starship into a parking orbit around the planet while he waited for authorisation to land. He didn't have to wait for long; the authorisation was rushed through giving him priority due to the nature of his cargo.

He took the starship into land at the main spaceport of

the military base, situated away from the populated areas. The population of the planet numbered close to four million, most of them living in the one huge city on the largest landmass. There were a few homesteads dotted about outside the city where those families who preferred to live off the land dwelled.

The military base was well away from any of these, situated almost on the opposite side of the planet, on the second of the two largest landmasses. It was a sprawling complex, low to the ground with only one floor at sea level but several floors below ground level.

As he landed, guards surrounded the craft the moment the engines were powered down and made secure. The hatches were opened and Marines stormed the craft.

"The engines have been cut and it feels like we've put down. Whatever they have planned will happen soon so stay close," Stryder said, standing between Hardy and the doorway to protect her from any intruders.

"What do you think they intend to do?" she asked as she came around him to stand by his side. If she was scared then she hid it extremely well and Stryder was proud of her, she was a fine Marine.

"I think they intend to extract what they can from me about the programme. How they intend to do that I'm not sure," Stryder replied, then his ears picked up a sound from outside the door. He turned his head so he could hear a little better.

"What, what is it?" Hardy asked, having heard nothing.

"They're coming, stay cool," Stryder said.

The door opened and three Marines entered the room.

They were all armed with assault rifles aimed at the couple in the room.

Norsky appeared from behind the Marines. His face had altered back to its normal physiognomy.

"Captain Stryder, you'll go with these gentlemen please," he said with a smug smile.

Stryder turned to look at Hardy, smiled, and said, "Don't worry, I'll be fine," then turned and walked towards the trio of Marines.

As they walked past Norsky Stryder said, "You touch one hair on her head and I'll kill you."

Norsky glanced at him and the cold stare from Stryder's cobalt blue eyes chilled his blood.

"You are in no position to make idle threats," Norsky responded.

"It's not an idle threat."

"Take him away," Norsky told the Marines, ending any further comments from his captive prize. He turned to Hardy and said, "You, my dear, will be coming with me."

"You've got to be joking right? If you think you're taking me anywhere then think again," she replied defiantly.

"You can stay here. The Marines will come back and lock you up, but God knows what they'll do to you. You're on your own behind enemy lines. You see, nobody knows where you are, so, my dear, there's no one who can help you. Or, you can come with me and I'll make your stay here as comfortable as I can. Your choice," Norsky replied.

"It doesn't look like I've got much of a choice; if I've got to be a prisoner then I may as well be a comfortable one," Hardy replied.

The Marines marched Stryder from the starship towards the interior of the base. They passed through several corridors until they came to a door that opened as they approached.

Inside the cavernous room was a large table at the centre. Straps were situated at the four corners, obviously to restrain whoever was forced to lie on it. At the head of the table was a row of monitors and three technicians, all wearing white lab coats, stood around waiting for the test subject, who Stryder knew to be him.

There was another person in the room, in the uniform of a General in the Alliance. He was huge, standing six feet six inches tall with the muscular build of a weightlifter, the bulges showing through his close fitting uniform. His hair was white and cut to military length. As they entered the room he turned and viewed them, a smile crossing his lips and his clear blue eyes showing his delight.

"Ah! There you are, you have no idea how long I've waited to meet you, Captain Stryder," General Solon said.

"I'm honoured, General Solon, in the flesh. I didn't realise I was *that* important for the head of Special Operations to come here personally just to tuck me into my new quarters. I feel very humble indeed," Stryder said. He'd recognised the man the instant he saw his broad back.

"So you know who I am. Of course, being in Recon Delta you would be aware of who commanded those opposite you. Well let's get down to it, shall we? You're here to help us find the solution to a problem that's been troubling us for a few months now."

"And that is?"

"Did the programme you took part in on your Research Station Five, render any repeatable results?"

"That's an easy one, so there was no need to go to all this trouble. All you had to do was ask and I'd have told you. The simple answer is, no, it was a complete failure."

"You'll excuse me if I don't believe you. There have been reports that you have exhibited signs of increased ability, which leads us to believe that it was the opposite in fact. We believe that it was an unqualified success and you're here to provide us with the samples that will allow us to repeat the process and form our own prototype."

"And what if I refuse?" Stryder asked.

A gun suddenly appeared in General Solon's hand, a Magerov M9. He said, "That isn't an option," and shot him. The blast of reduced pulsed plasma energy struck him in the centre of the chest stunning him. It sent him staggering backwards into the trio of Marines who caught him before he collapsed onto the floor.

"Strap him down on the table," Solon said to the Marines supporting Stryder then, turning to the lab techs, said, "He's all yours, get to work. I want results by sundown tonight." With that he left the room.

CHAPTER 20

Sinclair contacted Col Sec HQ on Earth via a secure link through his NI. The man he spoke to was his second in command and the man he most trusted. Colonel Abraham Gemmell, like Sinclair, was a career officer who had devoted his life to the service of the Confederation. He was the man who Sinclair relied upon the most to help run the Intelligence Division of Col Sec. Standing at six feet five inches tall with a slim, lean physique he set the example for the officers beneath him, regularly going on training exercises with the troops to keep sharp and abreast of the latest regime. Sharp grey eyes focused his keen intelligence on any task afforded him, which he faced head on with a fierce tenacity that bordered upon obsession. In his late forties, his hair, cut short to military length, had lost none of its colour and the dark lustre of the black hair contrasted with the light grey tone of his eyes.

He was at his desk in Col Sec HQ when he took the call from Sinclair. He had been waiting for a report from his superior, who had promised to keep him informed of the progress of that particular mission. It was a sticking point between them, as Gemmell argued that Sinclair should have delegated someone else to handle the op and not the head of the Intelligence Division. He thought that Sinclair was placing himself at risk and through him the entire security of the Confederation.

Sinclair had stated that he had a personal investment in the op because he had been in charge of the programme on Research Station Five, an investment that wouldn't allow him to delegate to anyone else. His personal involvement with the programme, and intimate knowledge of Stryder and the events that took place during the programme, made it imperative that he handle it. If there was any chance of rescuing anything from the ruins of that programme and getting Stryder to work with them once more, he had to take charge. He thought that Stryder might not take too kindly to just another Col Sec officer trying to persuade him to return, whereas if Sinclair approached him personally, he might be a little more receptive.

Whatever his arguments, Gemmell hadn't agreed but being only second in command – General trumps Colonel every time – he had to go along with it. What he did though was keep a close eye on things and have a starship on standby with a contingent of Recon Delta Marines on board ready to go at a moment's notice.

"We've got a major problem here Abe and I need you to do something. I'm not sure if it'll help the situation in time but this needs sorting anyway," Sinclair said once the connection was made.

"Go ahead, sir," Gemmell replied gearing himself for what he'd expected since the beginning.

"Stryder has been captured by Alliance forces. What I need from you is information. They captured him by accessing the codes for his tracker," Sinclair said, waiting for what he knew must come from his close friend and second in command – the inevitable "I told you so".

"How is that possible sir, those codes are accessible only to someone with Gold clearance?" Gemmell replied, controlling the urge to vent but instead focusing on the problem at hand.

"That's what I want you to find out."

"Now I understand what you meant about it helping the immediate situation. What are your thoughts if I manage to locate what you want? I'm assuming you think we must have a mole here at HQ?"

"That's right, it's the only possible answer. What I want you to do, and it'll be difficult I'm aware of that, made more so by the time constraints you'll have to work under, is find the mole without tipping your hand. I don't want them either running scared or going deep so we never find them, you understand? Once you have them I want them squeezed until they agree to work for us. We need their contacts so that we can work something out about getting Stryder back."

"I'm sorry, sir, but I don't see how getting the mole to work for us can help get Stryder back. The Alliance will just cut them loose; they'll never swap them for him."

"I know, but if we can get their contact in the Alliance we may be able to learn where they're holding Stryder and if, and I stress the word *if*, we learn that, we can hopefully mount an op to recapture him before it's too late."

"I understand about the time constraints you mention, sir, but there are also too many 'ifs' for my comfort sir."

"You'd better get to work then Abe."

"Yes, sir, I'll get my best man on it right away," Gemmell said.

"I knew I could rely on you for this Abe and I know I've got some serious 'I told you so's' coming my way from you, so I just want to say from the start, thanks."

"Look sir, the recriminations can wait until this is over. Let's just get this done, then you can thank me, okay?"

"You're right of course, do your best Colonel."

"Always, sir," Gemmell said, then the call was ended. He sat back in his chair and thought about what lay ahead and the best way to go about it. There was only one way to handle this delicate situation and that was with kid gloves. His top man was not known for his delicate approach, but he was the best he could think of. He would just have to adapt his approach to this particular problem.

Using a secure channel he called the person in question. Captain Matthew Hawk. He was on Earth at that moment training with a team of Recon Delta Marines in close quarter combat.

Standing six feet six inches tall with broad shoulders, trim waist and thick, muscular arms and legs, he faced three opponents. His ice blue eyes sparkled with a mischievous quality that was often mistaken for indifference. Those who faced him knew him well enough to not underestimate him.

They were in a chamber in Col Sec HQ, the Intelligence wing deep in the bowels of the building where most of the training took place.

"Okay guys, let's see what you've got," Hawk said with a smile, his deep bass voice booming in the confines of the room.

"Don't be too confident, Matt," said the leader of the trio who was in the centre facing him. Just then the two men flanking him rushed at Hawk who stepped forward, his arms open wide, and slammed both his log-like arms across the chests of the two attacking Marines in a manoeuvre called a clothesline, popular with pro wrestlers. The two Marines hit his arms and stopped dead but their feet carried on travelling at speed sending them spinning in the air to land flat on their backs.

"Oh, I'm not," Hawk said, his smile still in place. Kicking the last Marine in the stomach with his right foot sending him staggering backwards, Hawk followed and hit him across the back of his neck which sent him crashing to the floor.

The tingle he felt in his NI told him a call was coming through.

"Hawk here, go ahead," he said, instinctively knowing that it was a secure channel being accessed.

"Captain Hawk I have an urgent mission for you, I'll brief you in my office in ten minutes. Don't be late Captain, drop whatever you're doing now and get here," Gemmell said.

"Already have, sir, I'm on my way," Hawk replied.

"Thanks guys, we must do this again soon," he said with a smile as he left the chamber.

He went straight to Gemmell's office not bothering to get changed out of his training clothes and into something more appropriate. The call had said immediately and that's exactly what Gemmell meant. He knew better than to be late.

He walked into the office to see Gemmell seated behind his desk.

"Thanks for your prompt arrival Captain, believe me on this one time is of the essence," Gemmell said as Hawk approached the desk.

"What's up, sir?" Hawk asked as he sat on the chair in front of the desk.

"Are you aware of the project that took place on Outpost Station Five, the one involving Captain Stryder?"

"To an extent. I know that it was a failure and that Captain Stryder is on extended leave to recuperate."

"Well, the Alliance had other ideas. They're of the opinion that it was a success and have captured Stryder on Celeron. They did it by accessing the secure codes for the tracker integral to the NI. The fact that they've nabbed Stryder is bad enough, but the fact they now have the ability to access the codes means they can pinpoint any of the Recon Delta Marines either covert or not. It places our forces at a distinct disadvantage."

"What is it you want me to do, sir?" Hawk asked.

"It'll be a few days before we can implement the new codes which means all our operatives are in danger, including yourself and all the command staff. The only good news is that the Alliance will be too preoccupied with Stryder to implement any attacks. You, my boy, have the unenviable task of finding the mole in HQ. The only way they could've got their hands on those codes was from someone with Gold Access, that's someone in this building. I want you to locate whoever it was without their knowledge. We want them so that we can identify the person they passed it on to. General Sinclair wants to sweat the contact to find out where they're holding Stryder so that we can mount an operation to rescue him before he's told them too much."

"No pressure then, sir," Hawk said with a smile.

"Yea, I realise it's short notice and you'll have to work fast and quiet over this one, but it's come down from General Sinclair personally. He's requested my best man on it and here you are. There's a lot at stake here, Matt. I know you realise that and you'll do your best so I'll let you get on with it. Keep me informed. You have whatever you need to fulfil this mission, full authority on my command," Gemmell said his expression stern.

"Thank you, sir, I may need it," Hawk said, and getting to his feet turned to leave the office.

At the door Gemmell said, "Good luck Matt. Oh and no mess ups okay?"

Hawk turned back to face him and said, "As always, sir."

Walking away from Gemmell's office Hawk's mind was already on the problem. Whoever had gained access to the codes must have had Gold clearance, which meant that it was one of General Sinclair's staff. In a way that was advantageous in that it was a finite number and he would not have to consider the thousands of personnel who worked at HQ in total. Sinclair's staff numbered only a fraction of the total but he had to come up with a way to narrow the parameters of the search.

By the time he reached his office the germ of an idea had begun to form in his mind.

Norsky showed Hardy to her new quarters away from the main area of the complex. The silence between them was like a wall she had constructed as protection. She was a prisoner, that fact she was well aware of, but one thing puzzled her. During her capture Norsky had acted professionally, he had been courteous with just the right amount of steel to reinforce his control. Since they had arrived and Kurt had been handed over though, his attitude had altered slightly. It was almost as if his mission was over and he could relax. The way he looked at her and spoke to her gave her the impression that he treated this almost as if it was a date.

She knew he was attracted to her and she thought perhaps she could use that to her advantage.

"Here you are my dear, your new home for the next few days at least," he said at the door.

"And what then?" she asked, turning to look at him, trying to gauge him.

"That is out of my hands, but it won't be long before they have what they want from your Captain Stryder. Once that is completed then the balance of power will be reinstated. It may even have shifted into our favour."

"Do I hear the rattle of sabres in your words?"

"On the contrary Miss Hardy, just because I am a soldier willing to fight and, if necessary, die for his side, do not think I am an advocate for war. I pray for peace but I am unafraid to fight if war is declared."

"Nice words but I've seen little to back them up."

"What happens to your friend is inevitable, he went into the situation with his eyes wide open and if I'm not mistaken, he volunteered. The idea was to gain an advantage over the Alliance, isn't that, as you say, rattling of sabres? What we have done is merely an act of self defence, an attempt to restore the status quo."

"That's as may be, but if you seek to gain an advantage out of this, isn't that war mongering?"

"We could go around and around with this with no one gaining a clear advantage. One thing I am certain of is this; on either side are individuals who would seek any sort of advantage over the other to use as a weapon. Some would use that weapon to its full potential and an equal number would use that weapon as a deterrent. I pray it's the latter that wins any argument. You and I are soldiers and so are not privy to such arguments; we only have to act on their outcome.

"In the meantime, there is no reason for us to act like savages. I will treat you in a civilised fashion and even though I know you must try to escape, your quarters will be comfortable."

"And what about you? You've completed your mission. I suppose you'll be moving to your next mission, so why do you care if my quarters are comfortable or not?"

"Actually I have some leave owed to me so I can go wherever I please. To answer your other question, I suppose I'm eager to dispel the propaganda that surrounds the Alliance. We are no different from you; we have the same likes, dislikes, the same needs and fears. Borders are what separates us at this moment in time. We are all one race and despite colour, creed or spiritual belief, we are all human. We are not so unalike, you and I."

"If you truly believe that about us irrespective of merely being soldiers, why are you so concerned about this soldier?" she asked, her eyes boring into his until he looked away.

"Perhaps in the hope that one day the fighting will cease. Perhaps that end begins with one soldier laying down his arms," he said, looking at her again.

"Very prophetic, have you ever thought of resigning from the military and running for office? You'd have my vote," she said sarcastically.

Norsky glanced at the floor then placed his palm against the door lock so that the palm reader could identify him. The door opened with a soft whoosh.

"Your quarters may be comfortable but make no mistake, Miss Hardy, due to the nature of our profession it is still a cell."

As she slowly brushed past him, she looked into his eyes and said, "If I promise to behave, will you stop by to keep me company?" and then she was inside the room facing him with a smile on her face that hinted at the possible delights to follow, if he was brave enough to face the challenge.

He reached for the door lock but before engaging it said, "I am on leave, so I can spend it wherever I please." Placing his hand on the lock he looked at her and smiled. He said, "If I kept you company, would I want you to behave though?" and the door slid shut.

Hardy watched as the door closed separating her from him and she felt an odd mix of emotions. Norsky was her gaoler, of that there was no doubt, a very charming one but a gaoler nonetheless. He was passionate about what he was doing, of that there was also no doubt. She knew he was attracted to her but would that attraction outweigh his sense of duty? Would she be able to persuade him to swop sides purely on the basis of that attraction? She had her doubts.

If that attraction failed then she would have to resort to more tried and tested methods.

~

Matt Hawk sat at his desk staring at a computer monitor. For the past few hours he had been perusing the personnel records of all General Sinclair's staff, the only people with Gold clearance and therefore access to the stolen codes.

As he expected, each and everyone was beyond reproach as prerequisite for the position they held. Although they were civilian personnel, they were employed by a military body and therefore subject to military laws, rules and regulations, a fact they were made aware of right from the start.

One of them was at fault here though, he just had to delve deeper which was tricky because he had to keep his interest under wraps. If the person responsible found out someone had been going through their records they would do one of two things: either bring it to the attention of their superior or inform their contact, the real target of this investigation. If that were to happen the odds of capturing them would go from slim to none.

There was nothing at all against any of them. He had nothing to go on. His eyes felt like he'd walked through a desert sandstorm from all the hours staring at the monitor and he was about to close it down to pursue another avenue of investigation, when he noticed a comment placed on one of the files.

Zooming in on it he rechecked the file in question. The

comment had been almost a throwaway. A "something and nothing" event, but because of the nature of the work they undertook and the security involved, the shift supervisors were under orders to note any changes in behaviour, habits, work patterns in fact anything. It did not matter how slight or seemingly inconsequential. It was up to someone else to work out the significance.

The person in question had been flexible where breaks were concerned, always fitting her lunch breaks around the workload. The comment was about her leaving work after hearing some bad news regarding a relative.

Quickly he checked call logs to her and saw no mention of such a call, neither was there any follow-up action.

That was it; it had to be. There was no one else who even came close to looking like a suspect.

After closing down his terminal he quickly went to his bathroom, threw off his clothes and stepped into the shower. He let the hot water spray ease out the few aches and pains he felt from being stuck at his desk for so long, while his mind worked through the problem that lay ahead.

He stepped out of the shower and the water automatically switched off, and then he entered the drying chamber. By the time he was dry and getting dressed, he knew what he had to do.

~

Stryder opened his eyes and found himself in a small room. There was no window and only one door. He was lying on a simple bunk positioned by the wall to the right of the door.

Swinging his legs around and onto the floor he sat up. Taking stock of his position he quickly inspected himself. Not so amazingly, he could find nothing wrong. No injuries at all, so whatever they had done to him, they certainly hadn't tortured him?

There were no puncture marks on his arm, not surprisingly because they would have healed instantly anyway. If they had taken blood samples then there was no way of him knowing, unless he could get someone to talk.

Despite the position he found himself in, how hopeless the situation seemed not knowing what the Alliance had done to him or taken from him, he couldn't help but feel elated. Not just elated though, he felt good, never better in fact. He felt as strong as a bull elephant; his mind was sharp and focused so whatever they had done to him might have helped him in some way.

He had a clear and precise control over his senses and bodily functions. Not knowing how it had come about he was just aware that it had. He also felt something different about his mind, he couldn't quite put his finger on it but there was definitely something new going on in his head.

If all those changes had occurred during their tampering, how had his already enhanced immune system been affected? He could tell that it had not been diminished and if anything it had been improved even further.

Just what he was capable of now frightened, yet excited, him a little. A wonderful feeling of euphoria had come over him and he felt he had, despite all the odds stacked against him, a better than even chance of escaping. He had absolutely no idea how he would do it, he just knew he would. It was almost like he'd already seen it in the future and all that he had to do to allow it to happen, was not deviate from that path.

But before he could do anything he had to locate Hardy and without thinking an image of her popped into his mind and he knew instantly where she was.

Using his NI he contacted her through a secure channel.

"Hardy, are you alright? If you can't speak, clear your throat once," he said softly. Although he had accessed a combat channel that would piggyback the signal onto local frequencies, it would still be encrypted and transmitted directly to the communication centre of her brain, so that even if she were in a crowded room the call would not be overheard. It would only gain anyone else's attention should she reply audibly.

"I'm fine Kurt. Where are you? Are you alright? What have they done to you?" she said, concern filling her voice.

"I've no idea where I am, all I know is, it's a small cell with only one door and no window. I don't know what they've done, but whatever it was I feel great. Listen, we have to get out and back to Confederation space," he said, his tone upbeat and ebullient.

"And how do you propose to do that, Kurt? We're deep in Alliance space in a guarded facility populated by Alliance troops. Oh and we have no transport," she said, her voice rising a little with tension.

"I'm working on it, but first things first; we need to get out of this facility," he replied.

"Oh, when you say it like that, it doesn't sound so bad," she said her voice dripping with sarcasm.

"See, I told you I'd rub off on you. Just hold on and I'll have you out of there in a jiffy," he said calmly.

After getting dressed Hawk checked on the whereabouts of Joanne Watkiss, his suspect, who was still at home after being allowed to leave early the day before.

A sudden feeling of dread filled him. He knew how ops like this worked and he didn't think for one second that this data Joanne Watkiss had passed over was the first titbit. Her contact had probably started off with something small and worked up to this, the big score. Now that they had what they wanted from her they would probably close the op down, and to do that they would have to sever all connections and tie off any loose ends.

This meant that the moment she had passed over the codes was the moment she had signed her death warrant. They would wait for confirmation that the codes were useful before taking action. Once the confirmation came through then she was as good as dead.

His time might have just run out, he had to get to her and fast.

$\sim$

Pavel Temic had gathered all his things together in preparation to leave Earth. This had been his longest assignment and he had even leased a place of his own to use as an operations base. It was a small, yet plush apartment in the heart of New York. The allowance he was granted from the Alliance black ops fund paid for it, so he could maintain his cover as a playboy businessman. He made sure any meetings he attended were never anywhere near to where he lived, they were always in hotels far away.

Once he'd taken care of one last piece of business he was free to leave; that one piece was the last loose end he had to tie off. Nothing must be traced back to him; that loose end was the mole, Joanne Watkiss.

Having pre-booked a flight from Earth and put his bags in the ground car he'd leased, all he had to do was make a stop at her apartment to finish off, then straight on to the spaceport to catch his flight. It should be simple really; however these things rarely were. There were too many variables to contend with that could halt any carefully made plan. He'd thought it through as carefully as he could, given the time constraints he was working under.

He'd been ordered to return to HQ for debriefing once confirmation of Stryder's capture had come through. Events had unfolded at breakneck speed since he'd acquired and passed on the codes from the mole. Within twelve hours it was all over and he had to leave before any Col Sec investigation could be launched and eventually point in his direction.

Working feverishly, he'd severed all contacts, tied off all loose ends except one, the mole. He'd kept track of her, his most valuable asset, and knew pressure was getting to her. He had already decided to terminate her anyway so that she could not lead them to him, but now the order had been made official.

He knew she had gone home using some excuse and was still there. He planned to make it look like suicide due to her distress over the news of the relative, which tied in with her story.

Once that was done he could leave.

His flight left in three hours. He thought he had plenty of time as he envisioned himself sitting in the departure lounge sipping a cocktail while he waited for his flight.

With that thought still in his mind, he left his apartment.

CHAPTER 21

General Solon strode into the main lab eager for some good news. It had been a few hours since the samples had been taken from Stryder and he wanted to know what progress had been made. He could have contacted the lab from his office but he wanted to see first-hand what was happening. In his long experience he knew that a face-to-face consultation would yield better results from subordinates.

"So how's it coming, what progress have you made on the samples?" he asked with a sense of urgency that made everyone present sit up and take notice.

"Actually it's gone quite well. I've managed to isolate the genome responsible for…"

"In plain language, please! Have you got a workable serum?" Solon said cutting him dead.

"Well, obviously we would have to do some tests before…"

"Have you got a workable serum or not? Remember Doctor, these men are all volunteers."

After some hesitation he said, "I can't sign off on this until I'm sure."

"Then make sure, you have one hour, then you start injecting the team," Solon said, and with that he turned on his heel and walked towards the door. He stopped just before leaving, turned and looking at the dumbstruck lab technician and said, "Get to work Doc, the clock is ticking." He was gone and the door closing behind him emphasised the end of the conversation.

~

Temic arrived at Joanne Watkiss' apartment block and parked his car at the front. As he got out of his vehicle he called her via his NI.

Inside the apartment Joanne Watkiss was sitting on her bed still crying. She had been distraught since the news had come into Col Sec HQ that Stryder had been captured and that the Alliance had got hold of the access codes to the tracking chip in the Neural Implant every Col Sec employee had. The tracking codes were unique to the Delta Recon Marines and had been Col Sec's ace in the hole.

She knew, of course, how the codes had fallen into the possession of the Alliance, because she had handed them over. She was so distraught that she was considering suicide. She doubted she could face her employer, General Sinclair, who had placed his trust in her. The thought of being sent to a penal colony made her sick to her stomach.

She was contemplating what to do when the call came through.

"Joanne, are you alright? When you didn't show up for work I was worried." Temic feigned concern easily, he was a master at deception, having made it part of his job.

She was startled at first, wondering how he knew she

hadn't gone to work, then pleased that he was enquiring about her. She knew he worked for the Alliance, if she had had any doubts before, then his recent actions had destroyed them. She had given him the codes and Stryder had been captured. It didn't require a degree in Quantum Physics to work out that he had to be responsible. The question now though was what was he doing here, at her apartment?

Not knowing what to do, she replied carefully, saying, "I'm fine, what do you want David?" trying to keep the concern out of her voice.

"I've come to see if you're alright. Can't a man show concern for his woman now?" Temic replied, hoping that would suffice.

"Yes, of course he can, it's just that you've never called me your woman before and you've always kept your distance from my home."

"Well, I think it's about time to change that, don't you? It has been long enough, don't you think?" he said hoping that she would let him in. He could get in on his own, but he didn't want to leave any signs of forced entry for when the authorities arrived in a few hours.

Momentarily she allowed her emotions to get the better of her and she operated the lock on the outer door to the stairwell but by then it was too late.

Temic heard the door lock release and he pushed open the door to enter the foyer. In front of him was the stairwell that led up to the third floor where her apartment was located.

It will all be over very soon, he thought as he took the steps two at a time.

Matt Hawk arrived at the same apartment block just as Temic was half way up the stairs to Watkiss' apartment. There was a car parked outside the building and he knew instinctively that it belonged to whoever had come to kill her. He got out of his own car and ran to the door. Accessing a secure channel through his NI he said, "Miss Watkiss, my name is Hawk and I'm from Col Sec. I'm here to protect you."

"Col Sec? Why would you be here to protect me?" she asked, trying to keep up the pretence of innocence.

"I believe you may have handed over data to someone who works for the Alliance, data of a sensitive nature and now that person has come to kill you. I'm here to prevent that from happening," he replied.

"What do you intend to do, prosecute me?" she asked not denying her crime.

"Let's talk about that when I've got you safely out of there. Your safety is my main priority at the moment," he replied then added, "Now open the door."

"I can't go to prison," she said, her voice full of fear.

"Trust me; if you don't let me in that won't be a problem because you'll be dead. Now let me in!" Hawk said allowing his voice to rise at the end to emphasise the danger she was in.

She didn't want to believe him, yet found it impossible not to. She operated the door lock, allowing him entrance to the building.

Hawk ran through the door checking his pistol as he also took the stairs two at a time.

~

Temic reached her apartment at the same moment Hawk entered the building.

He rapped his knuckles on her door to indicate his arrival, startling her.

"Who is it?" she said before realising she'd spoken.

"Who do you think it is sweet one? It's me, the man of your dreams," he said injecting a note of humour into his voice hoping to put her at ease.

"David!" was all she could say. If what Hawk had said was true, and she had almost convinced herself of the validity of his words already, then she had to stall him until he got here.

"Yes, David, who else were you expecting?" Temic replied getting a little testy. He wanted this done and dusted so he could leave for the spaceport. Why was she acting like this? Had someone got to her? If they had, then it added a whole new dimension to the situation, one that he wasn't too happy about.

He took out his pistol, a Magerov P9, standard issue for Alliance armed forces. It was larger than the Sig P996 but worked on the same principle, delivering a larger shot capability. He pulled back on the slide at the top to prime the battery clip. Selecting full power he rapped on the door once more and said with a bit more force, "Come on Joanne, open the door."

Behind the door Joanne Watkiss was beginning to panic, her breathing was getting faster, her pulse rate was quickening and she was beginning to sweat. Accessing her NI she replied to the last call, Hawk.

"You'd better hurry he's at my door now," she said not bothering to keep her voice low as panic tightened its grip on her.

Temic heard her through the door and stepped away levelling his pistol at the door lock. His time had run out and his suspicions had just been confirmed. There was someone on the way to help her.

He fired his Magerov P9 at the door lock blasting it apart in a shower of sparks. The door slid open.

Joanne Watkiss stood in the centre of the room her hands bunched into fists near her mouth, abject terror in her eyes as she stared death in the face.

"Hello, Joanne, aren't you pleased to see me?" Temic said with a snarl across his lips.

She let out a scream as he levelled his Magerov P9 at her in preparation to fire.

~

Hawk was one flight down from them when he heard the door lock explode. Increasing his pace he powered up the last few stairs knowing that if he got there too late he had failed not only Joanne Watkiss, the unwitting pawn in this power play, but Captain Stryder too.

He was not about to let that happen.

The scream alerted him to her plight and he pushed himself to his absolute limit, sprinting up the last few steps. Reaching the top of the landing he saw a man outside a doorway aiming a pistol towards the inside of the room.

He'd already got his own pistol out and primed. If he shot the gunman, he'd lose his chance of finding Stryder; on the other hand he couldn't allow him to kill a defenceless woman.

Deciding what to do in a flash, he made his move.

Watkiss saw Temic's finger start to tighten on the trigger and she knew what was about to happen. She had hoped that her saviour would get there in time to help but it seemed that wasn't to be. She would die there and then in her apartment.

The blast of the pistol going off was as loud as anything

she had ever heard. She expected excruciating pain like she'd never felt before, but flinching reflexively as she expected the shot to hit her, she was amazed that she felt nothing.

She glanced up and saw a shower of sparks erupt at the side of the door next to Temic.

Temic was about to fire He had his target in his sights when he heard another shot. The plasma bolt struck the doorway at the side of his head showering him with sparks from the impact.

He turned to see a rather large man standing almost at the top of the landing with a pistol in his hand.

It must be her rescuer.

Turning quickly, Temic dived into the room just as his attacker fired once more.

Hawk fired another shot just to discourage and rattle him. The more he thought about his own safety the less he would think about killing the Watkiss woman.

He still had to get up there quickly though or he'd be too late.

Watkiss had flattened herself against the far wall as Temic came bursting into her room. The gun in his hand looked huge and powerful and the mere sight of it scared the crap out of her.

Temic rolled to his feet then ran farther into the room. He narrowly evaded Watkiss as she dodged out of the way and pressed herself against the wall to his left. He turned to face the door from where his immediate threat would come. Whoever her rescuer was, he would be coming through the door any second and he had to defend himself. The woman could wait until he'd taken care of this fool.

Hawk came storming up the last few stairs his pistol aimed ahead of him in a double-handed grip. He stopped as he had a clear view into the room. Temic was standing there in plain sight, his pistol aimed straight at him. Then he fired.

Hawk dived to the left. The pulsed plasma bolt flew past so close he felt the heat from the blast sear his flesh.

Hitting the floor he went into a roll and came up on one knee, his pistol out in front.

"This is not gonna be easy," he said to no one in particular.

Knowing time was against him he peered around the doorframe to see the gunman turn towards the woman, his pistol aimed directly at her.

Temic had fired at the hulking brute and was amazed at the reflexes of the huge man. No one should be able to move that fast, especially one so big.

He had to finish what he came for and then he'd take care of the big lummox.

Taking his eyes off the doorway he turned towards his original target and aimed at her head.

He couldn't miss.

Hawk fired around the side of the door jamb; deliberately aiming high, yet close enough to Temic to put him off what he was doing.

The bolt passed by him so closely it seared the cloth on the shoulder of his jacket. Spinning round just after firing at Watkiss, he aimed his pistol at where he thought the shot had originated.

Hawk dodged back behind the door jamb just as the bolt struck the wall at his side and passing through the open doorway.

Temic howled in fury at not being able to complete his mission and he stormed towards the doorway firing continually in an attempt to destroy the wall Hawk was using as cover.

Hawk had to get back behind the door jamb as fast as he could to evade the plasma bolt shot at him. He knew it had been fired blindly but wasn't about to take the chance of a random hit. Then the firing started and there was nowhere for him to go.

With each successive shot from the Magerov P9 more of the wall was blasted away along with any cover he might have had at the start. As chunks of masonry were blown apart, holes started to appear, getting closer with each passing second.

He had to do something, but his options were dissipating as rapidly as the wall in front of him.

"I have no idea who you are but you're going to die right now!" Temic shouted above the sound of gunfire. He continued to fire as he approached the doorway, each shot blasting away more and more of the wall. His next two or three shots would blow away what was left and he would be able to kill his attacker.

Hawk had to do something, he couldn't let this continue and he wasn't about to let this asshole get the better of him.

Rolling across the floor and into the doorway he fired his own pistol at the legs of his attacker.

Temic saw him come into view too late to do anything about it. The blast from Hawk's pistol struck him halfway between his right knee and foot knocking him over as the bottom half of his calf was almost blown away in a shower of blood and tissue.

Hawk continued his roll past the doorway and got to his feet the second he heard his attacker scream in pain. Framed in the doorway he had his pistol trained on the prone form of the Alliance soldier who was holding onto his bleeding leg.

When Temic saw Hawk he pointed his Magerov straight at him.

"Don't!" commanded Hawk as he aimed his own pistol directly between Temic's eyes.

It was a standoff. Who would fire first?

⁓

Believing it was safe her anger got the better of her. Watkiss had watched the exchange in abject terror. The thought that the man she loved had duped her to betray the Confederation and was now here to kill her was all too much. Her anger erupted like a volcano and she rushed at the prone form of her former lover screaming at the top of her lungs.

"How could you, you animal!" she shrieked punching and slapping at him as she fell upon him.

Temic fended off her attack and grabbing hold of her he pulled her down on top of him, one arm around her throat whilst the other held the Magerov to her head.

Hawk saw what was about to happen and was powerless to prevent it.

"Back off or she dies right here and right now!" Temic growled through the pain from his leg.

"Now just hold on. You know I'm not gonna let you out of this room alive if you harm one hair on her head. You know that right?" Hawk said. He kept his pistol centred on Temic's forehead.

"You aren't in a position to negotiate. I'm the one with the gun to her head, don't forget that."

"I disagree, you have nothing to bargain with. If you kill her then whatever leverage you think you have will be gone. I'm in control here, I have the power to either end your life or allow you to live. If you let her go I'll let you live, but if you kill her then you'll be dead one second later."

"You need me alive for what you think I can tell you about the whereabouts of your Captain Stryder. I know nothing, and even if I did, I'd never tell you."

"Are you telling me you have no idea where he's been taken?"

"Why would they tell me, that part of the operation was on a need to know basis?"

"I suppose they kept it from you just in case this happened?"

"You're not as stupid as you look are you? So you see I am in control."

"Wrong," Hawk said and shot him once in the centre of his forehead. The back of his head exploded backwards in a mist of blood and gore.

Watkiss was released and she screamed as she realised just how close she'd come to being killed.

Hawk accessed a comm channel through his NI and called Gemmell. "Sir, we have a problem," he said.

"Time's up Doc, we need to start the injections. You had better have them ready," General Solon said as he strode into the lab again.

"Yes, sir, we've got a batch of the serum ready but I can't guarantee the results, not without the proper testing," the lab tech replied with a trace of fear in his voice.

"That's what these boys are here for Doc, for the testing. Now let's continue shall we?" Solon said as he indicated five soldiers who had followed him into the lab.

The soldiers, having walked into the lab in single file, stood ready for whatever was going to be done to them. They were all hard faced, tough looking young men no more than twenty-five years old.

"Continue Doctor, the Alliance will owe you a great debt of gratitude if these tests are as successful as I hope them to be," General Solon said as he stood to one side.

The lab tech had readied a series of hypo sprays for

immediate use and with the General watching began to administer the serum to the neck of each soldier.

"Good, good. Let me know the second we have some results. Monitor them closely Doctor, your reputation rides on this, as does my career," Solon said as he turned and left the lab.

The lab tech watched him leave having completed the injections. He hoped they worked too; this was a huge risk. It was not one he would not normally take, especially when it involved someone else's life. The General though was not the type of person one said "no" to, not if life was something he wished to cling on to.

He turned to the lab tech standing just behind him and said, "Monitor their vital signs closely, the moment we have anything I want to be informed."

"Yes, Doctor," replied the tech as he watched his boss walk towards the door.

"I'll be in my quarters. I just need to lie down for a while," he said then turned and left the lab.

~

Stryder knew something was going on; he wasn't sure how he knew, he just did.

He'd pondered how to get out of his cell for the last few hours and all he'd come up with was that it was impossible. There was no way he could see of escaping without any weapons.

He would just have to wait until they came for him and hope that a chance arose once he was out of there.

~

Norsky was in his quarters contemplating the evening meal with Hardy when he was notified of new orders concerning Stryder and her, which would be issued to certain personnel on the base. It was a little bit of a shock even though he had half expected it. They had been listed for termination pending the results of the serum tests to be carried out by General Solon's personal guard.

The news hit him like a fist in the guts. Hardy was to be terminated! The feelings he felt for her came to the surface making him feel sick at the thought.

What could he do to prevent it happening? Wracking his brains for some solution to this new problem he began to pace up and down his quarters. Nothing seemed to work out of all the scenarios he came up with and each one was discarded with equal rapidity.

There seemed to be nothing he could do to prevent their deaths and then it occurred to him that if he approached the problem from a slightly different angle then he might just come up with something that could work.

The tests would be concluded soon. He had tracked the lab's progress through a remote monitor and so would have to move soon before the order to terminate was carried out.

The injections had been administered and they were simply waiting for the serum to begin taking effect. From the lab records he knew that would not be long. They must be expecting positive results because more of the serum was to be produced from the blood sample they had taken from Stryder. From this, a batch of replicated blood had been produced so that they had an almost endless supply from which to produce the serum.

Things were progressing quite nicely which could only be regarded as bad news for Stryder and Hardy.

If he was going to do anything, he would have to do it now.

Making a decision fast, he knew once he made his move there would be no going back. What he was contemplating was tantamount to treason and if he went through with it, he would end up a wanted man.

He had to ask, was she worth it? He would lose everything he had worked for, trained for and loved about the Alliance. It would all be lost to him, forever.

There was only one answer he could come up with. He had no idea how it had happened, but he had fallen for this woman, he loved her. He could not stand by and allow her to be killed, even if it meant he would lose everything he had. If he had her at his side then all the rest didn't matter.

The decision was made; he had to save her.

Foregoing all the plans he had thought of for the night, he left his quarters and headed straight to where he'd left Hardy.

Inside her quarters Hardy had been pacing the small room wondering what she could do. She felt trapped and it was beginning to get to her. Low in her stomach she could feel panic begin to bubble up and threaten to engulf her. It didn't seem there was anything she could do to escape. Having evaluated her situation she came to the conclusion that she was royally screwed.

After her brief conversation with Stryder her spirits had lifted slightly, but it had been a while now since she'd heard from him and despair was beginning to set in again.

When the door to her quarters suddenly opened she thought Kurt had been as good as his word.

Spinning around to greet him she exclaimed, "Kurt, you c- You!" as she saw who it was.

Norsky couldn't help but show the hurt he felt as he heard that name, and then as her expression changed, it was like she was turning a knife in his gut.

"No, Miss Hardy I'm afraid I can't help your friend, but I can help you," he said quickly entering the room.

"I don't understand?" she replied as she watched him.

"You will be terminated shortly, you and your friend. I'm here to help you escape," Norsky explained.

"Good, let's go get him then, no doubt we haven't much time," Hardy said as she made her way past him towards the door.

"Excuse me, didn't you just hear what I said? I can't help your friend but I can save you," Norsky reiterated.

"Well, that's not good enough, either we all go or we all stay. No, we all go or we all die!" she said stepping up to face him looking him in the eye, her gaze not wavering at all.

"You would die for him, you love him then?" he asked.

"We are both Recon Delta and we don't leave a fallen comrade behind" she replied evading the question.

"Yes, but do you love him?" he asked again.

There was a pause until finally Hardy said, "That's none of your business," watching for his reaction hoping that his feelings for her would outweigh his patriotism.

She readied herself to take action just in case he would not go along with her wishes. Balancing herself lightly on the balls of her feet, she was ready to move in any direction. She waited hoping that he would agree and help her to free Kurt, but if she had to she would attack him and then go to find Kurt on her own.

Norsky was going through hell in his own head. On the one hand, he wanted to get her out of there and out of danger but on the other hand, he was loyal to the Alliance. He had grown up and been nurtured by the Alliance his entire life and if he helped this woman he would be betraying all that he believed in. It was a quandary that seemed to have no answer. How could he choose between that which had nurtured him and the woman he loved? It seemed an impossible choice but he realised it was one he had already made just by standing there. He had chosen the woman he loved.

"Okay, let's go, we haven't got much time," he said.

They walked down the corridor and luckily for them, met no one. When they came to a corner Norsky stopped her and turning to her said, "Wait here, there will be guards outside his room. If they see you they will ask questions." Hardy nodded her approval and watched as he rounded the corner on his way to Stryder's cell.

The second Norsky was out of sight she accessed a combat channel through her NI and said, "Kurt, we're coming to get you out of there. The door will be opened in a moment, be ready to move."

Stryder heard the call and prepared himself, not questioning the veracity of it for he knew it to be true the moment he recognised the voice. All his senses went into overdrive, ready to move in an instant. His hearing picked up the approach of footsteps. He felt his pulse quicken as adrenalin flooded his bloodstream ready for the upcoming action.

Outside the door two guards stood dressed in battle fatigues with blast-resistant body armour and combat helmets. As Norsky turned the corner and walked towards them they turned to look in his direction eyeing him warily. When they recognised him their stances altered slightly, becoming more relaxed as they saw he was no threat.

"I've come to take the prisoner to General Solon's office; he wants to question him further," he said amiably.

"We'll have to check first, sir, you understand," replied the guard standing to the right of Norsky.

Before he could access the comm channels Norsky struck, slamming the heel of his hand into the throat of the guard to his left then punching the other guard full in the face slamming his head back against the wall. Both guards went down quickly and he opened the door to Stryder's cell.

"Come on Captain, it seems my loyalties have changed," Norsky said.

Stryder came at him with surprising speed, his right hand balled into a fist striking him square on the jaw rocking his head backwards with such force he was sent staggering across the corridor to slam into the wall opposite. Norsky was caught completely off guard by the speed of the blow and could do nothing to dodge or block it. His head hit the wall across from Stryder's cell further adding to the effect of the punch. He slid down to the floor as his eyes rolled up inside their sockets and he was out for the count.

Hardy came around the corner the second she heard the commotion just in time to see Stryder calmly strolling out of his cell. Without turning to look at her he said, "What took you so long?" He knew she was there without the need to look.

"I got caught up in traffic," she said with a smile beginning to blossom across her full sensuous lips.

He turned to look at her and smiled.

"C'mon, more guards will be coming soon so we need to get the hell outta here. Grab their weapons and let's go." He stooped down to retrieve the pistol and assault rifle from the nearest guard while Hardy did the same with the other one.

"Where to now, Kurt?" she asked

"I seem to remember the route we came in by, so all we need do is retrace our steps back to the entrance and the spaceport where we should be able to find our transport off this dump," Stryder said with complete confidence.

"And what if we meet some opposition en route?" Hardy

asked more than a little concerned by the simplicity of his plan.

"Simple, we remove it," he said as he started to walk off.

"Er, please tell me you're not planning on us taking on the entire base on our own?" Hardy said catching up with him.

Stryder looked across at her and his smile told her all she needed to know. He was just going to barrel his way through and anyone who got in his way had better watch out.

"Oh shit!" she said. She jacked the slide on the assault rifle to prime the battery clip and was ready to go.

"Have you any idea where we're going?" she asked as they steadily made their way down the corridor.

"Yes I do, strange but I seem to remember clearly everything from the moment when we arrived," Stryder answered.

"How do you mean, strange?"

"Well, I wouldn't normally remember details with this much clarity. I remember every step of the way in here and that's unusual for me. I've normally a good memory but this is like I've got double my normal capacity. Normally I'd remember certain details that blend together to give a mental picture that makes the whole, but this is phenomenal! Every single detail is etched into my memory like an engraving, a permanent record of our journey through this base."

"Well, it should help us find our way out but what good will it be if we meet any resistance?"

"We'll just have to cross that bridge when we come to it."

"That could be sooner than you think," Hardy said as they neared the end of the corridor.

Stryder put his hand up to shoulder height, his fist clenched in a Marine signal to stop the advance. He was using hand signals, which told Hardy they must be quiet so as not to alert the enemy. They both stopped in their tracks and Stryder's brow knitted as he concentrated. He was listening for something; Hardy realised he was listening for any sounds around the corner out of sight.

Stryder held up two fingers indicating that there were two people approaching from the direction they were headed.

Hardy brought up her assault rifle ready to fire and Stryder did likewise.

Norsky regained consciousness, saw the two guards he'd taken care of and knew he was in deep trouble. Stryder had got the better of him and was on the loose in the base somewhere. There were two courses of action he could take; the first was to raise the alarm and take his chances with General Solon and the subsequent consequences and the second was to find Stryder himself and carry out the termination order. In that way he might negate the consequences or at least lessen them.

Slowly he got to his feet, a little unsteady with the after effects of the blow from Stryder. Norsky was still trying to decide what to do when a third choice came to him. He could raise the alarm and still go after Stryder himself. With the alarm raised, the base would be closed off and it would make chasing him down a little easier.

With that choice he covered all the bases and kept his ass covered too, the best he could under the circumstances. Accessing his NI he called the base security centre and raised the alarm.

Within seconds the audible alarm was screeching throughout the integral speakers situated throughout the base.

When the alarm went off Stryder and Hardy looked at each other, an unspoken thought passing between them. They knew the shit had just hit the fan and an almost impossible task had just been made even harder.

Stryder went around the corner fast. There were two guards in front of him. They had stopped as they received instructions on the alarm status over their NIs. Stryder fired his assault rifle on burst fire sending several shots of pulsed plasma into the two unsuspecting soldiers. The energy blasts stitched across the two soldiers chests cutting them open as they were sent flying backwards in a mist of blood. They were dead before they hit the floor.

Hardy was just a step or two behind Stryder unable to match his speed. It was over by the time she reached his side.

"Wow! You don't take prisoners do you?" she said as she viewed the aftermath of his little action.

"Not got the time here. Things have just got worse," he replied, concentration knitting his brow as he listened, trying to pick out sounds beneath the strident alarm.

"We've got company coming?" Hardy looked both ways down the corridor to see what he meant; when she saw no one she looked at him quizzically.

"Some soldiers are coming at us from both directions. I can't make out how many, the alarm's messing with my hearing but I know they'll be here in less than a minute," he said when he saw her expression.

"You can hear that, above this noise?" she said incredulously.

"Yes, don't ask me how but my hearing, along with my other senses, was boosted with the original test and somehow they've gone off the chart since being here. Anyway haven't got time to ponder that now, we have to move."

"Where do you suggest if they're coming at us from both sides?" she asked urgently.

"We need a map of this base," he said stating the obvious.

"What if we try to access the main computer?" Hardy suggested. Stryder thought about it for a second then said, "Might work, but we'd have to distract them from searching for us, give them something else to think about for a while."

"What have you got in mind?" Hardy asked hoping he would come up with a plan soon because she had nothing to offer. All her training meant for nothing at that moment, her mind was a blank as panic was beginning to grow inside her.

"First things first," he said as he strode towards the edge of the corridor. He leaned back against the wall at the edge of the corridor, his assault rifle held high across his chest, and she could tell by the expression of intense concentration on his face that he was listening to the sounds of the approaching soldiers. Suddenly, he strode around the corner, his assault rifle aimed down the corridor and he fired a continuous stream of pulsed plasma bolts which stitched across the soldiers' chests sending them flying backwards in a mist of expelled blood. If they had been wearing body armour they would have survived the attack, as it was, they only wore regulation uniforms, which were no protection against the high intensity bolts.

Stryder walked down to them to check their vitals and to search for something.

"What're you looking for?" Hardy asked as she followed him down towards them.

"The security codes for their combat comm channels. If we can access them, we can cause all sorts of mayhem until they realise their system has been compromised," he replied from his squat position as he checked the fallen soldiers.

Standing to his full height he said, "Nothing, damn!"

"Have you tried accessing the comm channels anyway?"

Hardy asked what seemed to her an obvious question. He looked at her as if she had lost a cog, then a thought occurred to him.

"Never thought of that," he said and concentrating he accessed his NI searching through the comm channels available to him for one that he could use. All this information was downloaded directly to the brain so that it seemed like a thought.

"Any luck?" she asked and with a wave of his hand he quietened her. He probed the channels for one particular channel that would give him the results he required. They were slightly different to those used by the Confederation, similar in most ways but different enough so that any interloper or hacker would be spotted by the security protocols and it was these protocols that he was desperately trying to avoid. The particular channel he was searching for would give him access to all the security personnel on the base and he could direct them to bogus locations and, most importantly, away from them.

A smile suddenly crossed his face, followed by deep lines of concentration across his brow as he connected to the channel he had been searching for.

"All personnel report to the main lab area immediately!" he ordered. Then turning to Hardy with a broad grin on his face said, "Done!" Beads of sweat spotted his forehead, a testament to the fierce concentration and mental effort required to fulfil the task just completed.

"Are you sure?" she asked a little dubiously.

"I'm sure. I'm monitoring the channel so if anyone on the base uses it, I'll know, just like using our own combat channels when a unit is in action and the members of that unit are linked. I'm now linked to their combat channel with one notable exception," he explained.

"Which is?"

"They don't know I'm logged in."

"How is that possible? I thought it was set up so each member of the unit knew where the others were for logistic reasons?"

"Not sure how I'm doing it, I just know that I'm shielding my presence from the others. Don't knock it; if it works it can only be good for us."

"That means you have much greater control over your NI than they realise, you must be able to access parts of your brain that were never deemed possible before," she observed.

"You could be right; it's a fact that we only use ten per cent of our brain's capacity so perhaps with the enhancements I can now reach some of that hidden potential. Anyway that debate can wait until we're outta here. Let's concentrate on getting to the spaceport and off this planet. Once we've done that we still have to navigate our way through Alliance space."

"Yep; we've got to get to the border so Col Sec can come and get us," she said, which brought a surprised look from him.

"Are you serious? You know the rules; if we get captured we are forgotten. There will be no rescue attempt. They'll be changing all the security protocols we know in case they sweat them out of us. If they even thought about coming after us where would they start to look? We're deep in enemy space and any encroachment would cause an interstellar incident that would lead to all out war. Col Sec is not about to put all those lives on the line for two Marines. We know the score, you and me; we are on our own. As much as I hate to admit it, it's up to us."

Hardy was taken aback slightly, she had thought about what he'd said, knew the truth of it but had kept some hope alive that if they managed to escape from the base, that there was a chance they could be rescued. It was that glimmer of hope that had kept her going. Now though, that hope had been shattered by his harsh words, words that crushed every last vestige of hope remaining in her and she visibly collapsed from the inside.

Stryder saw it and reached for her placing a hand on her shoulder softly saying, "We're not dead yet though, I didn't say we won't get out of this, I just said we can't rely on Col Sec to come for us."

With tears brimming in her eyes she choked back the panic and fear and said "But what can we do?"

"We get the hell off this planet and then find our way home, or at the very least back to Confederation space, the rest will take care of itself."

She nodded her head slowly as the panic receded, warded off by his confident words.

"Okay," she said gathering herself again, summoning up reserves of courage even she didn't know she had. Once more, standing tall and proud, she was ready to continue the fight.

"Right, let's go," he said leading her on.

CHAPTER 22

"What the hell is going on?" shouted General Solon as he heard the alarm's shrill signal echo throughout the base. Accessing the comm channel through his NI he contacted the Security station. "Report," he said simply.

"We're investigating the cause as we speak, sir. Something has happened at the main lab, all personnel have been ordered there," replied the officer in command.

"Who issued the order?" Solon wanted to know.

The silence told him more than words ever could.

"We're investigating that also, sir. As yet I can find no officer who issued that order, I don't understand it," came the reply.

"I think I know," Solon said.

"Who sir?" asked the officer.

"Never mind that now, just get a team of your best men over to Stryder's cell and secure it immediately, is that clear?" Solon ordered curtly. The tone of his voice told the officer not to argue or question, simply to comply.

"Yes, sir, immediately," he replied as the call was disconnected.

"Damn!" Solon said angrily as he slammed his fist down onto his desk. He grabbed his jacket and left the office, he'd take charge of this personally but first he had to see what the commotion was down at the main lab. In the pit of his stomach he knew what had happened but he just needed to confirm it, then put in place actions to rectify it.

The lab would be the place to start.

He strode out of his office and what he saw sent a chill through him. There were soldiers milling around in disorder, rushing here and there seemingly following orders but from whom there was no way of knowing.

Anger rose within him like a volcano getting ready to erupt and he surged forward through the Marines. When they saw who was barrelling through them they soon made room for him to pass unhindered.

When he reached the lab he saw guards surrounding the exits preventing anyone from breaking the hastily erected cordon. Pushing his way through he entered the lab.

"What's the meaning of this?" he barked angrily indicating all the soldiers.

"An alarm went off; I thought you sent them here," replied the lab tech in charge.

"No, I didn't send them here, but someone did. Whoever sent them must have access to the private channels through their NI."

"Who could do that, surely not one of your own men?" replied the tech.

"Whoever did is in big trouble. The important thing now is are the test subjects ready to be initialised?"

"I've done all I can with them, we have to wait now to see if the serum actually works. From the initial scans, their autonomic responses have increased off the charts. They should have increased strength, agility and reflexes. As for anything else it's too early to say, I can't guarantee that anything else will generate within them so the results you're seeking may not be forthcoming."

"There's one sure way of finding out," Solon said turning to the five soldiers who had been given the serum. He stood in front of the leader, Captain Anders, and said, "Captain your first task is to bring me the head of Captain Stryder. I do believe he may have escaped, the how isn't important at this time, just bring me his head. I want him dead, is that clear?"

"Perfectly, sir! Is this mission for me alone, sir, or do I take the rest of the team?" Anders asked.

"This is a team mission which you will command. Now go, and report back to me directly," Solon said stepping aside while the team walked briskly out of the lab.

"Now we shall see if all this has been worth the effort," he said. Then, looking at the tech added, "Prepare another batch of serum, I want it ready for mass production within the hour." He then left the lab to return to his office.

Hawk had called a secure clean up unit to take the body away and remove any evidence of the shooting. He then escorted Watkiss back to HQ. Once he was sure she was secure he went to the morgue to view the body of Temic.

Doctor Marcus Randolph was the attending ME, a small man in his fifties with thinning grey hair and shrewd eyes. He was just about to start the preliminary exam before disposing of the body. A veteran of twenty years he had seen death in all its guises so nothing seemed to faze him anymore.

As Hawk entered his domain he looked up from the slab

where Temic was laid out beneath a cotton sheet, his slate grey eyes taking in the soldier as he entered purposefully.

"Come to view your handiwork I take it," he said returning to the job at hand.

"On the contrary, Doc, I'm here to see if we can salvage anything from this," Hawk replied shrugging off the jibe.

"Such as?" Randolph asked not bothering to look up. He was little concerned with the matters of the agents who sent a stream of work his way; he just had to deal with the after effects of it.

"Is there any chance we can save his NI? I need to salvage the call logs and anything else we can glean from it," Hawk replied.

"Intriguing; a post mortem interrogation," Randolph said finally looking up and smiling. Turning his gaze to the blown-apart head of Temic he said, "Well, my boy, you don't seem to have left me much to work with."

"It was a split second decision, I had to save a woman's life," Hawk explained earning a different sort of look from the ME; this one had a little more respect in it.

"I'll see what I can do," he said and set to work closely examining the blasted head of the soldier.

"We need the NI to see what we can learn from it. It may have valuable data stored which we can extract hopefully leading us to the whereabouts of Captain Stryder," Hawk said. He went on to say, "So we need to know what you can do as soon as possible. Do me a favour Doc, report your findings directly to me, no one else, okay?"

Randolph looked up at him not sure what he meant by his request, but decided it was none of his business and said, "Sure, I'll get right on it."

"Top priority, Doc. I'll take full responsibility so you need not worry about any flak that might come your way, I've got your back on this one."

Randolph looked up again and when he saw the expression on the big man's face he knew this was important.

"Okay, as soon as I get anything I'll contact you," he said with a new sense of urgency.

"Be quick Doc, but no mistakes, this is far too important. I'll be close by, just got to report in." Hawk left the room.

As he strode away he contacted Gemmell through a secure comm channel.

"Sir, the body is in the morgue," he said once the connection had been made.

"Okay Matt, well done. It's a pity that it worked out the way it did, we could really have used a break on this one," Gemmell replied.

"It's not over yet, sir," Hawk said cryptically.

"What do you mean, Captain?"

"Sir, I have a plan that needs your approval for it to go ahead. There may be a chance that we can pull something out of this," Hawk said.

"Then you'd better come to my office right away," Gemmell replied, intrigued by what Hawk had to say.

"Am on my way sir, be there in five." Hawk closed the connection. He was taking a gamble of that much he was sure. Having shot the Alliance soldier in the head, the only possible target presented to him at the time, he knew he was screwed. As soon as the body hit the floor his mind had begun to formulate a plan. It was tricky and dangerous and it all hinged on the fact that the one detail enabling the rest of the dangerous plan to go forward was locked inside the head of a dead soldier.

Gemmell was waiting for his arrival in his office and the moment Hawk entered he looked up and said, "So what's this plan then?"

"I've asked the ME to extract the NI and pass it over to me. With a little luck I'm hoping to access the memory of the device and see if there's anything pertaining to the whereabouts of Captain Stryder. There may be something in there that we can use, call log records, data about the mission. Once we have that we could plan a covert mission."

"Whoa, hold on there, how do you plan on doing that?" Gemmell asked.

"Once we have the whereabouts we put together a small team of Recon Delta people who are aware of Captain Stryder and his situation. We go in using a craft that the Alliance wouldn't suspect, something that can travel between the two zones of space with impunity, such as a freighter. We go in under cover and get him out."

"It sounds easy but there are quite a few details missing from your plan, Captain."

"I know, sir, but we can flesh them out en route to the destination once we have its location."

"So you intend to lead this mission?"

"I volunteer for it, sir. I would like to see this thing through to the end," Hawk said with conviction.

"What about the team? Have you any ideas who you'd pick?" Gemmell asked.

"I looked into the report from Research Station Five, sir, and there was a Recon Delta team heavily involved in the proceedings which was led by Captain Storm. I think his team would be the best as they already know Stryder and are familiar with the situation on Research Station Five. By all accounts Storm and Stryder became friends so the motivation is all there. I'm not sure of their location but I'm sure we can get them ready to go in time, sir."

"Okay, it seems like you have thought this through. I suggest you pitch it to General Sinclair. He's on Celeron, from where Stryder was snatched. If I'm not mistaken Captain Storm is there too. I suggest you make it a secure channel though," Gemmell said.

"Thank you, sir, I will straight away," Hawk said as he turned to leave the office.

"Captain, keep me informed of your progress," Gemmell said halting Hawk in his tracks.

Turning to face his commanding officer he said, "Of course, sir, it goes without saying."

"Well, I'm just saying, okay? I don't want anyone doing an end run around me so they can grab some extra glory for themselves," Gemmell said.

"This isn't about glory, sir; it's about getting two Recon Delta Marines home safe and sound," Hawk replied.

"Good man, let's just keep the focus on that then. There is a bigger picture here we have to be aware of and that's the interest the Alliance has in Captain Stryder. It makes him a very valuable commodity and one we must not allow to fall into their hands. Although they have him now I will do everything in my power to recapture him and I expect the same commitment from everyone under my command."

"You have it, sir."

"Good, dismissed," Gemmell said ending the interview.

Hawk left and went straight back to his own office where he could make the secure call to General Sinclair about his proposal. Once he had done that he would return to the morgue to see what progress the ME had made on retrieving the NI from the dead soldier. But first things first, he had a call to make.

Stryder came to a door and opening it went in dragging Hardy with him.

"What the hell are you doing?" she asked angrily, as his fingers bit into the flesh at her collar.

She looked around the small room; it had shelves across

the rear wall and down one side filled to capacity with cleaning products.

"This is a janitor's closet, what the hell are we doing in here when we're supposed to be finding our way out?" she asked, standing in front of him her fear and anger making her confrontational.

Smiling at her he said, "Quieten down for a sec."

She didn't know what to say for a moment then he went on with, "This place is still crawling with guards and unless you want to stand up against odds that we just can't fight, then we need another way out of here."

"Okay that makes sense," she admitted.

"I've learned that I can communicate with the central computer," he revealed. She looked at him askance, not sure what to make of that comment.

"Don't ask me how, but I know what the computer is doing and can actually communicate with it," he said.

"Don't worry, I wasn't going to," she said, then asked, "Do you mean you can talk to it?"

"Yes, I know everything that's happening inside this base but so far I've had to keep myself hidden or the security protocols will initiate and I'll be locked out. Actually, I'm not sure if it could lock me out but I'm not gonna take that chance, don't know what it would do to me."

"Can you give it commands?" she asked.

"I think so, would have to be subtle so as not to instigate any anti-threat measures against me. I have been thinking which would be the best diversion to use that would cause maximum confusion to help us get out of here," he said thinking out loud.

"Fire," she said simply as if it was the most obvious thing.

"You're right, that would open up all the fire exits and an evacuation would have to take place which we could use to our advantage," he said. He turned away from her and concentrated on placing a command into the central core computer that would fool it into thinking a fire had broken out in a vital location, one that had to be protected at all costs. Then the rest of the building would have to be evacuated for the safety of the inhabitants.

After a moment's thought he had the ideal location.

~

The fire alarm ripped through the building as an automated warning was sounded, urging everyone to stop what they were doing immediately and vacate through the nearest exit.

~

General Solon was just approaching his office when he heard the alarm. Swiftly he called security to see where the fire had broken out.

When he was informed where it was he screamed at the top of his lungs and ran from his office.

Within seconds he was outside the main lab. He could see through the Plexiglas walls that everyone was still trapped inside and that all the doors were locked to seal in the occupants and research materials from the impending blaze, except there was no fire.

Grabbing an assault rifle from the nearest guard he opened fire on the first lock. With the rifle on full power and at point blank range, all the energy from the pulsed plasma bolts struck the lock blasting it to pieces. The door slid open and he stood in the doorway.

"They'll be looking to leave the building along with the normal personnel through one of the fire exits. Get someone on the security monitors checking everyone. I want them found!" he shouted at the Marines inside the lab. The five test subjects led by Captain Anders had already left but there were still a few Marines guarding the lab.

Solon turned to the lab tech in charge and said, "Continue working, we'll soon get this situation under control. I want that serum ready to ship out to other Alliance bases as soon as possible. No excuses, is that clear?"

All the lab tech could do was nod his head in abject fear.

Solon turned on his heel and marched back towards his office. Changing his mind, he headed instead towards the security centre where the situation could be monitored more fully.

~

Stryder and Hardy were still in the janitor's closet when the alarm went off.

"We'll give it a few moments to let the chaos build before we join in and get the hell out," Stryder said, a look of concern on his face.

"What?" Hardy asked, reading from his expression anxiety about something other than the present situation.

"I'm getting something from the computer. I'm reading some reports that have been logged in from the lab area. They've manufactured a serum and administered it to five soldiers and are in the process of manufacturing it in large quantities," he said as the look of concern grew into one of deep resignation. He knew what he had to do and his escape plan had just been put on hold.

Hardy saw his expression change and knew what was coming.

"We're not going are we?" she said.

"I can't allow them to make more serum. I have to destroy it," he said with finality in his voice. His expression told her that he meant business. He had his game face on and was as determined as she'd ever seen him.

"What do you intend doing?" she asked.

"We have to get back to that lab and destroy all the samples of the serum, and to do that we need another diversion to draw all the guards away from that area," he replied. He went silent as his mind raced, analysing the problem he'd just outlined.

"Whatever you choose we'd better do it quickly, because considering what's already happened, their security will be on high alert. If we don't do something fast, we won't be leaving this place at all," she replied.

He looked her straight in the eye and said, "So be it. That serum is not leaving this place while I'm alive." She knew from his expression that he was determined, that if necessary would commit his life to the task ahead and he expected the same commitment from her.

Thoughts ran through her mind then, thoughts of her future, her career, raising a family, seeing more of the galaxy, becoming someone people could look up to and leaving her mark on the history of the Confederation. In that instant she knew that it could all end right here, right now. None of her dreams could come to pass except perhaps the very last. She would indeed leave her mark on the history of the Confederation but it would be an invisible one. These missions are invariably unreported in the annals of history but rather left to the vaults of secrecy.

First and foremost she was a Marine and upon taking the oath she realised that at any moment, in any mission, her life could be forfeit. It seemed to her that time could be now.

With the final resignation that comes with the knowledge that this is it, this has to be done, no matter the cost, she responded with a nod of her head.

"Okay, let's do this," she said and he knew he could count on her.

∼

Norsky had no idea where Stryder and Hardy would be, especially as the alarm had been raised. The base was in lockdown and they couldn't make it to any of the exits. One thing was certain, when he found Stryder he was in for a fight. It still worried him, the power of the man and how he'd taken care of him so quickly and easily.

As he was searching for him another idea was circulating inside his brain, one that could give him the edge or at least a fighting chance when he came into contact with Stryder. When he heard the fire alarm raised and learned of the location, the idea turned into a last minute solution, a desperate one but a solution nonetheless.

Stopping in his tracks he turned and headed for the main lab.

∼

Stryder and Hardy were about to leave the janitor's closet when he glanced up towards the ceiling.

"What?" asked Hardy when she saw where his gaze was focused? Right above their heads was a vent in the ceiling giving access to the shafts connected to the life support system.

"If we can fit inside there we can travel through this complex without them knowing where we are, straight to the main lab," Stryder said.

"Okay, let's do it, it's gotta be better than running around out there getting shot at by every guard in this damn place," Hardy replied, as she gauged the size of the opening hoping that the ducts behind the vent were large enough for them to crawl through.

Finding something to stand on he reached up and pulled the vent out of its recess with considerable ease then passed it down to Hardy. Within a few seconds he had pulled himself up and into the hole. Looking down and smiling he said, "Grab my hands and I'll pull you up," as he reached down towards her with both arms outstretched.

She joined him inside the vent amazed at how easily he had pulled her up. "Which direction?" she asked, a little disoriented in their new surroundings.

"That way," he indicated with a nod of his head.

"How can you be so sure?"

"I don't really know but it's like I've got a GPS fix and I know exactly to the inch where everything is inside this whole complex. Don't ask me how and I'm not even gonna try and think about it, just going to go with the flow and be thankful it works," he replied.

She smiled and said, "Okay, after you then."

❧

Norsky reached the main lab just as General Solon was leaving. Watching him turn the opposite corner he waited until he was out of sight then entered the lab.

The three Marines who had been ordered to remain behind and protect the lab looked up as Norsky entered. Even though they recognised him they were too slow to react as he brought up his Magerov P9 and shot them all in the head, each one sent flying backwards his head destroyed in a spurt of blood.

"Give me a dose of the serum, now!" he said turning to the lab tech nearest to him who was cowering in abject terror. This was not what he had signed up for. The research was what he loved but just lately things had got way out of control and here he was in fear of his very life, threatened from every quarter, or so it seemed.

"Okay, just don't kill me," the lab tech said his voice high pitched and shaky from terror. He reached for an injector gun and administered the serum to Norsky.

"How long before it starts to take effect?" Norsky wanted to know.

"Quite quickly," replied the lab tech, realising it was not what Norsky wanted to hear from the scowl he received. "It depends on the subject. Look, this part isn't an exact science. We've not had time to run the proper control tests so we're guessing most of the time," he admitted hoping his words would stave off any retribution.

"Give me some idea then?"

"The first batch produced results after as little as a few minutes, but I can't be certain."

"That'll have to do," Norsky said, then as he prepared to leave turned to the lab tech and said, "What has the General ordered you to do?"

"Get another batch ready for mass production," the lab tech blurted out.

"Get on with it then," Norsky said before leaving the lab.

~

Unerringly Stryder guided them to the main lab area taking less time than they had first imagined. The ducts were quite spacious and had afforded them enough room to crawl through unrestricted. When they arrived, Norsky had killed the Marines and they watched as the lab tech administered the serum. Hearing every word, they remained hidden behind a vent in the roof until the renegade captain had left in search of them.

"Well, that was interesting, to say the least," Hardy whispered when the coast was clear.

"Yea, in helping to solve our immediate problem he's given us something else to worry about," replied Stryder in the same tone of voice. "C'mon, let's get this done before anyone else comes in to complicate matters." He turned around and kicked the vent free so he could jump down into the room.

"Oh shit!" the lab tech exclaimed when he saw who it was.

Covering the inhabitants of the room with the assault rifle in one hand, Stryder reached up to help Hardy down with the other.

"If you want to get out of this with your skins intact I suggest you leave right now," Stryder said to the frightened lab techs who were only too pleased to be given the opportunity to escape.

Once the room had been evacuated Hardy asked, "What do you intend to do now?"

"Destroy this serum and any means of replicating it in the future," he replied as he looked around the room for the best means of accomplishing that task.

"How?"

"Fire is usually the best method. We set fire to this entire complex and destroy all evidence of the programme and the serum, everything, and then we get the hell out."

"Well, let's just hope that the knowledge isn't still with those lab techs you just let go," Hardy said.

Stryder glanced at the door they had just run through and realised his potential mistake.

"We'll just have to hope they were working from notes rather than from memory or knowledge they already had."

With that he set about erasing the records of the research in the main computer whilst Hardy went to where the samples of the serum were being replicated and increased the temperature in the chamber to dangerous levels. Within a few short moments the remaining samples were destroyed and all that remained to do was destroy the equipment.

"All done?" he asked when Hardy came to stand next to him.

"Yes, the samples are destroyed; we just need to destroy their ability to replicate anymore," she replied urgently.

He got up from the computer terminal and, picking up his assault rifle, sent a few well-aimed full power plasma bolts into the equipment around the room. After a short while the room was in a blaze from all the explosions erupting as a result of his shots.

As they watched the fire engulf the room, taking with it the Alliance's last chance of replicating the serum, they made their way to the exit.

"C'mon let's get the hell out, those plasma bolts will alert someone to what's just happened and bring the guards down on us," Stryder said. The two of them ran from the room, that part of their mission completed.

"How are we going to get out of here?" Hardy asked once they were free of the main lab.

"We need a different route that will bypass the guards surrounding us," replied Stryder thoughtfully.

"Well, if you've any suggestions you'd better make them fast because I've got a bad feeling that those guards you mentioned are gonna be all over us real soon," she pleaded.

Stryder's eyes glazed over, all colour bleaching from them for just a second as he accessed the files from the computer pertaining to the blueprints of the complex through his NI; areas he knew nothing about.

"I think we may have something," he said as his eyes regained their natural colour. Hardy didn't say anything, as she had never seen that phenomenon before when he used his NI in that way.

"This way," he said and led her down a different part of the complex towards the lower levels, going deeper inside instead of towards the exits. Pulling up short she stood, unsure of what to do. Stryder turned to face her and said, "You wanted a way out around the guards, and this is it, but you have to trust me." Holding out his hand to her he waited for her decision.

She looked behind her to where the obvious exits were. They were close but probably blocked by most of the security staff expecting them to go that way. If she followed him farther into the complex what would she be going in to? Only he knew.

Stryder waited for her to make her mind up. He needed her to be with him and not to question every decision he made, so he waited.

There really was no choice for her, he had been right on all the decisions he had made so far, so she just had to trust him once more. There was no way either of them could make it out of the complex alone but together they had a chance, a slim one, but a chance nonetheless, so she chose to go along with him.

With a sigh of relief he watched as she came towards him. He knew she would follow because as she had decided, there was a better chance for them together than alone.

As he turned back to face the way they were headed he was suddenly halted in his tracks by the voice of a guard who appeared from around the corner aiming an assault rifle in their direction.

"Freeze! Stand where you are!" the guard shouted.

CHAPTER 23

Matt Hawk had made all the necessary calls. He'd brought General Sinclair up to speed on what was happening and what he hoped to achieve and had received the man's blessing.

Once that was done he went directly to the morgue to retrieve the NI from Doctor Randolph.

"Here it is but I'm not sure it'll do you any good. It was close to the damaged area of the brain, what was left of it," Randolph said as Hawk entered the morgue.

"Thanks, Doc, it's up to me now to see if I can extract any data from it," Hawk replied gratefully.

"You can use that terminal over there; you'll need the nanoscope anyway to be able to read any data from something that small," Randolph said, indicating the terminal in question next to a piece of equipment that resembled a proton microscope.

Placing the slide with the Neural Interface containing all the encoded data into the nanoscope, Hawk waited while the information was downloaded onto the hard drive. Some of the data was corrupted due to the damage from the plasma bolt but there was some he could use. After a while he had what he wanted, the call logs. Scanning through them he found what he was looking for, the record of the call to Captain Nokorovic who Norsky passed the NI tracking codes to. Nokorovic was an aide to General Solon himself.

Turning to the ME he said, "Thanks, Doc, I've got everything that I need." He left the morgue and headed straight for Gemmell's office. This news he wanted to deliver in person.

"Sir, I think we may have something," Hawk said as he entered the office. Gemmell looked up from his screen saying, "Okay, tell me."

Hawk hastily went through everything he'd done with the NI to extract the data and his conclusions.

"And that helps us how?" Gemmell asked.

Hawk smiled. "Well, sir, I played a hunch and while I waited for the ME to extract the NI I placed a call to our closest monitoring station to Alliance space. As you know they monitor the comings and goings of all their top brass much the same as I'm sure, they do with us."

"Go on," Gemmell said, still not exactly sure where this was heading.

"Sir, the tracking codes were passed on to Captain Nokorovic who is listed as an aide to General Solon himself," Hawk said his smile still in place.

"But how does that help us in our present situation?" Gemmell asked.

"Shortly after the codes were passed on, the General made a trip to a small planet where they have a research facility. Now why would the man in charge of the Alliance Special Forces go to a research facility do you think?" Hawk saw the realisation dawn on Gemmell's face.

"He's gone to oversee what they can extract from Stryder," he said, adding, "Where's this planet?"

That's when the smile faded from Hawk's face a little.

"It's Toldax, sir, well inside Alliance space, they chose well."

"Right, well we've come this far and just because the destination is a little tricky doesn't mean we give up, there's just too much at stake here. I want you on the first available transport to Celeron where you'll rendezvous with General Sinclair. We can commandeer a freighter from local sources and refit her with stealth shields for your trip into Alliance space. We're going to do this Captain." Gemmell's enthusiasm was rising and contagious. Hawk had thought that once the destination was known the plan might have been vetoed and yet there he was standing in the office of his superior officer hearing that the plan was going to go ahead.

"Thank you, sir, I'm on my way," Hawk said as he turned to go.

"Good work Matt, and bring them back. Okay?" Gemmell said with a smile.

"You can count on it, sir."

"Your travel arrangements have been made and your transport is waiting in orbit as we speak. There's a shuttle powered up ready for take-off on the rooftop landing pad," Gemmell said. Hawk realised then that he'd had more faith in him coming up with the goods than he had himself. He left the office and headed straight for the elevator that would take him straight to the rooftop landing pad and his next mission. He dared not fail for too much was at stake. Not just the lives of the two soldiers he was going to help rescue, but possibly the lives of countless others including innocent bystanders who might get caught up in the conflagration should the Alliance manage to reproduce the serum that made Stryder so important to both sides. He didn't know what that was yet but he did know it must be important to warrant all this attention. The responsibility of the success of this mission therefore, lay squarely on his shoulders. If he failed now then everything he feared would come to pass.

So, no pressure then!

∼

Stryder had to make his move and do it fast. He brought up his own assault rifle and fired as he moved to the side.

The guard tracked his movement and opened fire at the same time.

Stryder's burst of plasma fire raked across the guard's chest sending him flying backwards whilst the guard's salvo went past Stryder harmlessly.

Hardy saw the movement, brought up her assault rifle and fired at two more guards as they appeared round the corner. Their attention had been on Stryder. Hardy's burst of plasma fire raked across their bodies sending them crashing backwards, their limbs askew as their torsos were blasted open by the salvo.

"C'mon we haven't got much time," Stryder said as he got up and continued down the corridor.

"Where the hell are we going?" Hardy asked, the recent bloodshed already a distant memory.

"Grab as many battery clips as you can," Stryder said as he raided the dead guards' pockets for more ammunition.

"That doesn't answer my question," she said as she stooped to the task as well.

"We're going farther into the complex," he said.

"I can fucking see that Kurt!" she answered him angrily. She was getting rather pissed off at his apparent reluctance to inform her of anything.

"Okay, well down in the bowels of this complex will be

the Life Support section of engineering. If we can access one of the tunnels there should be a way to the outside."

"'If we 'can' and 'should be'? Those are phrases I'm not sure I want to hear in an escape plan thank you very fucking much."

"C'mon, what do you expect here, I'm making this up as I go along; cut me some slack why don't you."

Just then they ran headlong into three more guards who appeared from around another corner. They collided and all ended up on the floor.

They all eyed one another before realising their weapons were scattered on the floor and that the first person to retrieve one of them would most likely be the victor.

Stryder kicked out at the nearest guard catching him full in the face, breaking his nose in a spurt of blood. He was on his feet in a flash followed by Hardy and the other two guards.

Hardy took the one on her right with a right cross to the jaw, snapping his head viciously to the side causing him to stagger slightly. She followed up with a kick to his midriff, which bent him double, then brought her right knee up to his face with such force it actually lifted him off his feet. He landed on his back, blood from his shattered nose leaving a trail in the air tracing his flight path.

Stryder watched this from the corner of his eye, assured she didn't need any assistance while he dealt with the other guard. The first attack was anything but subtle. The guard came rushing at him with his head down trying to take him across the midriff in a tackle. Stryder sidestepped out of range as the guard rushed past then came up short behind him. Stryder spun around to face him as the guard also turned and Stryder hit him with a back fist that had so much force behind it the guard was sent spinning through the air and landed heavily on his back temporarily winded.

Hardy was ready for her next challenge as the guard she had decked flipped onto his feet, rage clearing showing in his eyes. He wiped blood from his face and snarled in fury at her before rushing forwards. He swung a haymaker right cross at her head, which she easily ducked beneath, ramming her right fist into his unprotected stomach. A left cross to his ribs caused him to buckle so she followed with a right uppercut to his chin. As his head came up she sent her fist smashing into the side of his chin in a left cross, snapping his head sideways with such force that he left the ground and landed on the floor face first. He would not be rejoining the fight after that.

Stryder turning to watch and smiling at her technique and power was almost caught unawares by the first guard who had received the kick to the face. He'd regained his feet and was about to attack, when Stryder heard his approach from behind.

The punch from behind sailed over his head harmlessly and Stryder, ducking slightly, rammed an elbow into the man's midriff. All the air was expelled from his lungs by the blow and Stryder simply brought his fist up into the guard's face further damaging it. Broken teeth and blood were spat out from the blow and then Stryder spun around and smashed his left fist into the guard's face sending the man flying onto his back out cold.

The second guard was on his feet by this time and ready to continue the fight. Stryder saw his advance and, jabbing him to the face with his left, which stopped him in his tracks, he then finished him with a right cross to the jaw sending him to the floor also out cold.

"Cool," Stryder said to Hardy.

"Well, as much fun as that was, we still have to get the hell out of here," she replied with a hint of a smile because despite, or perhaps because of, the danger they were in she had enjoyed the brief struggle.

Stryder picked up both their weapons, tossed Hardy's to her which she caught effortlessly then, smiling, said, "Let's go then, oh and remind me never to piss you off, okay?"

~

General Solon heard the gunfire from his office. His NI was tied into the computer monitoring the facility's activities and he learned that a fire had broken out in the main lab area.

"Not again!" he snarled and he asked the computer to verify the incident, which it did by relaying real time video display to a monitor in his office.

When he saw the blaze, which by this time had completely engulfed the room, he was furious. Seeing all his plans literally go up in flames before his eyes was too much for him to bear.

Grabbing an assault rifle from a cabinet by the wall he stormed out of his office. Using a combat channel via his NI he called Captain Anders.

"Captain, are you any closer to finding Captain Stryder?" he barked.

"Not yet, sir," came the reply.

"I'm not surprised; he's just been back into the lab and destroyed all the serum and everything else there. I suggest you tap into those enhanced abilities of yours and get me some results." His voice was infused with anger and, ending the call abruptly, he left the captain in no doubt as to his mood.

Rage gripped him so fiercely that he couldn't think straight. He wandered the corridor looking for something to vent his anger on but when nothing presented itself he returned to his office. The blaze in the main lab was growing, but because he wasn't thinking clearly escape was not even something he considered. How could he rectify the situation, drag success from the very embers of defeat? There was only one way and that was to recapture Stryder and glean some more samples from him to reconstitute the serum and start all over again. There was only one flaw with that plan which was that he had already issued orders for the death of the very man in question.

"Captain Anders there has been a change in your orders," he said through the combat channel via his NI.

"Copy that, sir, I am ready to receive new orders," replied Anders.

"We need Captain Stryder alive. Your orders now are to capture him at all costs, but he must be alive, is that clear Captain?" Solon said.

"As crystal, sir. Does it matter if he's a little damaged, sir?" asked Anders. Solon could almost see the smile on the captain's face as he asked the question.

"As long as he's breathing I don't care if he's banged up any, just make sure you get him and quickly, this place is going up in flames and we're going to have to evacuate it very soon."

"Copy that, sir, we're on it. We'll keep you informed of our progress."

As his anger abated and clarity of thought returned, Solon had an idea. He said, "I'm inputting the tracking codes for the Recon Delta NIs into the facility's main computer which will be uploaded directly to your NI. Using these codes and the facility's interior sensors you should be able to pinpoint Stryder's location and find him."

Anders felt the tingle as his NI accessed the incoming data, and he smiled.

"Data received, sir. Copy your instructions. Will inform you when the target has been acquired."

"Good luck Captain and no slip ups," Solon said breaking the connection to leave the team to get on with their mission.

Smiling, he sat back and thought that perhaps he just might get a result from this after all. He had a team of enhanced soldiers looking for the source of the serum. If they didn't manage to capture Stryder he still had them. It might take a little longer to fabricate the serum from them, instead of from its pure form via Stryder's blood, but it could be done just the same. It was not a total loss after all, and this little exercise would prove the worth of the programme, demonstrating how the elite team performed.

~

Hawk had arrived at Celeron and was greeted by General Sinclair himself on the starship still in orbit around the planet.

The briefing had been simple and to the point.

"Bring them back, Captain," was all Sinclair had said. Everything else had already been stated, they all knew the vital importance of this mission and time was of the essence, so no one wanted to waste any more on pointless speeches.

While Hawk was en route to Celeron, Storm and his team were being briefed by the General about what would be happening when the team leader arrived.

They didn't know Hawk, but like the good soldiers they were, they trusted the General's judgement and followed orders.

A freighter commandeered from a company with whom Col Sec had dealings had been refitted in record time with some special fitments and renamed the Hyperion. The shield generators had been increased and some armaments had been installed and concealed so that they would not be suspected. The last item to be added was a stealth shield enabling them to pass through the border of Colonial and Alliance space without being detected.

When the munitions and hardware had been installed and all the briefings had been completed there was only one thing left to do and that was to board the ship and leave for Toldax.

Captain Reynolds' First Officer and certain members of his crew, now all suitably attired as merchant spacers, had replaced the original crew of the freighter.

It was a short jump through hyperspace to cross the border and then they were in Alliance territory. Another jump put them within a few light years of the solar system of which Toldax was part.

Hawk and Storm and the rest of his squad were on the small bridge of the freighter as it came out of hyperspace. Watching through the main viewer they saw Toldax in the distance, a small ball of blue against the obsidian backdrop of space.

"How do you want to play this, gentlemen?" asked Commander Park, the First Officer, as he turned in the command chair to see the small group standing just behind him.

"Commander Park, is there any way to get a transmission through to Captain Stryder's NI from here without us being detected? I need to inform him of our intentions," Hawk asked, not holding out much hope for an affirmative.

"It's very doubtful, sir, not without the planetary sensors detecting the transmission. They might not be able to pick out what the signal says or where it was going to, but they would certainly detect a signal coming from somewhere. As we are the only merchant craft out here, it would be just a matter of time before some bright spark wanted to know what a beat up old freighter was doing here anyway," replied Commander Park dubiously.

"Then we're just gonna have to get a bit closer," Hawk said.

"I was afraid you were going to say that," Cowboy muttered to himself.

"Button it, Cowboy!" Storm ordered.

Commander Park turned to the helm officer and gave the command to take them in closer using the sub-light engines.

Hawk said, "Guardian, are you and your men ready for immediate ship evac?"

"We are, sir. All munitions have been checked and we are as ready as we can be. We'd just like some hint of the plan so we can acquaint ourselves with it, sir." Storm replied.

"Ah!" said Hawk taking Storm to one side, "That's a good point but you see this is a rather fluid situation. We are just going to have to do the best we can with it."

"You don't have one do you?" Storm realised.

Hawk's face split into a rather sheepish grin and he slowly shook his head. "Not really, I'm making this up as I go, going with the flow as it were. It's difficult to plan for something like this when we have no intel on the planet or the facility down there."

"I see, sir," Storm said. "Well, sir, General Sinclair seemed to have enough faith in you to put you in command of this mission, so who am I to argue with that. We're with you sir, one hundred per cent."

"That's good to hear soldier. There are two Recon Delta Marines down there and I don't intend leaving here without them." He added, "If I just knew how though, it would be a help."

Storm huffed a short laugh that almost went unheard, but Hawk knew this officer would follow him even though this mission was absurd in the extreme. He would go through with it probably because of its absurdity. Times of battle were times of extremes and absurdity and it was this that brought out the best in some men and the worst in others. Hawk knew he had with him some of the best and he felt secure that whatever happened these men would give their all to help make this mission a success, or die trying.

He could ask for nothing less and want for nothing more.

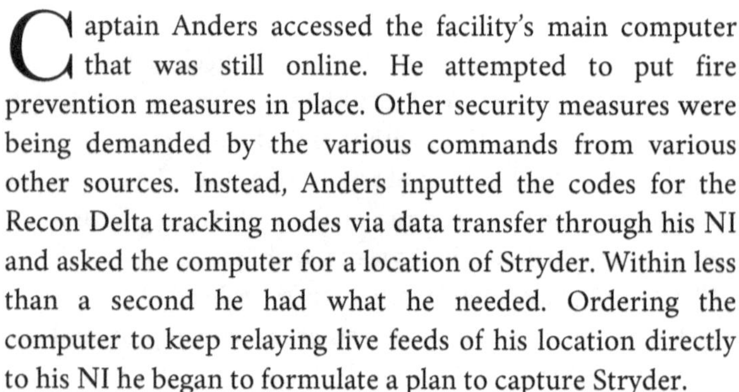

Captain Anders accessed the facility's main computer that was still online. He attempted to put fire prevention measures in place. Other security measures were being demanded by the various commands from various other sources. Instead, Anders inputted the codes for the Recon Delta tracking nodes via data transfer through his NI and asked the computer for a location of Stryder. Within less than a second he had what he needed. Ordering the computer to keep relaying live feeds of his location directly to his NI he began to formulate a plan to capture Stryder.

CHAPTER 24

Solon was in his office. He'd issued orders to Captain Anders and his team and all that remained was for them to complete their mission. The whole facility was coming down around his ears; the main lab was a complete blaze, a conflagration that threatened to engulf the whole building. Anders and his men would carry out their mission with complete disregard for their own safety for they belonged to the Special Forces known as the Black Knights. They were the Alliance's elite Marines; equivalent and maybe superior to the respected Recon Delta of the damned Confederation.

There was no reason he should remain inside the facility and put himself in danger; he had other concerns to concentrate on. He was in charge of all the Special Force missions for the Alliance and if this one was going to bite the dust then he had to resurrect his career by making sure no more mistakes were made in the other missions that were planned.

Even he had his masters to whom he was answerable, and

it was they who held the real power. He was just a pawn in a galactic game of chess spanning many solar systems.

Picking up his small travel grip, he headed out of the door and towards the nearest exit. He would wait at the spaceport landing pad for the arrival of Anders and his team, and hopefully Stryder. The woman, Hardy, was expendable.

~

Stryder and Hardy headed down the corridor and turned the corner to face yet another corridor.

"How many more of these things do we have to go down until we get there?" Hardy asked showing her frustration.

"Not far now. It's just down here," replied Stryder and just then his hyper accelerated senses warned him of danger from behind.

Stopping suddenly he spun around to see three guards turn the corner behind him all armed with assault rifles. Dropping down to one knee he fired a quick burst, which caught the lead guard across the chest. It opened up a series of wounds as the bolts stitched across his torso sending blood spraying outwards splashing the walls of the corridor. He was sent staggering backwards and the two other guards had to move to either side to avoid him delaying them using their own weapons.

Hardy turned when she saw Stryder spin around and took in the scene straight away. Her own reflexes immediately came into play. She brought up her assault rifle and fired at the two remaining guards. Her salvo caught the guard to her left in the centre of his chest and sent him crashing into the wall whilst Stryder fired another burst at the remaining guard with the same effect.

Within the space of a few heartbeats three more guards were dead. Stryder got to his feet and looked at Hardy, concern on his face, which she picked up on. This was something new.

"What?" she asked.

"They shouldn't have found us so quickly, the computer had the guards looking for us in the corridors around the main lab and heading towards the exits. How would they know to look for us here, and so quickly?" he replied posing the question that had sprung to his mind after the sight of the guards had almost caught him off guard.

"Could they be lost and it was just lucky that they found us, or unlucky for them?" she posited.

"Doubtful, I'm certain they were acting under orders, which can only mean one thing."

"What, that they were told to widen the scope of the search?"

"If that was the reason, why here, and why not somewhere else closer to the spaceport landing pad? If we wanted out of here we would eventually have to head in that direction. No, they've accessed the tracker inside my NI. That was how they found us on Celeron; someone gave them the codes. Sinclair told me when you had been taken. Now they're using the same codes to track us inside this facility via the internal sensors," explained Stryder and Hardy's jaw dropped open.

"Oh, this just keeps getting better and better. Anything else I should know before we continue?" she asked her voice fairly dripping with sarcasm.

"It's not as bad as it sounds, I may be able to cloud the sensor's search parameters," Stryder said slowly. His eyes had that thousand-yard stare again and she knew he was concentrating on something.

"If I can access the computer I may be able to readjust the internal sensors just enough to...."

"Pity you couldn't just turn off your tracker," Hardy said

as a throwaway comment not really expecting him to take her seriously.

Stryder looked at her and said, "Brilliant, why didn't I think of that?"

"What? You can't turn off your tracker that's why; it's a permanent signal so that we can always be located."

Stryder didn't answer, he just focused all his attention on what he was attempting to do. His eyes took on a glassy stare, actually going milky white, as his brain worked in overdrive. His mental powers expanded into unknown areas and then, his eyes returning to their normal colour, he looked at her and said, "Okay, done."

"Excuse me?" she said almost in apoplexy.

"It's off," he said in a matter-of-fact way.

"But that's impossible, how?"

"Don't know, I just concentrated on gaining control of the output and once that was done, I just turned it off. I can turn it back on just as easily too."

Hardy didn't know what to say. Stryder had just demonstrated an ability that should be impossible and yet he was convinced of it being successful.

"Cool 'eh?" he added with a smile, then becoming more serious said, "C'mon, let's move, I just hope they hadn't figured out which direction we were headed and send more guards to stop us."

"What if they were tracking both of us?"

"I'm banking on them only tracking me, no offence but they will need me now that I've destroyed their source of the serum and any future ability to recreate it. I'm hoping they only thought to track me."

"Hope you're right."

"Me too, c'mon let's get moving," he repeated.

〜

Anders received confirmation from the computer that the signal from the tracking codes was lost. For a second he was unsure what to do because he'd been assured the signal would be a constant. He asked the computer if the signal could be masked in any way, such as if the subject had entered an area where it could be interfered with, and received the same reply. The signal had just ended.

Having no other recourse but to change his strategy, he ordered the computer to correlate the data from the position where the signal was first intercepted to when it was lost and compute a possible destination.

Within a second he had the answer he was looking for and a location for Stryder, so no great harm done.

Using his NI he accessed the comm battle channels and, ordering the guards to surround the Life Support station, he told them to await the arrival of Stryder and to detain him until his team got there.

He had him now he thought, as he quickened his pace.

Stryder and Hardy carried on down the corridor until they reached the end where a door barred their way. It opened to Stryder's touch and they walked through onto a huge gangplank that stretched out for a hundred odd feet before them across a deep chasm. Hardy looked down and saw that they were standing on top of a walkway that was fifteen feet wide with a drop of over three hundred feet straight down.

"Whoa!" she said when she saw how high up they were.

"Yep, the reactor room is on the lower level and we need to get down there. There has to be an access panel to the vents for the exhaust gases from the fusion reactor.

"And how the hell do you propose we get down there?" she asked a little incredulously.

"I'm working on it," he replied as he looked around at the room.

Just then a plasma bolt was fired from beneath them. It just missed him, passing by his shoulder on its way up to the ceiling.

"Good job that guards a piss poor shot," Hardy said as they both dodged towards the centre of the walkway.

"Things have just become a little more complicated," said Stryder. Leaning over the edge of the walkway he returned fire to warn the guard against shooting again. As soon as Stryder fired his assault rifle over the edge three more guards took the opportunity to try and blast him off the walkway.

Plasma bolts whizzed past him and burned the very air as they passed so close to him that his clothes were singed.

"And how the hell are we going to be able to get down there now then?" asked Hardy once the firing had stopped. She was lying face down on the walkway to minimise her target profile. The guards down below on the balcony around the perimeter of what was in fact a huge shaft could not locate her.

"Like I said, I'm working on it," Stryder replied as he glanced over the edge of the walkway taking in more with one glance than a normal person could after studying the scene for several minutes.

"And how did they know where we are? I thought you said you turned off your tracker," Hardy asked. She was getting angry at the thought that the little hope of escape she had garnered from the seemingly hopeless situation was about to be torn from her and trampled under her feet.

"They must've guessed where we would go and sent guards on ahead," Stryder said.

More plasma bolts struck above their heads as the guards

below continued to fire at them. A few struck the edge of the walkway near Stryder and Hardy, forcing them to keep back from the edge.

Getting to his knees and shouldering his assault rifle he said, "Right, cover me."

"What!" Hardy gasped sensing he was about to do something absolutely reckless.

"I'm going to draw their fire to give you the chance to fire back. If you manage to hit any of them, that would be great. All I'm hoping for is that your covering fire will give me the chance to do what I have to. Trust me."

Before she could argue he had scooted down the walkway and then bobbed up into view of the guards below.

Their attention was drawn to where he was, farther down the walkway from where Hardy remained under cover so they opened fire on him.

He threw himself down on the walkway as plasma bolts struck the edge blasting chunks of plascrete away from it breaking his cover.

Hardy was up on one knee, her assault rifle up against her shoulder as she sighted down the barrel and fired a short burst at them.

Her first salvo caused them to cease fire and retreat to find their own cover.

"Go!" she said and Stryder sprung into action as she kept the guards pinned down with a burst of sustained plasma fire.

Stryder grabbed hold of the edge of the walkway and threw himself over, swinging out beneath it using his momentum to propel his body across the chasm and onto the balcony several feet below, the same balcony on which the guards were positioned.

The second he landed he retrieved his assault rifle from over his shoulder and positioned it to fire.

Caught in a vicious crossfire from both above and in front the guards died as the plasma bolts tore their flesh up in a mist of blood.

Once the guards were dead Stryder looked up at Hardy and said, "Well, what're you waiting for?"

A smile crossed her lips and as she was about to say something plasma bolts from behind her tore up the air. She leaped over the edge, flinging herself at the balcony below, narrowly evading the deadly weapons fire from above. As she landed a few feet from Stryder, she rolled exactly like her jump commander had taught her in basic training back at the academy. She came up on her knees still holding her assault rifle.

The guards who had fired at her from above followed her down with their assault rifles and were about to fire at her again when Stryder shot two of them. They went tumbling over the edge to spiral into the shaft below, their blood leaving a gory trail in the air tracing their descent into the shaft. The other two dodged back over the edge of the walkway to avoid being shot.

Glancing over at where the guards lay dead on the balcony Stryder said, "Go and see if they have any grenades on them."

Hardy turned and, crouching again to minimise her target profile, she ran as best she could over to where the bodies lay. In moments she was back with a handful of grenades, small, black and deadly.

"Great, just what we need," Stryder said.

He pushed the central rod situated at the top of the egg-shaped grenade, enabling the safety clip to spring free and thus armed two of the weapons. He then had five seconds before they exploded and he tossed them up onto the walkway expertly dropping them right next to the two remaining guards.

Seeing the grenades, the guards tried to run for it but hadn't gone more than a few paces before the explosions ripped into them shredding their bodies and tossing flesh and bone into the air in a shower of blood. The walkway was damaged and a huge chunk of it fell into the shaft.

Stryder and Hardy watched as the slab of the broken walkway passed by them and he said, "Well that will stop anyone following us from up there, unless they have grappling hooks."

"You're full of good cheer," she replied with the hint of a smile then she looked around and asked, "Now what do we do?"

Just then an explosion erupted from below sending a ball of white-hot flame up the centre of the shaft. The shockwave from the blast sent shudders through the walls of the shaft threatening to throw the two of them off the balcony into the ball of flame rising up.

Stryder saw the ball of fire coming and knew there was no way to outrun it. They would be dead in seconds if they didn't find shelter.

~

General Solon was just exiting the facility when the explosion shook the entire building. He spun around to look behind him and said, "Well, that can't be good."

He turned back and continued on his way. "Maybe waiting for Anders and his team will be a waste of time. If there are any more explosions like that then they might not get out before the whole place goes up in flames."

Seeing his shuttle in the distance on the landing pad, he quickened his pace. Accessing his NI he called Anders through a combat channel. "Anders, your time is limited, locate and capture Captain Stryder and bring him to my shuttle on the landing pad. Is that understood?"

Anders replied almost instantly, his voice seeming to echo in the General's brain, and he said, "Understood, sir."

~

Stryder dived to cover Hardy with his body as the wall of flame engulfed them both. The heat was unbelievable. He could feel his clothes burning and his skin begin to blister as the heat boiled away its moisture.

The second before he landed on top of Hardy he saw the terror in her eyes and heard her scream as she realised what was about to happen.

Pain assailed his senses as the flames washed over them. Unbelievable pain as the temperature soared to extreme heights in the space of a few seconds. The human body was not designed to withstand that kind of abuse as Stryder was well aware and trying to withstand the pain from the heat his thoughts dwelled on how he had failed his mission and in doing so had cost the life of a lovely young woman with whom he had fallen in love.

The fireball passed them by searing everything in its path and, amazed at the fact he was still alive, he rolled off Hardy screaming in agony as his clothes were still smouldering, nothing but rags left of them. Hardy was up in a flash rolling over to him, the thought that she was unscathed not even entering her brain. Her one and only thought was the safety of the man she loved, the man who had saved her life by risking his own.

Whatever she could do, she would, anything to help ease Stryder's pain.

Stryder was rolling on the balcony trying to put out the flames in his clothing, or what was left of it.

His back, which had been in contact with the flames, was a mass of blisters, but amazingly the rest of him seemed almost untouched.

After he had put out the flames he stopped rolling and looked up at her as she crouched over him.

"You're okay!" he said amazed at his success in keeping her alive and equally amazed that he too was still in the land of the living.

"How did you do that?" she demanded, knowing that both of them should be dead.

"I have no idea except to say that I'm not complaining," he replied as he got to his feet.

"It must be your enhancements, they work better than even they expected," Hardy said with the biggest grin across her face. They had both cheated death and perhaps, just perhaps, they might make it out of there alive after all.

"Does your back hurt still?" she asked amazed at being alive.

"It's easing off now. Wow! That was intense!" he said, and looking over his shoulder he saw the blisters begin to dry up right before his eyes. He was healing himself at an amazing rate, one he never thought possible.

Hardy saw the expression of wonder on his face and looking at his back was speechless at what she saw. The blisters were almost all gone by that time, having dried up and new skin forming over the burnt areas. As they both watched, his body formed new tissue to replace all the burnt and scarred tissue that moments earlier had covered his entire back. Within a few minutes he was as good as new.

"I think the greater the threat, the faster the immune system kicks in," Stryder offered as he got to his feet.

Hardy looked at him and smiling said, "I'm not complaining." It was then that he saw her eyes wander over his body and he realised that he was wearing nothing but tatters. All his clothes had been shredded by the blast of super-heated flame. His shirt hung from his broad shoulders in shreds exposing his muscular torso and washboard abs whilst his leggings were nothing more than strips of seared cloth hanging from his waist attached by the belt.

"Plenty of time for that girl," he joked. "Let's get off this planet first before we make any plans though."

"What do you think happened down there?" Hardy asked dragging her mind back to the job at hand and off his perfectly formed abs.

Peering over the edge of the balcony he looked down the shaft to where the fireball originated.

"It looks like the slab from the walkway damaged one of the Life Support generators," he said after assessing the damage below.

His brain was working faster than he thought possible dealing with many issues, multi-tasking faster than he thought a human brain was capable of, consciously at least. He was aware that the subconscious mind was capable of many things that the conscious mind could not even comprehend. Now though he seemed to be able to do more, concentrate harder about more than just one subject and correlate plans and strategies for each topic he was mulling over.

"Will that affect us in any way?"

"There's no way of knowing that until we get down there and look," Stryder said and led the way towards the elevator to the next level.

Elevator was perhaps the wrong word to describe what it was. A slab of plascrete attached to a belt at right angles that ran up the wall was all it really was. To use it you simply stood on it and the belt took you up to the floor you needed. On the other side of the belt it travelled in the opposite direction and took you down to the level you wanted.

They grabbed hold of the handles placed at head height and, stepping onto the ledge, they allowed it to take them down to the next level. Just one more level to go and they would be at the bottom where the Life Support station was. Smoke was billowing up from the blown generator and filling the shaft making it hard for them to breathe. Tears began to stream from Hardy's eyes as the acrid smoke affected them.

"Are you okay?" Stryder asked when he noticed she was struggling. His own eyes were coping far better than he thought possible, again another new development from his enhancements that he never expected.

"Can't see a damn thing through this blasted smoke, my eyes are streaming," she replied reaching out a hand to touch him for reassurance.

"You'll be fine, just keep hold of me and I'll make sure we get there okay," he said, clamping his hand on top of hers on his forearm to let her know he wouldn't abandon her.

"How come you can see where we're going and I can't?" she asked, almost knowing the answer before he gave it.

"Must be another advantage of these enhancements they gave me. I'm not knocking it if it helps us get the fuck out of here with both our skins intact," he replied.

"Me neither," she said through gritted teeth.

As they hit the bottom floor Stryder helped Hardy off the belt elevator and as he tried to get his bearings through the dense smoke he heard something that put him on edge. Grabbing Hardy by the scruff of the neck he pulled her down to the floor roughly just in time as a series of plasma bolts seared the air above them.

"What the fuck?" Hardy asked as she hit the floor.

"Guards," Stryder said as the bolts went harmlessly overhead striking the walls behind where they had been standing mere seconds earlier.

"How the fuck did you know they were there?" Hardy asked.

"Heard them," he replied quickly. Then, taking his assault rifle from his shoulder, he returned fire. His plasma bolts struck nothing except the far side of the chamber. He would have heard the shots hit bodies if his aim had been true.

"Damn! They're wearing visors," he said when he realised why he had missed them. The visors had increased visual acuity and because they were fixed to a full-face mask it enabled them to breathe in the smoke-filled shaft.

"We're screwed," Hardy said, when she realised what they were up against. They had no idea where the guards were, what they were armed with or even how many were there. The worst part of it for her was that in her present condition she could not help Stryder. She could not see anything at the moment because the smoke had rendered her eyes useless.

"C'mon, we have to keep on the move, they can track us via infra red and all I've got is my hearing to help us, my eyes may not hurt but this smoke is too dense for even me to see through," Stryder said as he grabbed her hand and pulled her after him. There was a doorway to his left, which he pulled Hardy towards. Although the smoke had not affected his eyes in the same way he still couldn't see anything farther than a few feet in front of him, so he did most things by relying on his hearing and his sense of touch.

Another burst of plasma fire struck the doorframe to the side of him helping him decide whether to go through the door or not. He went through as fast as he could, closing the door behind them.

Hardy was doubled over in a coughing fit as her lungs tried to purge the smoke from them. The air inside the room they had just entered was fresh and clean with just a trace of the smoke that had followed them inside when the door was opened. Stryder could see clearly again and quickly took in his surroundings as he waited for Hardy to get her breathing back under control. They were at the very end of a corridor, a few feet from a corner, and the thing that had niggled at him since the very first attack by the guards soon became apparent.

He had wondered why the guard's gunfire had been so erratic and unfocused. None of the shots had come close enough to warrant any danger. Certainly they had had to move out of the way for fear of getting shot, but the accuracy he had expected was just not there, almost as if they had been herding them in a certain direction. But why would they try to herd them in a direction when Stryder and Hardy were running away from them? It didn't make any sense until Hardy stood up. Two figures dressed in combat fatigues and armed with assault rifles walked around the corner and blocked their path.

Stryder recognised them instantly as two of the Marines who had received the serum. He had no idea how he knew, just that he knew. Almost like when a soldier recognises another in a crowd due to shared experiences and training, Stryder just knew that these two Marines had received the serum. It might not be the same serum that was administered to him, and it might not have the same effect on them as it had on him, but they had definitely been given a variation of it.

"Fuck!" Hardy said when she saw them. She too recognised that these were not just guards but soldiers like her and therefore would pose a bigger threat and harder obstacle to overcome.

"Don't move!" said one of them as they both brought their assault rifles down to aim at Stryder and Hardy.

Before any of them could react, Stryder dived at the two Marines so fast that even with their enhanced reflexes they didn't have time to react.

Their assault rifles went spinning from their hands as they were sent crashing into the corridor wall. Stryder landed heavily on top of them and aimed a fist into the face of the nearest one smashing through the Marine's helmet visor and breaking his nose and teeth. Blood spurted out and covered the man's face.

Snatching the Marine's dagger free from its sheath Stryder rammed it up into the chin of the other Marine, the blade penetrated the skin under his chin and thrust up into his brain severing the brain stem and killing him instantly. Pulling the blade free he slashed it across the throat of the other Marine before he had the chance to react after the punch to his face. The force of the blow to the throat slashed open the carotid artery sending a spray of arterial blood several feet into the air to splash across the walls of the corridor.

The entire action took less than three seconds and at the end of it two Marines lay dead. Hardy was absolutely amazed at the swiftness and severity of Stryder's action.

Getting to his feet Stryder said, "Couldn't afford to let them take us or to live. They had the serum inside them and with it the Alliance could make more like them. Soon we'd be facing an army of soldiers that can heal themselves and are faster and stronger than all of our regular troops."

"You don't have to validate your actions to me Kurt, I totally agree with you. I just never thought you could move so fast," she replied.

"Our only chance is that the serum hasn't taken full effect on them or they haven't yet learned just how to access their new abilities. Nevertheless, it's our only chance to be able to combat them as equals," Stryder said, running multiple scenarios through his mind as he spoke to Hardy.

"We'll have to be careful, I think the others could be close by," he said after a moment's hesitation.

"What makes you think that?" she asked

"It seemed strange that the guards' aim was so off when they fired at us. They had infrared visors don't forget so they could see us clearly. They should have hit us on a few occasions yet they didn't. They came close enough for us to think they were aiming at us but now I think that they weren't. I think they were simply herding us in the direction they wanted us to go and now we've made contact with the Marines it's obvious where they wanted us," he explained.

"Here?" Hardy said still not quite seeing the full picture.

"Yes, here, where the Marines could capture us. Don't you see they still want us alive to manufacture the serum from my blood?"

"He's right you know," Anders said from farther down the corridor. He appeared around the bend just as the first two had, and he also had his assault rifle at high port across his chest. "Captain Stryder is a very valuable commodity." Anders added then lowering his assault rifle said, "You, on the other hand, are not," and he shot her full in the chest on maximum power. The plasma bolt hit her square in the middle of her chest and burned through as it picked her up and smashed her against the door through which they had just come leaving a trail of her life's blood in the air. As she hit the door she bounced off leaving a gory smear of her blood over the impact zone. She died instantly, her young life ripped from her in the blink of an eye.

Stryder saw Anders drop his rifle to aim at them but never expected what was to come. He saw him tighten his finger on the trigger and in total disbelief saw him fire the weapon. His head spun around to see Hardy, the woman he had grown to love, struck by the full power of the plasma bolt and die before his very eyes.

A million emotions raced through him at the sight of the young woman being killed before him. The fact that he had been powerless to save her was etched on his mind forever. Firstly, total shock as he watched the plasma bolt strike her, lift her off her feet and slam her broken body into the wall, and watching her slide down that wall as her life's blood traced her path to the floor. Then disbelief as he couldn't conceive what his eyes had seen and finally a rage like he had never felt before, and probably never would again, overwhelmed him. A rage he could not control and which would only be satiated by the death of the man who murdered his love.

Slowly, he returned his gaze to Anders, the man he would soon kill.

"You will come with us Captain Stryder, you have no choice," Anders said.

"Wrong," Stryder said and he leapt at them covering the distance in a single bound. Landing on top of Anders he ripped the assault rifle out of his hands and as they crashed to the floor he hurled it from him. He was going to kill him, of that he was certain, and it would be with his bare hands.

Springing to his feet he spun around and with a spinning back kick kicked the first unsuspecting Marine squarely in the chest sending him crashing into the wall. Placing his foot down, he spun and kicked the other Marine sending him crashing into the other wall opposite. As he bounced off, Stryder struck him beneath his helmet across his throat crushing his oesophagus. The Marine went down clutching at his throat trying to force air into his lungs.

The other Marine lunged at Stryder, who blocked the attempt and grabbed his head in both hands then twisted it violently one hundred and eighty degrees snapping the man's neck like a twig. He died instantly and fell to the floor in a heap. Stryder stepped over to the choking Marine and dispensed of him in the same way. Then, stepping over the body, he stood in front of Anders who by this time had regained his feet and had been forced to watch the destruction of his team by one man. Unlike his teammates his helmet had fallen off when Stryder had collided with him so he had no protection for his head, something that bothered him even more in seeing how swiftly Stryder had dispatched his two colleagues who were both wearing theirs.

"See, I do have a choice," said Stryder.

Anders in desperation attacked Stryder with a series of punches.

Stryder carried on talking as he deftly evaded each punch with ease.

"You see if you had kept Hardy alive, that's the young woman you shot by the way," he said as he ducked beneath a haymaker right cross then blocked a series of left and right jabs, "then I might have had no choice but to do as you wanted to preserve her life. Killing her took that edge away."

Anders sent a straight right punch aimed at his head and because the serum was beginning to take effect the power he put into it would have demolished a normal person's face. Stryder simply swayed to one side allowing it to sail past his face. Grabbing the wrist and twisting to force the arm to go against the joint, he brought his other hand down on the upturned elbow, smashing it.

Anders let out a howl of agony, but instead of falling down in pain he threw another straight punch with his left arm with the same result. Stryder caught, twisted and then broke the elbow leaving his foe with two useless arms.

"Now then, I'll give you the same choice you gave Hardy shall I? Oh and by the way, if you're wondering who she was, I'll tell you. *She was going to be my wife!*" His voice rose at the end so that the last seven words were shouted in rage into the face of the man before him.

Stryder struck Anders on the point of his nose in an

upward palm heel strike which pushed his nose straight up into his brain killing him instantly.

"I wanted you to suffer, to feel my pain, but I don't have the time," Stryder said as he watched him fall straight-legged to the floor.

"Besides, I'm going to kill everyone else in this building and that's gonna take some time," he added as he stepped over the dead body and walked away down the corridor holding an assault rifle in one hand, a Sig P996 in his other and hate and rage in his heart. He intended to do harm to every man he saw who belonged to the Alliance.

CHAPTER 25

"I can't wait any longer. We have to do something," Hawk said as he came back to the bridge of the starship.

"Have you formulated a plan yet?" Storm asked as Hawk came to stand by him.

"How good are you and your men at orbital jumping?" Hawk asked with a smile.

"Cool, now we're talking." Private William (Hacker) Ives said. Although his speciality was computers, he was also somewhat of an adrenalin junkie.

Storm and Wayne were standing there also, the only other members of the squad that had been picked to come along, and they looked at Hacker with a puzzled expression.

"What?" Hacker said when he saw them. "It's about time we did something positive instead of sitting on our asses up here like we have been doing."

"Commander Parks, will we be able to initiate an orbital drop from one of the hatches if you get us close enough?" asked Hawk.

Parks spun around in the command chair and said, "You

do realise we'll have to drop our stealth shield to allow you to leave the ship?"

"Of course, but with luck we'll be gone and clear in less than a second, hopefully you won't show up as more than an anomaly on any sensor screen that might be looking in our direction." explained Hawk.

"Okay then, I'll get as close as we can without making it too easy to spot us when we drop the stealth shield. You get ready guys, we'll wait on your call for pick up, although I have no idea how you intend to get back here," Parks said.

"Come on guys we need to suit up for the jump. Oh and Commander, about the return trip, I'll let you know as soon as I figure it out," Hawk said as he turned and led the way off the bridge.

"How did I know he was going to say that?" Cowboy said.

"Button it, Wayne," Storm said with a slight smirk in his voice.

"Commander, contact Stryder and let him know we're coming," Hawk said. Then he left the bridge.

~

Stryder hadn't gone far when the call came through to his SNI on a combat frequency. "This is Commander Parks in orbit around the planet. Captains Hawk, Storm and two Recon Delta Marines from Captain Storm's team are coming to help you and Miss Hardy off the planet."

"Hardy is dead. How are they coming and how long before they arrive?" Stryder asked quickly, wanting to know all the details.

"They are making an orbital jump and should be there in moments, sir. They will contact you as soon as they get planet side."

"An orbital jump, that means they'll need transport off

this planet. What contingencies have they made to get off the planet?"

"Captain Hawk will brief you on arrival, sir. Please stand by, Parks out."

Stryder was more determined than ever to destroy the place and everyone in it. If Col Sec were here to rescue him then Sinclair had plans for him, probably just as bad as those the Alliance had. He was not going to allow himself to be used or abused any longer. There was no way he would allow this team to take him with them which meant he would have to make plans to ensure they got off here safely but without him. His previous plan of destroying the place and remaining inside was now out of the question and thinking about it brought him to his senses a little. Why should he sacrifice himself just to prevent them making use of the serum inside him? He would just have to think of some other way of depriving them of it.

He couldn't let Storm and this Hawk die though as they had probably come to rescue him because he was a Recon Delta Marine same as them and the Delta lived by a code. One of the tenets stated was that they never left a soldier behind. If they had come to save him, then he would have to do what he could to ensure they got off the planet safely. Hardy's death was already laying heavily on his mind. He might not be able to cope if his presence cost the lives of any more Delta Marines. That was something he might not be able to live with.

Using his NI he linked into the main computer once more and after a quick search found what he wanted.

"Okay guys, if you're coming, the least I can do is prepare a welcome for you and arrange a way off this rock," he said out loud to himself.

Norsky had accessed the computer and had been listening in to any available comm chatter to see where Stryder and Hardy were.

Explosions were going off around him as he made his way to Stryder's last known destination. He was well aware that the facility was going to self-destruct soon. Somehow he had obtained that knowledge through his NI from the computer, and he also knew that General Solon was awaiting the arrival of Captain Anders' team who had been sent to collect Stryder. He wasn't sure how he had obtained all that information because surely any comm chatter between the two parties had been through closed, encrypted combat channels, unless his enhanced abilities had somehow enabled him to hack into the channels in question without him knowing. However, it had happened and he was not the type to look a gift horse in the mouth. He knew General Solon was waiting for him and it was common sense to assume that he had transport ready and waiting to escort them away from the upcoming conflagration.

It also made sense for him to make his way to the General's location, take Stryder away from the Marines and hand him over to Solon personally and thereby regain his position with him.

The four Marines were suited up with the jumpsuits incorporating the Rapier battle helmet, full face visor with breather unit that attached to the jump suit's main breather unit, which was in the back pack they all wore. It also held the combat parachute made from light, durable material, which would open when the release button was hit and on landing retract back into the backpack.

Across their chest they each wore the Mk II Remm assault rifle and in a holster strapped under their left armpit they each had a Sig P996, both standard issue. Finally, in a sheath strapped to their left forearm was the Howell combat knife.

Their NIs would interface into the battle helmet's computer which would then give them a HUD display on the inside of the helmet visor showing all relevant data they would want to call up, such as weather conditions and battle group deployments. Comm channels would be connected using the small, integrated transmitter.

Hawk gave the command and the stealth shield was dropped. The hatch opened and as one, they jumped. The hatch closed up immediately after their evacuation and the stealth shield was raised simultaneously.

Quickly they fell, fanning out into a delta wing formation their heads angled forward, their arms at their sides and legs together to minimise their radar silhouette. It also cut down on any drag so they would plummet through the upper atmosphere at an alarming rate. The suit would prevent friction or the freezing temperatures from being that high up in the atmosphere being a problem, keeping their core temperatures at normal as the onboard computer in the Rapier battle helmet monitored their vital signs constantly and relayed the data to the heating unit inside the jumpsuit.

Buffeted by the atmosphere, the four Marines fought to keep their silhouette stable and prevent themselves from going into a tumble. Should that happen at the speed they were travelling, the chances of them being able to regain control of their descent ranged from slim to none.

Closer and closer their descent brought them to the surface of the planet. Through the upper atmosphere, through the clouds and out and down until the ground below came rushing towards them at a fantastic rate. Lesser men would have baulked at the idea of jumping out of a starship whilst still in a low orbit, but not these men. They knew this was the only way and they agreed to it without a second's hesitation.

The readout in the helmet counted down their altitude as they rushed towards the ground:

20,000 feet
    Not yet,
10,000 feet
Just a little closer,
5,000 feet
Just a little more,
3,000 feet
2,000 feet
1,000 feet
Almost there
900 feet
Now!!

Each chute was deployed and instantly snapped open catching the air in its canopy, dragging the wearer's speed down from terminal velocity to almost nothing by comparison in the blink of an eye. It was at this point where most injuries occurred, due to the sudden deceleration.

Literally within seconds they were down on the ground, rolling to the side to lessen the impact with the hard surface, their chutes automatically retracting inside their backpacks. Up on their knees they kept low, minimising their chances of being seen from any lookout post situated near the facility where they had targeted their landing.

"We're down! Will report back once our objective is in

sight and has been achieved," Hawk said through the comm link that had been established prior to their evacuation from the starship in orbit.

Storm was at his side in a flash, "Okay, sir, it's on you, what are your orders?" he asked.

In the distance they could see the facility. They had come down close to it but on the opposite side of a small copse of trees, which they had used for cover. The facility was being wracked by explosions from the inside and they could see quite clearly chunks of debris being flung high into the air as each new blast destroyed more and more of it.

"Whatever you decide, it had better be quick, while there's still something of that place left for us to search," Storm added.

Hawk's keen eyes then saw something and he pointed over to the far right.

"There, it looks like a landing pad with a shuttle waiting. My guess is Stryder will make for that. So, first order of business is to take control of the pad and the vehicle on it to ensure that when Stryder finds us we have a way off this rock," he said.

"And what if he can't get to us?" Storm asked.

"Then we'll have to find a way to get to him, but first things first, let's capture that shuttle," Hawk replied. He unhooked his Remm assault rifle, pulled the lever to prime the battery clip then turned to Storm and smiled, "Time to rock and roll," he said.

Inside the rapidly self-destructing building, Stryder was dodging falling masonry and mini explosions that were erupting everywhere. They were becoming more frequent as time went on.

The information from the computer about the location of key personnel inside the building told him where General Solon was.

The lab had been destroyed along with any workable samples of the serum, so even if any of the lab techs survived this catastrophe the chances of them being able to recreate their findings here would be impossible. The key to all this was his blood. That only left General Solon; he was a danger to the Confederation and his drive to gain an ascendancy over them would push him to do anything. That was something he could not allow to happen. Enough lives had been lost to this experiment and it was about time it came to an end.

It would end here, today, with the destruction of this facility and with the death of General Solon.

~

The wait for Captain Anders' team to bring the damned Stryder to him was becoming interminable. Solon used his NI to access the computer to locate Anders but he refused or was unable to respond to his call. What the computer told him brought a chill to his blood. Apparently all Anders' team were dead and the facility was just less than an hour away from the fusion reactors going critical and destroying not only the entire facility but the surrounding area up to a one hundred mile radius. At least the planet's population would be spared but this facility would be totally destroyed. It would be a great loss to the Alliance, one they could ill afford.

He staggered from the enormity of what his desire to gain an advantage over the Confederation was about to do to the lives of the people he had hoped to improve. He was about to cause a catastrophe that would rock the Alliance to its very core. The loss of life and this facility was bad enough, but for it to be caused by one of the top ranking Generals was just unacceptable.

The worst thing was that he was powerless to prevent it.

If Anders' team were all dead then Stryder must be responsible, which also meant that by now he had figured out an escape route. The only way off here was in Solon's shuttle. Stryder was coming to him.

If he could capture him then perhaps he could lessen the loss of life here, perhaps swing the blame somehow onto him, if his honour would allow him to do that. Either way he needed to take measures to attempt Stryder's capture.

Using his NI he called all remaining guards and soldiers who were not helping to evacuate, to come to the landing pad immediately. He just hoped there would be enough left and they would get there on time to stop Stryder so they could get away from there before the entire region was blown to atoms.

An idea formed in his mind and he contacted the nearest starship in orbit to inform them of the impending disaster and order them to send a troop carrier down to his location to start a full evacuation of the facility.

Hawk brought up his right hand with the closed fist sign that told his teammates to halt. Palm facing down he motioned for them to hit the dirt. They dropped to the ground as one, face first into the dirt. They all heard the roar of the engines as the troop carrier swooped down overhead towards the landing pad of the military base.

Things had just got worse.

"I love my job," Cowboy said quietly, yet they all heard through the integral comm units in their battle helmets.

They watched as the troop carrier hovered over the landing pad at the side of the building and then ropes fell out of an open hatchway in the side and Marines started to rappel down to the ground.

"Things just got a little more interesting," Hawk said as they all watched ten soldiers debark down and take up positions close to the shuttle.

"We have to take them out," he added and motioned them onwards. "We need to take control of the landing pad and shuttle. That part of the mission hasn't changed, it's just become harder but we'll still carry it out," he said. Then, crouched low to avoid detection, he led them slowly towards their objective.

Stryder saw his objective getting closer; through his NI he had accessed detailed plans of the interior of the facility and without realising and almost subconsciously, he was plotting his way through the maze of corridors unerringly to his final destination.

He had learned something else that brought him to a complete halt, something that chilled his blood. General Solon had issued an evacuation order to a starship in orbit. A troop carrier had arrived to drop off more troopers to aid with his capture, which made his escape almost impossible. It also made the danger to Hawk and his team that much more deadly.

He was almost at his destination when he stopped to re-evaluate his situation. The only way out of the building was through the entrance to the spaceport landing pad that was close, but by this time well guarded by the new influx of troopers. He would have to get past them and find some form of transport away from there.

That could be tricky.

∾

Norsky had anticipated Stryder's intentions and got there first. The hiding places were few and far between so he waited in plain sight for him to arrive. Because the serum was taking effect he found his hearing had increased and could hear his approach.

He waited at the last corner of the corridor, behind him was the doorway to the spaceport landing pad.

∾

S omething was not quite right. He felt a presence, heard a heartbeat not too far away from him.

He was not alone.

Someone was waiting just around the corner of the corridor he was in.

His objective was around that corner so he had no choice but to follow his course and go around it and face whatever challenge was waiting for him.

~

H awk accessed a combat channel via his NI and spoke to Stryder. "Where are you Captain? We have extra troopers in sight at the landing pad of the spaceport. If you're planning on coming that way let us know when, so we can arrange some sort of diversion for you to slip past them," he said.

Hearing Hawk, Stryder stopped in his tracks before rounding the corner and replied, sub-vocalising so that no one close could overhear, "I'm close to the exit and am about to approach it. If you can either, engage the troops or give them something else to think about, then it'll give me the opportunity to do as you suggest and slip past them."

"Will do, sir, just give us five minutes then make your move," Hawk replied.

"On my mark then Captain, and good luck," Stryder said.

"Good luck to you too, sir. We'll be waiting for you to give you any assistance you may need."

"Thank you Captain and here we go. Mark," Stryder said then the connection was ended, his internal clock would unerringly count down the time to make his move. Whatever was around the corner waiting for him, he had given himself five minutes to deal with it and get to the exit of the building.

He was confident that it wouldn't be a problem so he stepped around and saw…

"Norsky!"

"Hello Captain Stryder. My, my, you seem to have been in the wars as they say," replied the Black Knight as he stood facing him, legs slightly apart with his hands folded across his broad chest. An air of confidence exuded from the man.

The second Stryder laid eyes on him he knew he had been changed and the only way that was possible was if he had been given the serum.

Staring deep into the eyes of the man before him, he knew the task before him had just got much harder and that he might have underestimated the time allowed for him getting to the exit. That having been said, he wanted nothing more than to face this challenge alone. To test his abilities against a possible equal and with that in mind, he placed his weapons down on the floor.

"It seems you've proven to be a problem to our forces Kurt, I can call you that can't I? I feel that I know you quite well by now, brothers under the skin, as it were." Norsky had a smug smile across his broad, flat features as he watched Stryder place the weapons on the floor.

"Well, if you think having the serum administered to you makes you my brother then you are sadly mistaken. We are nothing alike you and I. We fight for opposite causes. We are opposite sides of the same coin," replied Stryder, hoping to dent his confidence, rattle him somehow and therefore force him into making a mistake. He had little time and could ill afford to waste it on idle chatter, he had to get past this last obstacle, and fast.

"I should have realised that you would intuit that I had the serum coursing through my bloodstream making you my equal," Norsky said, unfolding his arms and slapping his own chest to enforce his point.

Stryder stepped forward and punched him full in the face sending him reeling backwards to stumble over his own feet and fall to the floor.

"You talk too much. Are we going to fight or not?" Stryder said looking down at the fallen Black Knight.

Norsky was enraged now. He flipped back to his feet and rushed at Stryder his anger controlling him, wanting nothing more than to destroy the man before him.

Starting with a series of blows aimed at Stryder's head Norsky attacked holding nothing back. His hands moved with incredible speed and were almost a blur, yet Stryder blocked or evaded them with relative ease. His hands moved with a preternatural ease almost as if they had a will of their own, moving to block before the blow was even delivered as if he knew where it was going to strike before even Norsky.

Countering this barrage would be difficult he knew that. Waiting for the right moment would be the key and could take longer than Stryder was prepared to wait. And then it came.

Frustration began to set into Norsky's attacks; he was not getting the results he had hoped. He had not been able to land a decent punch, a telling blow onto Stryder. The opportunity came when Norsky threw a haymaker right cross at Stryder's head. Ducking beneath the blow as it passed by harmlessly, he rammed a right fist into the solar plexus of the man before him. All the air was forced from Norsky's lungs with an explosive "whoosh!" as he was bent double. Stryder hit him again and again with three rapid-fire blows to the stomach and kidney area forcing him to bend over and frantically cover up that exposed and damaged target area. Then, with his other hand, he hit the point of the Black Knight's lowering chin with his fist in a tremendous uppercut that lifted him off his feet to land squarely on his back dazed and confused.

Stryder stepped over Norsky's momentarily inert form as he headed for the exit picking up his weapons on the way.

~

Not having a great deal of cover hampered Hawk's team as they approached the landing pad. They had to mount an offensive against the troopers there but at the same time protect themselves, which was going to be difficult.

"Mark," Hawk said and readied his assault rifle. They were all lying flat on their bellies in a pile of shrub grass, the only cover they had.

"Pick your targets carefully gentlemen and fire when ready," Hawk instructed firing the first shot.

The troopers were positioned around the shuttle facing away from it, all looking in the direction of the exit of the building. When the first shot was fired, the trooper on the furthest guard position from the shuttle was sent flying through the air as the plasma bolt from Hawk's assault rifle struck him. As soon as that happened the rest of them took up defensive positions, with half of them remaining facing the exit while the rest turned to face the new threat.

Two more went down before they took shelter behind the shuttle and started to return fire in the direction of the muzzle flashes.

"Try not to damage the shuttle; we will need it to get off this rock," Hawk said as he continued to fire at them.

~

Stryder came through the exit and shot the first guard he saw. The plasma bolt struck the guard and blasted him back to collide into the hull of the shuttle. Glancing around, he quickly took in his immediate surroundings. The shuttle was in front of him guarded by the six remaining troopers, some of whom were facing away from him taking refuge behind the shuttle as plasma bolts were striking all around, obviously the covering fire from Hawk and his team. To the right of him was a set of Ground Haulers, huge eighteen wheel trucks used to load and offload shuttles with cargo or personnel.

That was his way out.

"I'll draw them away from the shuttle. You capture it and come after me, you can pick me up en route," Stryder said through his NI to Hawk then sprinted off towards the nearest Ground Hauler.

Inside the shuttle General Solon had been monitoring the proceedings and when he saw Stryder leave the building and shoot the trooper he got in touch with the pilot of the troop carrier who had just dropped off the troopers. He ordered him to return to the facility immediately.

He was determined to prevent Stryder from escaping at all costs, using whatever means were at his disposal.

Jumping behind the console in the flight deck he powered up the shuttles engines ready for take-off.

CHAPTER 27

Stryder approached the Ground Hauler from the near side. The empty driver's cab was situated high above the ground sitting in a protected cabin above the engine block slightly behind the front two tyres, each as tall as a man. Positioned just behind the tyres was a set of steps embedded into the walls of the vehicle, which he used to climb up into the cab.

Hawk saw Stryder dash across the gap from the shuttle towards the Ground Hauler then, as the shuttle's engines burst into life, said to the rest of his team, "Time's run out, we've gotta move, now."

He brought up his assault rifle as he stood up, sighting down the barrel. Holding it tightly against his shoulder he fired as he ran forward towards the shuttle. The recoil suppressor fitted into the weapon had to work overtime to keep it steady as he fired so that he could both run and keep it on target.

Storm saw Hawk jump to his feet and immediately followed suit, as did the other two members of the team. There was no question of them not following him, they were

Recon Delta and they stuck together no matter what, and they would rather die than leave one of their own behind.

Seeing the four, armed soldiers rushing them, the troopers tried to fire at them but had to seek cover behind the shuttle to avoid being hit by the incoming plasma fire.

General Solon saw what was happening outside the shuttle and bellowed at the troopers to stop them. His voice carried through the comm channel directly into the troopers' brains via their NIs almost causing neural shock from the overload. One of them was spurred into action and was promptly shot through the head by Storm the moment he appeared from his cover, which gave the others more cause for concern.

Norsky came to his senses with a start. Sitting bolt upright he looked around and knew that Stryder had got the better of him, again. This made his blood boil. Getting to his feet he ran through the exit almost straight into a burst of plasma fire.

Assessing the situation he quickly found all he needed to know, tapping into all the comm chatter he learned that Stryder had made his way to the Ground Hauler to his right. As he watched he saw it pull away from the landing pad and with it went any chance of capturing it.

Overhead he heard a troop carrier returning, he caught a glimpse of figures approaching at a full run from across the open area directly in front of him. He heard the shuttle's engines coming to life and knew that was where General Solon was. There were troopers hiding behind the shuttle just waiting for the opportunity to return fire on the approaching soldiers but at the moment they were pinned down.

As the Ground Hauler pulled away rapidly gaining speed, Norsky spotted a second vehicle, another Ground Hauler and a plan came to mind as his accelerated thought patterns assessed the situation and came up with a solution to his dilemma.

After a second or two he saw a pattern in the plasma fire and knew he could get across to the second Ground Hauler if he timed it perfectly. Now that he was gaining more and more control of his enhanced capabilities he was confident in his ability to do just that.

Waiting for just the right moment he set off at a full sprint, his legs pumping, his feet pounding the ground and his arms pumping through the air as he covered the ground between the exit and the vehicle in almost record time. Jumping onto the steps behind the front tyre he pulled himself up into the cab and sat himself behind the controls.

"You won't get away again Kurt," he said as he started the engine.

~

General Solon saw the approach of the four soldiers and knew they were here for Stryder. He couldn't figure out why Stryder was running away from them though.

The troop carrier was returning swiftly and as it was armed he knew he had the best chance of stopping and recapturing Stryder if he was aboard that, rather than on an unarmed shuttle. Leaving the cockpit he made his way back to the exit to wait for the arrival of the carrier.

Using his NI he opened a comm channel to the troops guarding the shuttle. He said, "This is General Solon; I want you to hold this position against those hostiles. Prevent them gaining control of this shuttle by any and all means necessary," and without waiting for confirmation, ended the call.

The troop carrier hovered overhead just to the rear of the shuttle. A ladder was lowered from an open exit hatch, which Solon sprinted towards and swiftly climbed onto. He pulled himself up with his powerful arms as the carrier took off again before he was even fully on board.

Once he was through the hatch he said through the comm channel to the pilot, "Get after that Ground Hauler and persuade the driver to stop."

"Persuade sir?" was the confused reply.

"Yes, I want the driver alive, is that understood?"

"Perfectly, sir. You want him alive, copy that, sir!" The pilot knew that to disobey an order from the General was tantamount to career suicide.

~

Hawk saw the figure of the General vacate the shuttle and said, "C'mon, guys it's ours for the taking. We need that shuttle so we can complete our mission."

The troopers guarding the shuttle continued to fire at the advancing soldiers but their aim was terrible. Whether it was the threat of the facility getting ready to blow a hole in the planet making them nervous, or the fact that the General had just retreated to the troop carrier leaving them behind, the Recon Delta Marines weren't sure, but they weren't the type to look a gift horse in the mouth. They advanced quickly, picking their targets carefully. They ran forward in a staggered pattern so that the troopers couldn't easily draw a bead on them. They though, were experts at firing on the run so it didn't present a problem to them.

Another trooper went flying backwards in a mist of blood

as a plasma bolt from Hacker's assault rifle caught him square in the chest.

Storm got another and Hawk killed one more leaving three left to defend against the four advancing soldiers who seemed unstoppable.

Panic took hold and they came out from behind the shuttle, their assault rifles on sustained fire hoping for a lucky hit when Cowboy hosed two of them with his own assault rifle and Storm shot the last one. All three were sent flying in a shower of blood and gore as the full power plasma bolts tore up their bodies at close range. They stood no chance of survival.

"Right, get on board! Fire up the engines and let's get after them!" Hawk commanded.

~

Stryder was travelling along in the lead Ground Hauler at a dangerous pace over the uneven ground. It took him all his control to keep in his seat while he steered the massive vehicle and yet he couldn't seem to shake whoever was in the other Ground Hauler. It actually seemed to be catching him, closing the gap between the two vehicles slowly, yet undeniably. It could only be Norsky, the soldier who had received the serum, whose hatred of him had almost sent him over the edge of sanity into the abyss of madness. He would do anything to catch up to him.

The road ahead was rough; it wasn't really a road at all, not even a track, just part of the landscape that he was travelling over to get away from the base. It was pitted and uneven and directly ahead lay the desert with its loping dunes and rocky outcrops. It would undoubtedly slow him down but it would do the same for Norsky in the trailing Ground Hauler, or at least that's what he hoped.

Suddenly a massive jolt from the rear of the vehicle caused Stryder to be almost thrown clear from his seat. When he looked in the huge wing mirrors he saw the cause of the jolt. Norsky had somehow closed the gap between them and rammed the front of his Ground Hauler into Stryder's.

He just had time to brace himself before another huge jolt almost threw him against the front windscreen as Norsky rammed him again.

There was nothing he could do to evade the other vehicle. Somehow Norsky had managed to find a way to increase the speed of his vehicle and use that to his advantage to catch up with him and now he was using the vehicle as a weapon against him.

～

Norsky had found the Turbo Boost feature on the control panel that was utilised when the vehicle needed that extra bit of power for heavier than usual loads. For example, pulling other vehicles such as other Ground Haulers, if they had broken down or Shuttles that needed moving from one bay to another and their own engines could not be utilised in safety. The feature was not meant for continuous use as Norsky was doing, as it would eventually burn the main engine out through overload, but Norsky was willing to take that risk to catch up with Stryder.

Putting the engine on Auto Pilot, controlled by the onboard computer, a very basic design, he left his seat and headed for the door. He climbed out onto the side panel using hand and footholds in the side of the vehicle he had used to climb aboard, then allowed the door to close just as his vehicle collided once more with the rear of Stryder's. The force of the collision almost threw him from his perch and if it had not been for his enhanced strength he wouldn't have been able to hold on. Somehow though, he did and once he had got his breath back under control he started to climb up onto the roof of the vehicle.

Sitting crouched down on top of the driver's cab, Norsky waited for the right time to make his move.

Stryder watched as Norsky got out of the side of the vehicle just before it rammed the rear of his own, once more almost throwing him clear, and he wondered what the hell he was trying to do.

With one eye on the road ahead and another on the wing mirror he watched as Norsky climbed up the side of the vehicle and reached the top of the cabin.

What was he doing he wondered as he sat atop the cabin, waiting and watching like a cat ready to pounce on an unsuspecting mouse, then it hit him exactly what he intended to do.

The huge vehicle came rushing forward again and on the point of impact Norsky hurled himself into the air.

By the time Stryder realised what was about to happen it was almost too late to take action. As he saw the trailing vehicle come hurtling towards him he tried to avoid it by turning the controls to the left and away from the oncoming collision. The massive vehicle had only just begun to turn when the collision happened and he saw Norsky fly into the air across the space between the two Ground Haulers.

The impact at the rear of Stryder's vehicle helped turn it even more, forcing the rear end to skid a little and in so doing altered the landing area Norsky was hoping for.

As he landed on the top of the vehicle the sideways movement of the surface beneath him forced him into a slippery slide, which almost threw him off the top onto the ground several feet below.

He tried to grab hold of anything available to prevent

himself from falling. He saw the edge getting closer as he slid towards it and his arms flailed about searching for a handhold, any handhold to prevent his inevitable slide off the top.

As his legs slid out over the edge into space he felt his stomach getting closer as well and he knew he would fall to his death.

He fell sideways off the roof and his right arm fell across the wing mirror. Instinctively he held on stopping himself from continuing the full length to the ground beneath him. Ignoring the pain in his shoulder from the jarring halt to his fall he punched his left fist through the door window shattering the Plexiglas so that he could open the door.

The cabin was quite large with a flat bench seat that the driver and at least two others could sit across and when Norsky had got the door open and climbed inside Stryder was at the other end waiting for him. His hands were still on the controls desperately fighting to steer the vehicle out of the skid and away from the following vehicle, which was still on autopilot and continuing to ram it from behind.

"Where do you think you're going?" Norsky said as Stryder wrestled with the controls. He made a dive to grab him but Stryder's peripheral vision was such that he caught the movement the second he made it. He blocked his advance, sweeping his arm in an arc knocking Norsky's arms to the side pinning them to the back of the seat. Taking hold of the controls with his left hand and holding Norsky's arms with his right, he spun in the seat and lashed out with his feet. Kicking Norsky in the stomach and releasing his arms, he sent him flying towards the doorway again.

Having his arms freed once more Norsky found he was quickly exiting the cabin. To stop his retreat he grabbed hold of Stryder's legs before he could pull them back.

Stryder struggled to free his feet and control the vehicle

at the same time, something that was becoming increasingly more difficult as the terrain was getting rougher the farther they got from the facility. Dragging one foot free he managed to kick Norsky in the head, only a glancing blow but strong enough to free his other leg a little more. Stamping down again and again with increasing force he felt his foot coming free and his attacker weakening as he pushed him closer to the door of the cab.

General Solon was on board the troop carrier sitting directly behind the pilot and co-pilot. The space was cramped and generally used by the weapons operator. It was fitted with two plasma cannons – one on the roof and the other on the underside of the craft. They could be operated either individually to fire on two different targets or in unison against the same target. The General was now in control.

From the screen mounted on the controls he had seen Norsky get on board the Ground Hauler Stryder was driving and he ordered the pilot to close in on them. Taking the control stick in both hands he took careful aim at the vehicle. He wanted to persuade Stryder to stop without destroying the vehicle and killing him. Norsky had proven to be somewhat of a liability, unable to follow orders and in the future could prove to be a problem. If he survived this encounter he intended to deal with him at a later date. If he failed to survive this skirmish then that would be one thing less for the General to worry about.

The targeting controls of the plasma cannons had locked onto the rear section of the vehicle; all he needed to do now was fire the weapon.

~

Cowboy was seated at the pilot's controls of the shuttle. The engines had started to cool down after Solon had left it but not too much that when they were kicked in again they reached optimum efficiency within seconds. Initialising the thrusters, Cowboy steered the shuttle up into a hover then, realigning the thrusters for horizontal flight, he set off after the troop carrier.

"We could have a problem here guys," Hawk said as they all watched through the front viewport at the troop carrier in the distance.

"I know what you're going to say, sir, that thing's armed and we're not," Storm said highlighting the problem they were about to face once they caught up with them.

"Any ideas?" Hawk asked as he was rapidly becoming aware that things were beginning to unravel before his very eyes.

"Well, we can't face off against that thing, that's for sure, but we could outrun it if need be. We just need to get Captain Stryder over here so we can use that advantage," Cowboy said, not sure if his suggestion helped.

"Yea! How the hell do we get him over here?" Hawk said almost to himself as he pondered Cowboy's words.

"I think I might have an idea," Storm said and they all turned to look at him as a smile slowly crept across his features.

~

Solon fired the lower plasma cannon once, nothing more than a warning shot really. The bolt struck the ground just to the rear of the vehicle kicking up a cloud of dust and pulverised a rock. The blast rocked the Ground Hauler so that it was almost thrown sideways; the rear section actually lifted off the ground by almost three feet then fell back down to the ground with a bone-jarring whump!

Connecting through his NI Solon said, "That was just a warning shot Stryder, pull over or the next one will send you into orbit."

Stryder was not intimidated and he let it show. He said, "Go fuck yourself General, you want me alive so I don't think you'll risk killing me."

"Are you absolutely certain of that Captain? What I want is your blood. I don't need you alive for that, do I? Now stop that vehicle and surrender to the inevitable." Solon tried to keep his voice calm and not let Stryder see just how angry and frustrated he was getting.

"If that's the case then General, take your best shot," Stryder said without hesitation, letting him know he wasn't bothered by any threats from him.

Solon was seething, he had hoped to intimidate him into at least slowing down but that wasn't the case. He detected no slowing of the vehicle they were chasing so, taking the controls of the plasma cannons firmly in his hands, he took careful aim once more.

If that's the way he wanted to play it then that was fine by him. He would drag his stinking dead carcass from the wreckage of the Hauler himself.

~

"Close that gap!" Hawk ordered as they all watched the troop carrier open fire on the Ground Hauler holding Stryder and Norsky. Turning to Storm he said, "Whatever you have in mind it had better work, we've just run out of time."

Turning away from Hawk, Storm said, "Cowboy, get us as

close to that carrier as you can. Alongside it if possible so we can get a clear shot."

"Copy that, sir," Cowboy replied increasing power to the shuttle's thrusters. They all felt themselves pushed back in their seats as the shuttle leapt forward.

Hawk's brow creased as he wondered what his teammate had in mind.

Leaving his seat Storm grabbed his Remm assault rifle from the rack and headed for the hatch.

"What the hell do you intend to do with that?" asked Hawk.

"I'm going to try and even the odds a little," Storm replied. Hawk smiled knowing exactly what he had in mind.

"I'll lend a hand, it might work better if we all join in. Hacker you're with us." Hawk got out of his seat reaching for his assault rifle and followed Storm to the hatch.

Inside the cab of the Hauler, Stryder turned to Norsky who had overheard the conversation between him and the General and smiled. "Hang on," he said with a wink.

The rear of the vehicle was lifted off the ground again and almost overturned as another plasma bolt struck the ground behind them. Inside the cab the two men were thrown from side to side as the concussion wave from the blast struck.

Stryder saw his chance and hit Norsky full in the face with a back fist strike from his right hand. Norsky's head was rocked back as blood from the impact sprayed out over the windscreen. Grabbing the back of his head with the same hand Stryder rammed Norsky's face into the dashboard again and again leaving a bloody smear across it. Releasing his hold, he pushed the dazed form of his attacker away from him and lashed out with his right leg in a sidekick that struck Norsky in his side and sent him hurtling towards the door. The force of the kick sent him colliding with the door causing it to fling open and in the next moment he found himself flying through it into the open air.

At the very last second, when he became aware of what was happening, Norsky reached out with a flailing right hand and his fingers closed on the edge of the door gripping tightly to prevent him leaving the vehicle.

His legs swung free of the cab and collided with the front of the vehicle then he swung back, his shoulder almost tearing from the strain.

While Norsky was thus engaged Stryder dived across the bench seat, feet first and slammed both feet into Norsky's face as he swung back. The blow landed squarely on the Black Knight's face knocking his head backwards with such force that it would have broken the neck of a normal man. Norsky was forced to release his tentative grip on the door as he was sent spinning through the air to land on the gnarled and pitted ground away from the vehicle.

Just as he landed another blast from the plasma cannon on the troop carrier struck the ground close to him. The blast tore up the ground mere feet from him and showered him with debris from the impact. Heat from the blast seared his flesh, burnt his clothes and engulfed him in agony. All he knew for the next few moments was a world of pain until blackness took him.

~

"Coming up on it now, Guardian," Cowboy said as he steered the shuttle closer to the troop carrier, his voice carrying over the NI link they all shared.

"Hold her steady," Storm replied as he got himself into

position in the open hatchway. Either side of him were Hawk and Hacker. They were all strapped onto a harness so the buffeting from the wind outside would not drag them through the hatch into the air and to their certain deaths.

The wind dragged at their clothes as it tried to grab and pull them out of the opening, but the straps held them secure.

They were slightly above the troop carrier matching its speed and then Cowboy lowered the shuttle down until they were alongside it.

"Hacker you aim for the flight deck, try and get the pilot, Captain Hawk and I'll take care of their cannons," Storm said as he took careful aim. He then added, "Fire when ready."

Solon saw a figure come flying out of the cab of the Ground Hauler just as he fired the lower plasma cannon again. The blast caught whoever it was and flung the body high into the air before it came down in a heap on the uneven ground.

"Hope to the Almighty that wasn't you Stryder," he said more to himself than anyone else, then fired again. This time the plasma bolt hit the rear section of the Ground Hauler throwing it several feet into the air to land with a bone jarring "whump!"

An explosion wracked the vehicle and flames slowly began to spread out from the already damaged rear section by the previous near misses from the plasma bolts.

"I've got you now," Solon said when he saw the effects of his handiwork.

Storm and Hawk opened fire on the plasma cannons on the troop carrier. Solon was only using the one situated on the underside of the craft, as he couldn't target the Ground Hauler properly from his position in the air with the topmost cannon. This made it difficult for Cowboy, who was piloting the shuttle, because he had to drop it down below the troop carrier slightly so that his men could target the lower cannon more accurately.

The plasma fire from the two assault rifles hammered into the plasma cannon immediately destroying it. It caused a fireball as it exploded, pushing the troop carrier higher up into the air.

Hacker missed with his first salvo aimed at the pilot's cockpit as the craft was pushed upwards by the explosion on its underside, but keeping his wits about him he tracked his target with his assault rifle and kept firing until his shots landed on target. The plasma bolts burst through the Plexiglas windscreen of the troop carrier killing the pilot in a shower of blood and gore.

Immediately the craft lurched and shuddered in mid-air as the death of the pilot meant all control of the craft was lost. Swiftly the co-pilot regained control, pulling it up moments before it crashed into the uneven ground below. As it was held it in a hover, General Solon saw the shuttle to their side and turned the remaining plasma cannon on top of the troop carrier around ninety degrees to aim at their attacker.

Storm saw the action and screamed at his teammate, "Take evasive action NOW!"

Cowboy steered the shuttle, banking the craft away just as General Solon let loose with a salvo from the plasma cannon.

"Get us back around on that troop carrier, we have to stop it," Hawk said through his NI to Cowboy.

~

Stryder wrestled with the controls of the huge ground vehicle after it hit the ground once more. There was a fire in the rear section that had almost been totally destroyed by the plasma bolts from the troop carrier.

He knew he would have to get out of it and soon. There was a real danger of it all blowing up with him still in it.

"I might need a lift a bit sooner than I thought," Stryder said through his NI to Hawk.

"We're working on that as we speak Cap, we're trying to get this troop carrier off your tail but it's proving a bit of a nuisance," Hawk replied through the same medium.

"This Ground Hauler is about to blow, if you can force it down close to me, the blast when it does go should take care of it for the both of us," Stryder suggested.

"Good idea, I'll see what I can do," Hawk said, relaying what had been said to the rest of the team and a plan was rapidly formulated.

Stryder kept the huge vehicle on as straight a path as he could, mindful of the time running out for the facility and for the Ground Hauler. It was getting dangerously close to the time when the fusion reactor back at the base went critical and wiped out everything around it. He knew he had to finish this as fast as he could and get off the planet with the Marines who had risked their lives to rescue him.

Norsky was out of the picture. He was in no doubt he had been killed by his own men when he was thrown clear from the vehicle, then blasted by the plasma cannon. All that was left to do was take care of General Solon who was in the troop carrier above him and he could do that with the vehicle, but he had to get off first.

Setting the autopilot, he opened the door and grabbed the

rim above and pulled himself up onto the roof of the huge vehicle.

"Okay guys do your stuff but be quick!" he said through his NI, hoping they could force the troop carrier down close enough for his plan to work or he could end up staying here with the rest of those doomed to die when the fusion reactor blew.

~

"Cowboy, position us over the troop carrier, right over the top of her and stay there, don't let her grab any air," Hawk shouted through to the pilot's station.

Cowboy steered the shuttle down over the top of the craft in question right over the plasma cannon and, as it had a limited elevation for the barrels, where they sat was the safest place to be. The plasma cannon's barrels could rotate three hundred and sixty degrees but only had an elevation of forty-five degrees.

~

"Get me a clear shot at that shuttle," bellowed the General, even though he was seated close by the co-pilot. The air rushed in at them through the shattered Plexiglas windscreen as they powered forwards gradually being forced lower and lower.

"I can't, sir, she's sitting right on top of us. I can't take us higher without crashing into the shuttle."

"Then crash into it, just get us up and away from that Hauler, she's about to blow," Solon said as he watched the flames on the ground vehicle begin to reach the engine compartment just beneath the driver's cab.

~

"Don't let them gain any altitude till I tell you to move, okay Cowboy. When I say move, take us away from here and as fast as you can, is that clear?" Hawk said.

"As crystal, sir! Holding her steady until you say otherwise," Cowboy replied.

Hawk turned to Storm and with a smile said, "It's about to get interesting."

~

Stryder saw the troop carrier try to gain some altitude and knew his time was running out. He had to move and fast. He saw his opportunity and braced himself. Crouching down with his powerful legs bunched beneath him like coiled springs, he hurled himself upwards towards the troop carrier almost ten feet above him.

He timed his jump so that he caught hold of the landing strut closest to him, wrapping his arms around it and swinging his right leg up to throw that over it too, to secure his hold. He pulled himself up so that he was standing, albeit in a crouched position, on the horizontal strut. He then proceeded to clamber up the outside of the troop carrier.

As he reached the top he sank down so he was the same height as the plasma cannon. He needed to crouch down as the shuttle was close by and the downward thrust from its engines threatened to throw him from his precarious perch.

"You need to move off slightly so I can come aboard and quickly as the Ground Hauler will blow any second," he said through the link initiated by his NI.

As Cowboy brought the shuttle away a short distance the troop carrier instantly started to climb and Stryder was pressed down onto the roof. Then, at that precise moment, the vehicle beneath it exploded in a cataclysmic fireball.

The co-pilot of the troop carrier vainly attempted to outrun the fireball and the occupants of the shuttle watched helplessly as fire engulfed the craft tearing and destroying everything and everyone on board.

"Holy shit," exclaimed Hawk as he saw the event unfold before his very eyes and he knew that they had failed in their mission.

Just then, the fireball expanded outwards even more, as if something was pushing through from deep within the interior. Then a figure, engulfed in flames, came bursting through screaming at the top of his lungs flying straight at them. Their first instinct was to back off in fear, but then they all realised at the same time just who the figure was.

"Stryder!" Hawk said incredulously. They all watched as he leapt from the troop carrier, which by that time was completely engulfed in the exploding fireball, to themselves a distance of over twenty-odd feet and getting wider with every second as Cowboy banked the shuttle away to avoid being blown up.

On the flight deck Cowboy felt the shuttle being hit by something and asked, "What the hell was that?" He received no answer, as the others were all busy helping the unrecognisable form of Stryder on board through the shuttle doors.

Their own combat suits were flame-retardant and afforded them some protection against the living torch that was Kurt Stryder. His screams of pain were almost unbearable to them, but being the true professionals they undoubtedly were they set about the task of dousing the flames that were eating away at his flesh.

"Go, go, go!" screamed Hawk to Cowboy. "Get us the hell out of here." The young Marine needed no further encouragement, he steered the shuttle away from the exploding vehicle and up into the skies heading towards the ship in which they had arrived.

Inside the shuttle the flames had been extinguished and they kneeled by the smoking ruin that was the man they had come to rescue. Each one was deep in thought thinking about what he had gone through in his last moments before life had left him.

So close, they had come so close to succeeding only to have victory snatched from their grasp in the very last few seconds.

Hawk was about to say something, lend words to the thoughts in all of their minds, when Stryder suddenly took in a sharp intake of breath, like a swimmer breaking through the surface of the water to take that first satisfying breath. He opened his eyes and then the miracle happened once more, right before their eyes.

Flesh started to heal at an alarming rate, blistered and burnt flesh started to regenerate, hair began to grow again and within seconds he was returning to a more recognisable figure.

After a few minutes, while the three Marines watched in total fascination, Stryder sat up and smiled at them, he was totally renewed.

"Boy, was that hot!" he said.

"And that's why Sinclair wanted you brought back," Hawk said finally truly understanding the importance of the naked man sitting before them.

"Yea, he has suspicions about my party trick, but he doesn't know just how well his little experiment worked. I was trying to keep that little fact from him for as long as I could. Guess that idea's out now that you boys have seen what I can do," Stryder said with some remorse.

Storm glanced at Hawk with a look that said – it's your

call.

Hawk looked at Storm, then Hacker, before finally turning back at Stryder. With a blank expression he said, "I have no idea what you're talking about Cap. I've seen nothing. How about you two?"

Storm and Hacker both said in unison, "I've seen nothing either."

"Let's see if we can find you something to wear then let's get you home," Hawk said as he got to his feet.

Stryder looked at Storm and said, "Did Sinclair ask for you personally to come here because of your knowledge regarding what happened on Research Station Five?"

"As far as I know Captain Hawk asked for me and the team personally. He said you'd feel more comfortable with us coming, seeing as how we were there when the experiment went sour."

"I think Captain Hawk knows quite a bit more than he's letting on," Stryder observed as he got to his feet. Just then Hawk returned with some clothes he'd found in a locker in the storage section.

"Here, don't know if they'll fit but it's got to be better than nothing," Hawk said as he tossed the bundle to him.

"I'd love to see Sinclair's face though if we returned with you as we found you," joked Hacker.

"Everyone brace yourselves!" Stryder said with a sense of urgency. The three of them turned to look at him in confusion as he was gripping the webbing attached to the side of the shuttle used to secure any cargo.

When it hit, the shockwave threw the small craft end over end and the three others had to scramble to grab hold of anything to prevent being dashed against the bulkhead.

"The fusion reactor just blew!" shouted Cowboy above the din inside the shuttle.

"How the fuck did you know that?" Hawk wanted to

know as he struggled to hold onto the webbing alongside him.

"He's tied into the computer down there, or was until it blew apart," Hacker said before Stryder had time to reply.

After a while, once the immense shockwave had washed over them, Cowboy got the shuttle back under control and had her on an even keel as he continued their journey up towards the transport they had arrived in.

"There will be other craft escaping same as us as they evacuate whoever was left in the facility, so be careful Cowboy, it could get a little crowded," Storm said to his teammate.

"What happened down there?" asked Hawk.

"They tried to duplicate the results of the experiment," was all that Stryder would say at first.

"And did they?" prompted Hawk. "Sinclair will want to know," he added.

"They manufactured what they thought was the serum and administered it to five Marines."

"I'm assuming they didn't survive that explosion down there."

"They didn't get the chance, I killed them before the serum had any chance to take effect."

"What about Hardy, you said she died?"

"Yes, they killed her, said she was expendable so I killed them too. I'd have killed them anyway once I knew they'd been given the serum. I couldn't take the chance that the Alliance had the capability of making soldiers with my ability. I would have destroyed the facility too but our fight took care of that. I also destroyed any samples of the serum they had left and the destruction of the facility has taken care of any chance they may have had of replicating their findings."

"Who was that guy you threw out of the Ground Hauler?"

"He was the guy who brought Hardy and me here. I think he had a soft spot for her and when he found out they were going to terminate her, he released her. She persuaded him to release me too, so I knocked him out and made our bid to escape. He took it badly and somehow got them to give him the serum too. It was beginning to work on him as we fought, but General Solon took care of him with the plasma cannon when he was trying to stop me, and then of course the explosion of the reactor will have finished off any chance of him recovering. I don't think it had had the time to affect his immune system as it has mine. So that just leaves me with the full effects of the serum."

"Sinclair will be pleased," Hacker said.

"He must never find out. As far as I'm concerned everyone who knew about the experiment died in that explosion down there, which just leaves those present. If General Sinclair finds out that it was a success to the extent it is, then he would put me in a lab under close guard while they did endless tests on me to learn just what had happened so they could reproduce the effects in countless others. I can't let that happen. I won't let that happen," Stryder said vehemently.

"I can understand why you wouldn't want that to happen, but just think of the advantage that we could gain over the Alliance," Hawk posited.

"And just who are we to say that we should? The status quo exists between us at the moment. How many do you think would die if they could make more like me? If Sinclair could make an army like me who could heal on the battlefield, do you honestly believe he wouldn't put it to use? There would be war, total all-out war in which the Alliance would be routed. Once they saw what we could do, what do you think their response would be? Lay down their arms in surrender or fight to the bitter end? Whatever they did, the outcome would be the same, more and more deaths. I don't know about you, but I can't have that on my conscience."

"What do you suggest? As we've seen you come back from being roasted alive it's not like you can kill yourself to prevent them doing all the things you said. What do you intend doing?" Hacker asked.

"There's only one thing I can do really, and that's carry on as if it didn't happen," Stryder answered.

"How do you mean?" Hawk asked.

"All along I insisted that the experiment was a failure. I just need to continue with that argument and until they get undeniable proof to the contrary there's nothing they can do," Stryder explained. He looked at each of them to gauge their reaction.

Storm said, "Well as far as I know, you were damned lucky you got off that troop carrier before the Ground Hauler exploded or you might not have survived."

"Yep, damned lucky," Hawk added with a smile.

"Coming up on the Hyperion," Cowboy said as they cleared the atmosphere of Toldax.

"Let's get back to the flight deck, we're not out of this yet and it could get a little hairy," Hawk said leading the way forward.

"Commander Park we'll be coming up to your location soon. Please be prepared to drop your stealth shield so we can come aboard," Hawk said through a combat channel.

"We'll be waiting, Captain. We've been monitoring the section and travel has become quite congested as the evacuation of the facility got under way," Park replied.

"I'm expecting that as soon as you drop the stealth shield you will become a target. Once we're on board make the jump to hyperspace."

"We have the coordinates already locked into the

computer, weapons systems are being manned and we're ready to take you on board on your command Captain."

"That's good to hear Commander, stand ready on my mark," Hawk said. Then he asked Cowboy, "How soon?"

"Now!"

"Mark!" Hawk said through his NI and almost instantly an outline of a starship began to coalesce in front of them, taking shape from the inky blackness of space until it was fully formed and they recognised the Hyperion.

"Ready to take you on board Captain Hawk," Commander Park said, his voice carrying clearly through to the shuttle.

Just as the shuttle made her run to the freighter's docking bay, some of the other craft in the area noticed what was happening. Commands were issued through the ether and a plan of action was formed.

Two starships veered off from their flight plan and took on an attack vector. Their target was the Hyperion.

"We have two craft coming in hot Cap, suggest you get on board as fast as you can, things are about to get interesting," Commander Park said.

"You heard the man, Cowboy, let's see just how good a pilot you are," Hawk said to the man seated before him.

"Hang on to your balls," Cowboy said as he applied full thrust to the engines sending the shuttle hurtling towards the freighter at an alarming speed.

Plasma blasts from the two attacking starships began to explode all around them as the two crafts closed.

The Hyperion was the main target of the attack but when the attacking ships realised what was happening the shuttle too became a target.

"You'd better make this fast, Cowboy, as this bird doesn't have sophisticated shielding and if we take a full hit then we're toast," Hawk said stating the obvious.

Cowboy threw the shuttle into a series of complicated

twists and turns to evade the plasma blasts as they neared the Hyperion.

"Commander Park you have my permission to engage the enemy to protect the ship," Hawk said, wondering why they had not returned fire.

"Sir, I'm under orders from General Sinclair to only engage as a last resort. In my opinion we have not reached that stage yet," Park replied sternly. Hawk knew that no matter what the commander would obey those orders.

"You are in command of the ship, Commander; I'll stand by your decision. Make it a good one, for all our sakes," Hawk replied, placing a reassuring hand on Cowboy's shoulder and saying, "Take us home."

The closer they got to the Hyperion, the more intense the firepower from the attacking ships. The shuttle was buffeted from the shockwaves caused by the plasma blasts and it was clear to all those inside that it was just a matter of time before the targeting computers on the attacking ships actually got a firm lock on them and blew them out of the sky.

The docking bay of the Hyperion loomed large in the front viewport of the shuttle as they neared it in preparation to make their final run.

Plasma bolts erupted all around them as they flew in a straight line for the Hyperion's docking bay. A bolt scored a glancing blow on a rear port side thruster just as they were about to enter the docking bay, which forced Cowboy into some serious flying to counter the change in their trajectory. As it was, they impacted with the side of the bay as they entered and came skidding to a halt not quite where they were supposed to be, but safe nonetheless.

"We're on board Commander," Hawk said. On the bridge Commander Park went into action.

"Target those attacking ships and fire, but just enough to

discourage any further involvement, then make the jump to hyperspace," he said, his voice commanding in the confines of the freighter's bridge.

The crew manning the weapons fired the hastily installed plasma cannons in short rapid bursts targeting the weapons systems of the attacking craft. Then, while they backed off to reassess the situation, the Hyperion made the jump into hyperspace.

As the ship's trajectory smoothed out the occupants breathed a sigh of relief, all except Hawk.

"Commander Park, what's our status?" he asked.

"We've entered hyperspace and we'll be entering normal space quite soon, then it's another short jump to Colonial territory. We've detected no ships following us. You can relax a little Cap, you did it," replied Park, with a smile in his voice.

"I'll be able to relax once we're in Confederation space and *we* did it Commander, it was a good team effort."

The Hyperion returned to Celeron where General Sinclair was waiting. Commander Park parked the freighter in a close orbit and the general came on board alone to debrief Stryder.

Stryder was still dressed in the borrowed uniform when Sinclair came to see him.

"Glad to have you back, Kurt," he said as he shook his hand.

"Not as glad as I am to be here, sir," replied Stryder with a half smile. "I can't thank those guys enough. If it hadn't been for them I'd still be there."

"Well, we can go into that at a later date, for now you need to get some rest before you return to work."

"Excuse me?" Stryder said taking a step back putting some distance between the two of them.

"You'll return to duty as soon as you're fit and ready and have undergone a full medical. We need to know exactly what was done to you while the Alliance had you," Sinclair said.

"I can tell you exactly what was done to me – nothing."

"Well, you'll have to excuse me if I don't take your word for it."

"That's your prerogative, General, but let me assure you that is all you'll get."

Sinclair looked at him for a long time assessing how far to go with this, wondering what he would do if pushed.

"You know I can't just leave this like you want me to, don't you. You have to realise that I have to take you back with me. You've become too valuable a commodity to just be allowed to wander around like any normal citizen."

"Why? You know as well as I do that the experiment didn't work. So why can't we just leave it be and move on."

"But that's just it Kurt, I do know it was a success, to some degree anyway. The rest I'm sure we'll learn with some testing."

"Okay, let's just say for arguments sake that it was an unqualified success. What would you do?"

"We'd try to reproduce the effects in others," Sinclair said with an expression of mild surprise. "Don't be naive Captain, you know exactly what I would do."

"And then what, invade the Alliance? Let's just say you could reproduce the effects of the experiment. That the experiment actually yielded the results you'd hoped for. What would be your plans for the Alliance – an initial strike to cripple their military capability for retaliation perhaps? And what would their response be do you think?

"Don't you see, that would only lead to all-out war with neither side ever gaining an advantage because to defend their way of life they would fight to the bitter end. Maybe even come up with a plan of their own to obliterate as many Confederation colonies as possible.

"How many lives, General? How many lives would it cost to prove the experiment a success?"

"But what would you have me do?" Sinclair asked after a

pause. He could see the future that Stryder had painted for them all and in his heart knew it to be true. Oh, maybe not by him, he had the same view as Stryder, but there would be others who would outvote him to make that awful dream a terrifying reality.

"Just let it go. Allow me to resign my commission and report that the experiment was a failure. Everyone who knew absolutely anything about this on Toldax has died, that just leaves Hawk, Storm, Cowboy, Hacker, you and me. I know they'll keep it quiet, they can't tell anyone about something they know nothing about anyway. You know I'll say nothing as I maintain it was an unparalleled failure, which just leaves you General. The ball is in your court."

Sinclair turned away from him while he thought through what had been said.

The nightmare scenario that Stryder had painted so eloquently was a viable one. The question was, would he sanction it and if he did, could he live with the consequences?

Turning back to face Stryder, just one look into the eyes of the man before him and he knew. His decision had been made.

The nightmare scenario was alive and living inside him and would continue to do so for as long as he lived. Seeing the anguish in that man's eyes at the horror he could envisage, he knew he could never let that vision become a reality.

"Your resignation is accepted forthwith," Sinclair said and held out his hand in friendship.

Stryder relaxed for the first time since he could remember and took the offered hand in a vice-like grip.

"Thank you, General, you have no idea what this means," Stryder said smiling.

"Oh, don't think I've done you any favours my boy. You're

a soldier and as a soldier you will be called upon to act, maybe not in an official capacity but act you undoubtedly will."

"If I'm a soldier then I'll be one who serves no master, like the Ronin from Japan's past, a samurai who served no Shogun," countered Stryder.

"Ronin 'eh? I like that. Well, I'll keep a watch on you Kurt. You've become more than just a soldier who served under me, you've become, and dare I say it, a friend. Look after yourself."

"Thank you, sir, you take care too."

"I'll organise a shuttle to take you back to the surface. Oh and finally, I'd just like to offer my condolences about Hardy; I understand you two were close."

"Yes, sir, we were. She deserves to be remembered with honour. She died a meaningless death but should be remembered for being not only a good soldier but a decent human being."

"We will, I'll see to it personally, my boy."

They parted then with nothing left to say. Stryder boarded the shuttle that took him down to the planet's surface close to his home. The home he had been brought up in, where his parents had lived to a ripe old age and now would be his sanctuary.

As he watched the shuttle leave, he wondered what the future now held for him. No doubt it would be interesting; there would be many adventures to come mainly because he was not the type of person to sit back when he saw an injustice. He remembered a quote, one of his father's favourites, "For evil to triumph all that is needed is for good men to do nothing"

He joined Col Sec so that evil would not triumph, as his father had wished, now though he would face it alone.

Sinclair had said that they would keep an eye on him, no

doubt via the tracker within his NI. With a thought, he turned off the tracker, a little trick he'd learned back on Toldax, he could do it with ease now.

"Try and keep an eye on me now, General," he said as he strolled back inside his home.

THE END

ABOUT THE AUTHOR

Jan Domagala was born in Staffordshire, England to a working class family where at school he discovered the joys of reading. Jan was a big fan of sci-fi books but would read almost anything he could get his hands on. His mother took him to join the local library as soon as he could read and from that day on, if it had words on it, he'd read it.

In the early 70's there wasn't much choice for employment where Jan lived so he ended up in an apprenticeship in screen printing for the ceramic industry. In the early years of his apprenticeship he had the pleasure of a trip on the schooner Captain Scott, a training ship as part of the crew. They sailed around Scotland and even up as far as Stornoway in the Outer Hebrides.

Jan is still in the same trade after a forty year career, but his passion is and has always been writing. After several abortive attempts, he started the Col Sec series, which is an action-adventure series set in the twenty fifth century.

Jan is currently working on the next book in the series.

Join Jan by subscribing today!
   http://eepurl.com/dLM3gk
   Follow me on BookBub! https://www.bookbub.com/authors/jan-domagala

And on Facebook: https://www.facebook.com/ColSecSeries

www.ingramcontent.com/pod-product-compliance
Lightning Source LLC
Chambersburg PA
CBHW061557190726
48288CB00007B/2073